Praise for Charles McCarry

THE
MULBERRY
BUSH

Other Novels by Charles McCarry

The Shanghai Factor
Ark
Christopher's Ghosts
Old Boys
Lucky Bastard
Shelley's Heart
Second Sight
The Bride of the Wilderness
The Last Supper
The Better Angels
The Secret Lovers
The Tears of Autumn
The Miernik Dossier

THE
MULBERRY
BUSH

A Novel

Charles McCarry

The Mysterious Press
New York

First Grove Atlantic hardcover edition: November 2015

First Grove Atlantic paperback edition: January 2017

Published simultaneously in Canada
Printed in the United States of America

FIRST EDITION

ISBN 978-0-8021-2557-6
eISBN 978-0-8021-9080-2

The Mysterious Press
an imprint of Grove Atlantic
154 West 14th Street
New York, NY 10011

Distributed by Publishers Group West

groveatlantic.com

17 18 19 20   10 9 8 7 6 5 4 3 2 1

To Otto Penzler

He who seeks vengeance must dig two graves: one for his enemy and one for himself.

—Chinese proverb

Prologue

On a midsummer day in January, Luz Aguilar, the love of my life and the only child of the legendary Alejandro Aguilar, martyr of the revolution, and I met for the first time at first light in a rose garden in Los Bosques de Palermo. The vast park was empty. Dew sparkled on the roses. Beyond its gates, felt but unseen and still abed, Buenos Aires stirred and coughed as it awakened. As Luz approached, details of her face came into focus. I saw the color of her eyes, glimpsed the even teeth beneath her upper lip, her piquant face, her dark hair, which gathered the light. Short skirt. Memorable legs. She squinted into the sun, trying to make me out. She had been told I would be carrying a copy of the financial newspaper *Clarin* in my left hand and wearing a Brigade of Guards necktie—the one with the broad diagonal red and navy blue stripes.

As scripted, we bumped into each other lightly as we passed, and then murmured the sign and countersign:

Me: *"Un hermoso día, señorita."*
Luz: *"Buenos Aires es siempre soleada, señor."*

For operational reasons I had studied Spanish with a Honduran tutor. Argentineans are famous for their linguistic snobbery. She looked at me as if I were speaking her mother tongue with an Inuit accent.

Like the citizens of many great capitals, the *porteños,* as people who live in or around Buenos Aires are called, have their own way of speaking the language. Among other peculiarities, they habitually use the formal *usted* and almost never call even the closest relatives or friends *tu,* but address them instead with the archaic *vos.*

In English—I knew she spoke it fluently—I said, "Follow me."

She did as she was told. Luz was already a marginal asset of the intelligence service I worked for, ostensibly because she held a minor post in her country's foreign ministry but actually because she had grown up with her father's terrorist friends, many of whom remained persons of interest. Because it is the business of an intelligence service to stay in with the outs no matter how odious the outs might be. Because we wanted to keep tabs on her honorary uncles and aunts who were still terrorists in their hearts—sleepers waiting to be reawakened by a messiah waving a red flag. Because in their imagination, this savior would resemble Luz's late father, Alejandro Aguilar, the One—enemy of mankind, murderer, traitor, hero of the romantic left.

Actually, for the final weeks of his time on Earth, Alejandro was systematically betraying the revolution to its enemies. At that point I knew little about him and did not need to know more, or so I then thought. He died before Luz was old enough to be trusted with the truth. It was also good for his cover that Luz's mother, herself a beauty, had been disappeared. It was said that she had been thrown out of an airplane, probably after being tortured until her bones broke. Even now, as I would later learn, Luz dreamed of her, naked and falling, falling in cold darkness, hearing the airplane's throbbing engines, smelling the sea, not knowing until impact the exact moment when she would hit the frigid water and die.

Once a month Luz met her Yanqui case officer and handed over a thumb drive loaded with useless information. For this, and because Headquarters was partly responsible for her father's early and violent and famous demise, we paid her a monthly stipend, in cash, that covered her hairdresser, her clothes and shoes, her beautician, her wine, her holidays, her impulses. And theoretically bound her to us because she signed for every payment with a thumbprint and this gave us the power to denounce her as a traitor to her country or to her father's memory. This was not a diabolical threat that applied to Luz alone because she was who she was. It was standard procedure—just the way we did the thing we did.

Thanks to her upbringing among people who played at danger, Luz knew enough tradecraft by the time she was ten to realize that if she was ever caught leaving a clandestine meeting with a blackened thumb, this treasonous smudge would be all the evidence military intelligence or the national police would need to gang rape her while they waterboarded her and administered electric shocks to her genitalia before locking her up for life or dropping her from an airplane into the Atlantic Ocean. The federal police and military intelligence were no longer supposed to do such things now that democracy had been restored, but who knew when they might revive old habits, or if they had ever really given them up?

Owing to our good relations with the Argentinean intelligence services, Luz had less to fear from exposure than she imagined. Nevertheless, the memories and the fear with which she had grown up lingered within her. Headquarters didn't require her to take large risks. Like the superfluous ingredient in a recipe, she was being reserved for another purpose.

I led her to a coffee bar where they were just rolling up the shutter. We sat down at a corner table. For the moment we were alone except for the cashier and the skinny kid who ran the coffee machine. For show, still following the script, Luz smiled at me as if for a lover just home from the sea. She squeezed my hand and passed me her monthly flash drive. She had downloaded onto this drive an entire digital folder of the useless gibberish that is generated daily by the inconsequential ministry of an irrelevant government. The moment it touched my fingers, its new life as a valuable commodity began—valuable not because it had any actual value, but because it was secret and because it was purloined. I would pouch it to Headquarters. Some wretch in Virginia would be required to translate it, another wretch to read it and yet another wretch to analyze it, and yet more wretches tasked to follow up on the analysis. The value of secrets, like the value of money, is in the mind. A strip of paper the exact size of a hundred-dollar bill is worth nothing in itself, but smear it with green ink and the portrait of a dead president and presto, it's worth two tennis shoes.

While we drank our coffee we talked about movies for the benefit of eavesdroppers. I claimed to admire the work of a certain radical Argentinean director. In riposte Luz quoted the pope on the subject of Mel Gibson's S-and-M epic about Jesus of Nazareth: "It is as it was." Despite this readiness to quote the Holy Father, Luz was no Catholic. Her father and mother had immersed themselves in their roles as godless Communists, so their child was raised as a heathen as part of their cover. Still, a small gold cross nestled in her cleavage.

I scratched my right ear with my left forefinger—a signal, absurd like all tradecraft, that it was time to break contact. Luz got out her stamp pad, which was disguised as a compact, and surreptitiously inked her thumb. I handed her the receipt and she thumb-printed it. I gave her a foil packet containing an alcohol swab with which to clean the ink off her thumb. She smiled a tiny smile at this small gallantry. Then she picked up the folded *Clarin*, in which her money was cleverly concealed, and rose from the table.

In the mirror behind the coffee bar as she walked away, Luz noticed my eyes glued to her bottom, and she gave me, in the mirror, the same minimal smile as before.

Much later, she told me that the thought that brought a smile to her lips was *Possibilities.*

Two minds with but a single thought.

1

Although I am, for the time being, hiding something from you when I put the matter so simply, I became a spy because my father before me was a spy. He was recruited during his final semester in New Haven. Being chosen in this way was the culminating honor of an early life filled with promise. He had been a star athlete at school, he was a popular man on campus. He posted good marks, was tapped for one of the more desirable secret societies, held his liquor and his tongue, smiled when the situation warranted it. He was presentable in an all-American way, and even the prettiest Seven Sisters girls would not have refused a proposal of marriage if he made one. He was a fine tennis player and a fairly good midfielder in lacrosse. In other words, he was the whole package.

In those days, as the Cold War waxed, many of Headquarters's most alert talent spotters were professors at Harvard, Princeton, and Yale and at smaller eastern colleges that specialized in producing a type that thought alike, spoke alike, and behaved with predictability. Though I suppose he had his suspicions, Father never knew which of his mentors recommended him or why exactly he had been singled out. It didn't really matter. He had been tapped for membership in the most exclusive fraternity in American life, and that was enough for him to know. He accepted the invitation to go undercover without a moment's hesitation.

The Korean War was in progress, and to his surprise, Headquarters sent him to the Marine Corps instead of straight into the heart of darkness as he had hoped and expected. No one told him the reason for this detour (he assumed it was just a detour), and mindful that he was being watched by invisible judges, he did not ask. He completed officer candidate training at Quantico with his usual brio and was commissioned in the Marine Corps reserves as a second lieutenant. His commission was, in the jargon of the intelligence community, a "genuine-false" credential—that is to say, the commission was genuine, but its purpose, its only purpose, was to provide him with a convincing résumé.

While the other new second lieutenants with whom he had trained went off to risk their lives in the mud and snows of Korea, Father was sent into quarantine at a secret installation on a locked-down military base in Virginia. There he was trained in the techniques of espionage and absorbed into the culture of the craft, which was not so very different from the culture of the secret society to which he had been elected at Yale—or for that matter, from that of a summer camp of the Boy Scouts of America. The Plantation, as this installation was called, was an incubator, a place so closely guarded, so profoundly secure that not even his real name was at risk. He and his fellow trainees were called by their "funny," i.e., fictitious, names. They were told that even the instructors did not know their true identities. Father and his classmates were assured in many small ways that they were now on the definitive inside, immunized against risk or even visibility—safe, protected, nonexpendable. Glamorous.

Meanwhile, one in every four of Father's Quantico classmates were being killed or maimed on the battlefields of Korea. In later years the gnawing guilt he felt about his own escape from combat tended to emerge in fits of anger, usually after the third martini. Suddenly he would become a different person—angry, loud, wild-eyed. Mother called these drunken tantrums "the escape of the lout." She hated these non-U outbursts, and over the years decided, as his career spun downward and their marriage crumbled, that the lout was the real him.

I don't really know what, if anything, the ghosts of dead or mutilated classmates had to do with the first step in Father's self-destruction, but it began with something he did at the Plantation. The training course for apprentice spies was a game, something like military maneuvers, with a clueless rabble of students pitted against a disciplined, battle-tested Wehrmacht of instructors in a series of exercises that the Wehrmacht always won. The pedagogical goal was to teach the students, through repeated failure and humiliation and constructive criticism, to learn from their mistakes, and like children learning to talk, to master tradecraft by absorption rather than by precept.

The emphasis was on the tried-and-true: proven methods brought desired results, reckless innovation bred disaster. The final exercise in the cycle was a mock operation in which the students attempted to penetrate a Wehrmacht target and neutralize it without arousing suspicion. It was a given that the students would fail to achieve this impossible objective, be captured by the Wehrmacht, be interrogated with realistic brutality, and in some cases be broken and give up their service, their country, and their honor, and be weeded out before it was too late.

For my father, this contrived failure, this suspension of his natural worth, no matter how brief, was a bitter pill to swallow. His upbringing and his education had endowed him with a belief in his own value, in his natural invulnerability. No one could be his puppeteer, no one could touch him without his permission—especially not those who were not his equals and could never be his equals. The instructors, or some of them, affected the manner of the underworld: tough talk, uncouth accents, Neanderthal politics, contempt for hapless rich kids, a manner that suggested that their street smarts were a hell of a lot more useful than the dead language of literacy the neophytes had learned in Ivy League classrooms.

Father, along with other students—these young men were not where they were because they were stupid—understood that the outcome was designed to humble the students. He decided to teach the instructors a lesson about the danger of making false assumptions. What happened next became part of Headquarters lore. Under Father's leadership, a core of the smartest students turned themselves into a gang and put together an operational plan to turn the tables on the instructors. In a preemptive strike, the students captured the instructors, interrogated them, broke a couple of them, and infuriated all the rest.

The chief instructor, a revered figure who had done great things behind enemy lines in World War II, was gagged and tied to a chair and denied bathroom privileges, a standard interrogation technique. He fouled his pants. When his gag was removed he shouted that Father had a lot to learn about playing the game. With maddening insouciance Father replied that the chief instructor had just learned that playing the game was a matter of not always playing the game.

This anecdote was passed on to me years later by a lofty superior, a friend and admirer of the chief instructor, who had known Father at the Plantation and who had prudently refused to take part in the coup Father engineered. Father himself never mentioned the episode to me, or for that matter, anything else having to do with his work. His early education had taught him to keep secrets from those who had no natural right to know them.

Father's schoolboy prank, which placed so many assumptions in question, split Headquarters into two camps. The old guard wanted to fire him and blackball him from all other employment that normally was reserved for men of his social class in the outside world. The positive thinkers and those with a sense of humor, a minority at Headquarters but at the time a powerful one because it included an imaginative director, thought that Father was exactly the kind of young fellow Headquarters needed—unafraid and smart and daring and, above all, creative.

He was retained, even promoted a little ahead of time. Had he been as smart as his admirers thought he was, he would have at that point resigned with his laurels intact and gone back to the real world. Apparently he liked the glow he now gave off as a result of his wonderful joke, because he elected to remain inside. This was a fateful decision. For the rest of his career his admirers pushed him into assignments where they believed he would shine. But when he got to where he was going, the chief of station almost always was an avenger of the chief instructor who saw Father's arrival in his shop as an opportunity to put out the bastard's lights.

Consequently, Father never became the star at Headquarters or in the field that he had been for that brief moment at the Plantation, or before that in college, home, and school. It is difficult to pinpoint the reasons why a man who seems destined to succeed fails to live up to expectations. Father could have dispelled the mystery by telling his own rollicking story at dinner parties, but he never emerged from his tomb of discretion to set the record straight.

Never apologize, never explain, he counseled me, his only child, over and over again. I listened to this precept, and as you will learn, it cost me, in the end, almost as much as it had cost him.

My mother also paid a steep price for his folly. She married Father expecting to become, in due course, the wife of the Director, dining with the world's most powerful men and playing bridge and gossiping on the telephone with their wives. It was Father's fault that this did not happen. He had misled her into marriage, he had betrayed her in a way that was a hundred times worse than adultery. Obviously he had something wrong with him, a skeleton in his closet, a genetic defect he had failed to disclose to her. He was imperfect. He had hidden this from her. He deserved no sympathy. The important thing to her, the central fact of her life, was her own crushing disappointment.

Another of my superiors, who had known Father in his youth and afterward shunned him as damaged goods, summed it up with cruel brevity.

"Your old man," he said, "was all sizzle and no steak."

Maybe so.

Father was what he was, and like so many others in all walks of life, he is remembered for his worst or best moments, depending on your point of view. He was living proof that there are no second acts in American lives. If in fact he was incompetent except for that one brief Fitzgeraldian flash of brilliance when he was twenty-three years old, he had plenty of company.

My own experience of the world of intelligence and the wider world is this: 90 percent of the workforce feigns effort, and of the 10 percent who do put their hearts and minds into the job, no more than one in ten is any damn good.

My own ambition—and I had no illusions about my chances of success—was to do one great thing to clean up Father's reputation before I used up my life and its opportunities.

Like father, like Quixote.

Father crashed and burned for good when he was about twenty years into his blighted career. His own opportunities, as we have seen, were severely limited. Over time, his fitness reports portrayed his work as acceptable, nothing more, and he had risen in rank in step with those findings. Promotion at Headquarters tends to be fairly rapid in the early years. Headquarters does not use military rank, but most intelligence officers (there were very few women on board in Father's time) reach a level equivalent to the military rank of major by their early thirties. Some advance to the equivalent of colonel around their fortieth birthday, and then, for most, promotion stops.

At forty-five Father was posted to Moscow, an assignment in which he had almost no chance of succeeding. He spoke no Russian and had no background in Soviet affairs or expertise in communism, which he regarded as a sham religion, modeled on Christianity, that was mainly interested in controlling the poor as a means of accumulating wealth.

At the time, Father's civil service pay grade was that of a lieutenant colonel, the tombstone rank of officers who are neither successes nor failures. The Moscow assignment would be his last before he was shooed out the door. He knew this, and the knowledge that the end was in sight plunged him into a midlife crisis. He who had once, long ago, been a somebody in the fabulous somewhere of his famous university, had become a nobody. His colleagues regarded him as a drone. His wife treated him as if he were invisible and hadn't granted him access to her body in fifteen years. Other Headquarters wives, who seemed to smell this rejection upon him, treated him like a eunuch. His friends had surpassed him and fallen away.

He and his only son, myself, had barely a nodding acquaintance. I imagine him, three sheets to the wind after the fourth martini and all alone in his bugged, shabby, underheated Moscow flat, uttering a loud *Fuck it!* into the empty air and deciding to wing it in whatever time and identity he had left.

In the months that followed, he drank too much at diplomatic receptions and often showed up at the office smelling of booze and seemingly incapacitated by hangovers. The chief of station ignored him but sometimes gave him a meaningless assignment. When tasked to meet a potential asset, a female Muslim from Kazakhstan in whom the station had no real interest, he embraced her on the street and kissed her moistly on the cheeks and (or so it was said) squeezed her left breast. She fled in outrage and was never seen again.

He slept with the first sparrow, or trained sex specialist, the KGB put in his way, and was photographed by hidden cameras committing Kama

Sutraian acts with her and two of her coworkers, one of whom was male. Father himself told me this story during the brief moments toward the end of his life when after years of estrangement, we became friends. After the encounter with the sparrows, he knew that he had not seen the last of the KGB. In his fertile mind, a plan took shape—he would entrap the Russians who were trying to entrap him. In one last prank, he would turn the tables on them and on his own service and make his enemies at Headquarters shit *their* pants.

He began to take long, lonely nighttime walks, knowing that the Russians would take notice and see an opportunity. They would follow him, watch him, and in due course attempt to hook him. What fun.

To record the approach of the apparatchiks, he wired and miked himself and wore on his tie clip a tiny camera that took clear pictures in very dim light. All of this gear was his own property, not the station's. He had bought it in a spyware store in a Virginia mall before leaving for Moscow. His plan worked. He was followed, monitored, watched by teams of sidewalk men wearing overcoats that resembled grocery bags with sleeves attached and fur hats like sawed-off shakos pulled down to their eyebrows. In his who-gives-a-shit state of mind, all this amused him tremendously. His intention, fueled by alcohol and disdain for his tormentors at Headquarters and the sheer boredom of having operated at 10 percent of capacity for twenty years, was that this joke would be the way his world would end: not with a howl but with a giggle.

The KGB's approach came as he sat on a park bench at two in the morning under a flickering light standard. Snow was falling, fat flakes of it tinted yellow by the artificial light. He knew, of course, that there was someone behind him, someone with a different tread and a different feel from the usual gumshoes who shadowed him, and he had chosen this bench because there was light enough for his camera, and because the snow-muffled silence was perfect for his microphone. Father crossed his legs, took off his fur hat, and scratched his head, coughed, as if signaling the all clear to a contact. When after a long interval no contact appeared, a Russian sat down beside him. He had an un-Slavic face—shaggy eyebrows, large brown eyes, nose like a doge.

"May I join you?" he asked in competent American English.

Father grunted and offered him the silver flask of bourbon he had stowed in an overcoat pocket. The Russian drank it down like vodka. He coughed and made a face.

"*Awful* stuff."

Father said, "True, but it gets the job done."

The Russian chuckled. He said, "I am called Vadim."

Father said, "Bob"—not his true name, but Vadim already knew that.

"I have brought the photographs you ordered," Vadim said, and handed over a large envelope.

It was already addressed to my mother in McLean, and bore the correct Russian postage.

"Very kind of you," Father said, tapping the sealed envelope with a forefinger but not opening it. "How much do I owe you?"

Vadim waved a hand in dismissal of this small favor.

"Our pleasure," he said.

With a smile, Father said, "Mine, actually."

It began to snow more heavily. Vadim's hat and overcoat were coated with the stuff, so that with his great nose he looked like an emaciated snowman.

At length Father said, "Maybe you'd like to come to the point before they have to shovel us out, Vadim."

"I would like to ask for a favor in return for the photographs but I do not want to be misunderstood," Vadim said. "You can refuse of course, but it is a small thing."

"Don't worry," said Father. "Spit it out."

"I have great difficulty remembering American names because they are such a hodgepodge of names from all over the world—English, German,

Spanish, African, Arabic, Jewish, who can count them all? So what I was wondering was this. You work in the American embassy, so could you possibly obtain a copy of the embassy telephone book for me?"

In his first days at the Plantation, Father had learned that this approach had been a fishhook of recruiters since the invention of the telephone: bring me this trivial little thing and Topsy will grow.

Father said, "The phone book? Why?"

Vadim laughed apologetically. "It's a silly hobby, Bob, but I collect foreign telephone books. They fascinate me. Like novels."

"You like character-driven stories, is that it?"

"Something like that. I just like telephone books. There's a certain romance to them. By the way, I happen to have Natasha's phone number in case you would like to have it."

"I'd love to have it. Natasha has an amazing twat. It *squeezes*. Do you happen to have that number on you? "

"Unfortunately, not at the moment. But I could bring it next time we meet."

"Sounds good," Father said. "When and where would that be, our next meeting?"

Vadim named a different Moscow park. "Same time, eleven minutes after the hour, a week from tonight."

Vadim took back the envelope containing the pictures. "I will keep this for you so the snow will not blur the ink," he said.

"Do take good care of it until we meet again," Father said.

Father played Vadim for the rest of the winter, recording every second, every word of all their meetings with his trick ring and tie clip, but without delivering the embassy phone book or any other secret or official U.S. government document or tidbit of information.

Gradually, subtly, he turned their conversations around, so that by the end of April, Father had become the seducer and Vadim the reluctant virgin. Father offered the Russian the turncoat's equivalent of marriage:

legal sex, security, safety, a new name, escape into a happier, easier life in which the other person paid all the bills and, in case the union did not work out, made a down payment of half his net wealth.

Father had always been good at recruitment. Even the clique that had ruined his career conceded him that. Vadim, whether he was playing a role or playing it straight, wavered like a man who knew that his grip on his most precious possession, his virtue, was loosening with every encounter in the dark and haunted parks where the two men met in the small hours of the morning.

Finally Vadim said maybe, but first he wanted to talk to someone higher up in the chain of command than Father, someone who could make promises that could be kept. Father had not informed the chief of station or anyone else in the Moscow station about this off-the-books operation. Keeping his own counsel had been no great feat, since almost no one in the station or the embassy or in the American community, not even fellow old Blues, had the slightest interest in talking to a drunken outcast like him.

Because the case officer manuals for the KGB and Headquarters and practically every other secret espionage service in the world contain the same hoary truths about handling potential traitors, Father understood that Vadim's behavior—he was a little too compliant, a little too willing to part his knees—was likely to be a theatrical exercise. Routine skepticism suggested that Vadim's masters had seen an opportunity to penetrate Headquarters, to dump a mother lode of false information on the American service, to have a good laugh at the stupid Americans' expense.

That was the beauty of Father's prank. It would present the clique that ran Headquarters, the people who had banished Father into outer darkness, with an all but irresistible temptation. Whichever course they followed, they could never know if they had missed a bet or brought a disaster down upon themselves. In either case, they would remember

Father, they would remember what they had done to him, they would never be rid of him.

As retaliation goes, it's hard to do better than that.

On a night when the silence in Sokolniki Park was so heavy that it seemed that it made you imagine you could seize it like fabric between thumb and forefinger, Father looked deep into Vadim's eyes, which in the feeble light seemed as large as a horse's eyes, and said, "My friend, this flirtation has gone on long enough. This is the moment of truth. Decide now or we forget the whole thing."

He laid an encouraging hand on Vadim's coat sleeve and said, "Do what's best for you and your family, my friend, whatever that is."

Vadim tried to speak but like a stutterer reaching in vain for a word he can pronounce without inviting ridicule, he stood mute.

Father shrugged and said, "OK. It's been good to know you."

Then he spun on his heel and walked away.

In a voice that cracked, Vadim said, "Wait."

By then, however, Father had turned his back and stepped behind yet another curtain of falling snow. Because they were reading with different eyes from the same sheet of music, both men understood that this was not the end. Whether Vadim was behaving honestly (a possibility, after all) or dissembling, he would not, could not back off. If he honestly wanted to defect, he was already so compromised that he was a candidate for the KGB's standard penalty for treason: to be placed naked in a coffin and cremated alive. If, on the other hand, he was under orders to feign defection and was this close to success, he would have to go through with the operation.

Time would tell. Father and Vadim had the means to get in touch with each other. All either man had to do was chalk the Russian letter that looks like a mirror image of *R* on a certain lamppost on Tverskaya Ulitsa and they would meet at the time and place agreed upon.

Father was ready first thing the following morning to spring his joke on the chief of station. He asked the chief's secretary for an appointment.

In an expressionless voice she said, "I'll tell him you want to see him."

This happened on a Tuesday. It was Friday, during the last minutes of the workday, when the chief, a famously foulmouthed man who bore the Dickensian name of Amzi Strange, sent for him.

Amzi Strange had never smiled in Father's presence, nor did he smile now.

In a toneless voice he said, "What?"

Father handed him a bulging manila folder. Skilled bureaucrat that he was, he had organized a meticulous file on his mock operation.

Amzi Strange said, "What's this supposed to be?"

Father said, "I think you should read it, and read it yourself instead of handing it off to someone else, and then if you want to talk about it, we can talk."

Strange tossed the file into his in-basket and said, "Right. We're done."

It took Amzi Strange more than two weeks to read the file. He called Father on a Sunday at seven in the morning and said, in his grating voice, "My office. Now."

The chief was already at his desk when Father arrived. He did not invite his visitor to sit down.

He said, "Have you completely lost your mind?"

Father said, "I don't think so, Amzi, but if I have, I guess I'd be the last to know."

The Vadim file lay on the Strange's otherwise bare desk. He tapped it with a forefinger.

"This is real? It's not some kind of sick joke?"

"It's genuine."

"You've been meeting a KGB officer clandestinely, in public parks in the middle of the night, and playing along with a recruitment pitch for two fucking months without telling me, without telling anybody what you were up to, with no authorization from Headquarters and without its knowledge?"

"Yep."

"'Yep?' *Yep*, you frigging imbecile? Why? What in God's name were you thinking?"

"I didn't know we acted in God's name in this business," Father said. "But to answer your question, I was thinking that we had a good chance to turn this guy—I still think we will be able to do that if we play him right, and that that would be a feather in the station's cap, inasmuch as we've recruited not one single local asset in the year and a half you've been in charge here. Or for many years before."

"Thanks for sharing," Strange said. "You never wondered if this target you found with such ingenuity was a dangle, that this was a KGB operation, a threat to security, a quick feel?"

"Why yes, Amzi, those possibilities did cross my mind. But there was the other possibility, the one where with a little help from us, he could become a threat to *their* security."

"Pretty fucking slim possibility. So I ask you again, why didn't you let somebody know that you were singlehandedly putting at risk every single operation we're running and every single officer in this station, not to mention the family jewels back home?"

"I just did that."

"After the fact. I ask you again, what were you *thinking*? Tell me. Please help me understand."

"Basically, I was trying to keep busy," Father said. "You haven't asked me to do so much as to sharpen a pencil in the months I've been here, so I figured you'd be unsympathetic to any project I proposed. On this particular one, you'd tell me to cease and desist."

"You're fuckin' A I would have."

"And besides that, Amzi, I have no reason to care whether you like this or not. It's an opportunity to run an asset inside Lubyanka—"

"There is no Lubyanka anymore, my dear fellow. They've moved to the country."

"Well then, I guess Vadim would have to commute, supposing you and Headquarters have the guts to consider this, to take a chance."

"What chance, you fucking nutcase?"

"Amzi, really. Instead of hurling obscenities at me you should be thinking about the benefits you might reap."

"Benefits? Like what for example? Dismissal? Disgrace?"

"If all goes well, admiration of the nation, possibly a medal, almost surely a promotion—branch chief, chief of division, eventually. I'm on my way out. You can run this op, reap the glory, without ever mentioning my name."

Amzi Strange locked eyes with Father. Neither man yielded. By his own account, Father was calm, in control, enjoying himself. Strange was red in the face, breathing audibly, teeth clenched.

Trusting his voice at last, he said, "You're so fucking right about being on your way out. Get your sorry ass out of here. You're toast."

2

Father had committed the ultimate Washington sin of baring the ass of the Establishment. His Moscow prank made his betters look foolish, exposed the hesitancy of an agency that was chartered to be bold, and made it the jest of the month at Georgetown dinner parties. At Headquarters, a full internal investigation began. Amzi Strange was summoned home to be debriefed by the inspector general, who was in charge of this exercise. The IG operated on the assumption that everyone at Headquarters except him was a potential if not an actual double agent controlled by the intelligence service of a hostile power. Father thought that the IG was a psychopath in desperate need of treatment. The IG thought that Father was a dangerous saboteur who should long since have been fired—or, better yet, prosecuted for his antics at the Plantation.

Downfall in Washington among the mighty and the obscure alike typically stems from a trivial incident. In a cubbyhole outside the Oval Office, a president undergoes fellatio by a woman not his wife or discusses ways to cover up a Keystone Kops burglary, and thereby provides his enemies with an opportunity to destroy him without revealing their real purpose, which is to reverse the outcome of an election they lost but should have won if the voters had not been deceived by the political Beelzebub they feel it is their moral duty to overthrow.

The same rule applies to more humble figures, like Father, who discomfit the elite. Whether you are carrying out a coup d'état or the shaming of a nobody, it is essential that you be perceived as the virtuous avenger, and that your victim to be unmasked as the evil person he is and always has been.

In Father's case, kangaroo justice was swift and thorough. He was reduced two civil service grades in rank, fired for cause, and threatened with prosecution for violation of federal espionage laws and for cheating on his expense account. Father was not deprived of his pension, a pittance based on a percentage of his pay and his years of service, but the IG ruled that he had to wait until he reached retirement age to start collecting it. Meanwhile he had no income, and as a result of the divorce, few assets.

He was unemployable in any profession where Headquarters had friends. Former colleagues who had gone into business as government contractors shunned him. So did everyone else he had ever known at Headquarters. He was a fluent writer, but he soon discovered there was no market for his memoirs (which in any case would have to be cleared by Headquarters before publication), so he wrote a comic novel about undercover life, casting the leading character, based on himself, as the Little Tramp of espionage. The manuscript was rejected by twenty different publishers, none of whom read past page ten because they saw nothing funny about the unspeakable doings of the satanic thugs who, they devoutly believed, worked at Headquarters.

Finally, when Father was down to his last few dollars, he got a job working for a shady private investigator, but he had been a spy by trade, not a cop, so this didn't work out and he was let go after the probationary period. In letters to me he joked about buying a used taxicab and becoming a mobile philosopher.

As I have already reported, he and my mother, who was a lawyer at a backwater government agency, had led separate lives for many years. She had long since stopped accompanying him on foreign assignments, so I hardly ever saw him after the age of twelve, though he wrote me monthly letters and every summer he and I got together for two weeks wherever he happened to be posted. We went on safari in Tanganyika (I shot a kudu), hiked in the Himalayas, toured three-star restaurants in France. Among other ancient ruins, we visited Angkor Wat and the Taj Mahal and the ruined architecture of the Roman Near East, sailed in the Mediterranean and dived in the Red Sea.

He had real affection for me, I now realize. He made an effort to be amusing. Little shit that I was, I never laughed at his jokes.

When he was home he and Mother slept, while the marriage endured, in separate bedrooms and dined in silence. They never went out as a couple. Mother had an active social life, Father had none in the United States outside of bars. It all ended when, after his return from Moscow, he showed up at the house with his luggage. Mother shut the door in his face. From the Headquarters grapevine she had heard all about his latest outrage. She wanted no part of his disgrace, and besides, because of his heartless neglect, she had fallen in love with someone else.

Under the terms of an estate plan, executed years before, when my parents were still on speaking terms, the house was in her name, and Father's bank accounts were held jointly with her. Mother's own name—she was a lawyer, after all—was the only one on the bank accounts in which she deposited her earnings and the profits on the stocks and bonds she had inherited from her parents. When they divorced, she was awarded alimony and somewhat more than half of what remained of Father's paltry wealth.

When the final decree was handed down, I was studying in Beirut, and when I asked Mother over the telephone what Father was going to do now, she said, "I really have no idea. Maybe roam the world naked with his begging bowl."

In a way, Mother's quip about the begging bowl came true. Father was not left naked by the combination of disgrace and divorce, but he had exhausted his savings and sold everything of value that he still owned. After Mother and his lawyer took their share of the spoils—including, in Mother's case, thirty-six months of alimony in advance—he was literally penniless. He had three years to wait for his pension to start, and even after that happened, he would be left after taxes and alimony with a net annual income that was only slightly above the poverty line. Meanwhile he was well below it with no prospect of escape because the job market was closed to him. He applied for positions for which he was well qualified—he spoke four languages, had contacts all over the world, and was a capable manager—but never received a reply.

He bagged groceries at the Safeway where Mother's friends shopped, washed dishes in a restaurant and cars in a car wash. He begged for coins on the street, ate in soup kitchens, slept in shelters for the homeless in winter and in doorways in warm weather, and sometimes when the police were rounding up vagrants, spent a night in jail. He stopped writing to me, maybe because he couldn't afford the postage.

All this I learned later on. Mother, my only source of information about him, never mentioned Father in her breezy notes, invariably dashed off on tasteful blank greeting cards from the gift shop of the National Gallery of Art. The handwriting on these missives was slightly askew, as if she had written to me while waiting for traffic lights to change on commutes to and from the office.

Although I knew he was in trouble and adrift, I had little idea what was happening to Father—for all I knew he was dead or in prison—and to be truthful, I was not interested in knowing more. He was long gone from my life. Except for our annual quality time together, he had been absent since I was twelve years old. In theory I knew he loved me, or wanted to love me, but I gave him little encouragement and almost no thought. His face flickered in my memory as if I only had seen it, like that of a passerby, for a split second. I seldom bothered to read his letters, though I always opened them promptly to see if money was enclosed. Usually I found a twenty, or at Christmas and birthdays, a fifty. The bills were always fresh from the bank, crisp and new and good to smell. I seldom answered his letters. They were, I thought, false, contrived, presumptuous because the intimacy between us that they suggested did not exist and had never existed.

A couple of years passed before I completed my studies and went back to America. I had a knack for languages. Because I spoke and read and after a fashion wrote Arabic and Hebrew and three major Persian languages spoken in Iran and Afghanistan and had lived among Muslims in the Near East and knew a few who were educated and well placed, I was deluged with job offers from multinational corporations and government agencies. Billions were being poured into the war on terrorism, and everyone in Washington, it seemed, wanted to listen in on the enemies of the United States or interrogate them. Among other degrees—I prolonged adolescence for as long as I could—I had a PhD in Islamic studies and a passing acquaintance with a few people who counted in Muslim countries. My ambition was to teach languages and Islamic history and culture at a reputable small college and live in a large gingerbreaded Victorian brick house with a good-looking, good-natured, intelligent wife whose appetite for sex was as insatiable as my own and who wanted no kids.

Soon after I got off the plane in New York, a former professor introduced me to a friend, ostensibly a venture capitalist, who wined and dined me and one night offered me a handsome salary, a rent-free apartment in Washington, a leased car, and the opportunity to travel a lot and do good in the world and for myself in return for, as he put it, encouraging in their own languages certain persons in the Middle East to look kindly on his firm.

We were dining, just the two of us, in a New York restaurant where dinner for two cost five hundred dollars even if you ordered the second-best wine.

I had about as much interest in accepting this offer as of lying down on the FDR Drive at rush hour. However, my connection with Father had not left me in a state of total naïveté, so after listening to his pitch I said, "By the way, what's the name of your firm? You've never mentioned it."

"Actually it doesn't have a name, just a reputation. Ambiguity is an asset in my business."

"I see. Does your nameless firm ever do business with a large ambiguous enterprise with headquarters in northern Virginia?"

He smiled. "You ask the right questions," he said. "That's one of the things I like about you."

But he didn't answer the question.

I said, "Let me ask you this, then. Do you know who my father is?"

"I know a little about him. Very able man, as I understand it. A bit too able for some tastes, some say, and that was the problem."

At that point in the conversation, knowing the little I knew but also knowing what was coming next, I should have laid my silverware on my plate, dropped my napkin on the tablecloth, and left. Instead, because I had been living on kebab for a long time and I wanted to finish this elegant meal.

My suitor smiled. I had given him the key to my room.

"Be patient," he said. "There are better ways than taxable salary to be compensated for good work."

I told him I needed time to consider the offer.

As we parted on the sidewalk I said, "These people who talk about my father. Do you think they know how he can be found?"

"Let me get back to you on that," he replied.

A few days later he called me with the answer to my question.

A couple of weeks after that I found Father outside the Metro station at Gallery Place. He was begging for coins. He had stationed himself at the top of the escalator. When he saw me rise like an apparition from the underground, he took an exaggerated step backward and, still kidding, looked furtively right and left, as if seeking an escape route.

He was dressed in stained corduroy trousers, runover sneakers, tattered golf cap, worn-out tweed blazer torn at the shoulder. He carried a large khaki rucksack that was much the worse for wear. It was the same one he had bought for our two-week climbing expedition in the Alps when I was sixteen. I still owned its duplicate. I realized that the rucksack contained all his worldly goods—sleeping bag and overcoat, clothes and whatever other street person's essentials he carried around with him because he had no other place to keep them. He had lost weight, he had grown a full beard or let it grow for want of a razor. He looked beyond me, as if expecting someone more interesting to rise into view.

I said, "Hello, Father."

He said, "Hi. Is this encounter a stroke of fate or are you acting on information?"

"Someone told me you might be here at this time of day."

"Anyone I know?"

"He says not."

"He would say that. How do you know this person?"

"A friend introduced us."

"In that case," Father said, "beware. What time is it?"

I looked at my watch, an entry-level Rolex he had given me as a graduation present when I was eighteen. "Quarter after twelve."

"Have a seat over there, will you, and give me half an hour to work the crowd. That's why I'm here, to catch the lunchtime rush. Then *we'll* have lunch."

Despite the threadbare affect, he was behaving as if he still wore a tailor-made suit and shirt, a Sulka tie and Allen Edmonds shoes, and would be taking me to the Metropolitan Club for the midday meal. I sat down on a bench and watched him beg. He was good at it. He looked like what he was, a former somebody who had had a great fall. Most people gave him quarters. A few who perhaps saw him for what he used to be or what he was now or what they themselves might become, handed him dollar bills.

When the crowd dwindled, we walked down to Constitution Avenue, where lunch wagons were lined up at the curb near the National Gallery. He ordered two of the fat spicy hot dogs that Washingtonians call half-smokes, two bags of chips, and two bottles of spring water. When I tried to pay, he pushed my hand aside and counted out the money in quarters. We found a bench on the Mall and ate our half-smokes and Fritos in silence. Father gathered up our empty bags and plastic bottles and threw them into an overflowing trash basket.

He said, "So what prompted you to look me up?"

"Curiosity. Concern."

"In that order?"

"I haven't sorted that out."

Father spread his hands. "Well, here I am. Don't leap to conclusions. This is not such a bad life once you get over the surprise of having ended up a derelict. Simplicity, the absence of possessions, really does have more good points than bad. I used to think that was goody-goody bullshit, but it's true."

"You don't miss anything about the old life?"

"Hot showers, tennis, king-size beds with warm female bodies in them. Cleanliness. Being dirty all the time is an itchy way of life."

"You look thinner. Do you get enough food?"

"Oh, yes. Do-gooders supply plenty of day-old bread and soup and canned beans and venison—Park Service hunters secretly shoot the deer in Rock Creek Park at night and give the meat to the shelters. They say it's beef stew—otherwise the bums won't eat it. The experience is something like wandering bare-ass with a begging bowl in India, except not many people in this culture mistake the homeless for holy men."

"Funny you should say that about the begging bowl. Mother made a similar reference."

He lifted his eyebrows but made no comment.

I said, "What about conversation, the company of the like-minded?"

"Actually I never ran into many like-minded people," Father said. "But you might be surprised. Some of these outcasts are credentialed. A larger percentage are crazy, of course, but the demented can sound learned, and some of them *are* learned. You run into alcoholic ex-professors, disbarred lawyers, drug-addict doctors who have lost their licenses for selling prescriptions to pushers or jumping on their female patients, a few former wheeler-dealers who owe the Mob money. All sorts, all of them interesting in a one–dinner party kind of way."

"You don't mind living without money?"

"But I don't live without it. On a sunny day—never beg in the rain, son—I can make fifty bucks. That's where I stop. For one thing, fifty dollars' worth of quarters weighs a lot. That's one reason to spend them right away. Also, because of the addicts, it can be dangerous to go to sleep with money in your pocket. I work the crowd in different locations—Dupont Circle and the Zoo are good—two or three days a week, depending on the take, and have more than I can spend, tax free. You can buy cooked food and canned stuff and salads in supermarkets, so I eat a healthful diet. I have no expenses, no wants, no mortgage. No family obligations. No possessions anyone would want to steal. All very liberating. I'm sorry to have cut you off without a penny, but you look like you're doing all right."

Father was perfectly relaxed, as he always had been, and for the first time since early childhood I saw him for what he really was. As if some sort of psychic curtain had been pulled aside, I realized that I had disliked and resented him as an adolescent because, as I saw it, he had left Mother and me. Rejected us. Rejected me in particular. I wanted to pay him back, to let him know that there was no chance, none whatsoever, that he would ever recover the love he had forfeited. His only child would never come back to him. Take *that,* you bastard!

Seeing Father as he was now and always had been, watching as his original face became ever more visible through the grime and the beard, I realized all of a sudden how deeply I loved him and what powerful reasons I had to do so. He had put up with me when I was at my worst. Long before I was a man, he had treated me like a man. He might not have made a man of me, but he equipped me to make a man of myself without once letting me know what he was doing. Now he was showing me how to lose everything with effortless grace.

This was—I am going to come right out and say this—a religious moment. Something came over me. Some invisible savior in whom I had never believed had laid his invisible hands upon me. Mixed with this total stranger of a thought was a sudden resolution: now that I had found my father, I wanted never to let him go. On the spot and in this mystical moment I decided to take the job in Washington that the venture capitalist had offered me.

I said, "Look, there's something I want to tell you."

Father nodded amiably. *Go right ahead.*

"I'm taking a job in Washington," I said.

"Congratulations. May you be happy in your work."

"Here's the thing. I'll have a good-size apartment. I hope you'll move in with me."

"Oh, my," Father said.

He didn't ask who I was going to be working for or what I was going to be doing. After a moment he looked me in the eyes again.

"The prodigal to the rescue," he said. "How good of you to invite me. I am touched. But really, I think not."

"Why not?"

"We just got through discussing that. I am otherwise engaged."

"Don't worry about being a burden to me," I said.

"Why would I worry about that? You were a burden to me. But really, I couldn't. I don't want to. I'm where I want to be."

"Jesus!"

Father grinned. "I hate to ask," he said, "but have you found Jesus? Is that what's going on here?"

"Not even a brush contact," I replied.

"'A brush contact.' You remember the lingo, I see."

"Actually I remember almost everything you ever tried to teach me in spite of my best efforts to ignore it. You won't change your mind?"

"No. But thank you."

Clearly this was his last word.

I said, "I hope you don't rule out our staying in touch."

"Of course not. Maybe I'll drop by every now and again for a shower and the use of your washing machine. But let me make the moves. I have no fixed abode, so finding me may not be a simple matter."

I scribbled my cell phone number on a scrap of paper.

Father took the number and buttoned it into a pocket.

"Thanks, I'll keep this," he said. "But it's hard to find a pay phone nowadays, so actually calling you might be a problem."

He held out his hand. The nails were rimmed with black. I knew I might never see him again. I did not take his hand, but instead embraced him. He hugged me back, patted me consolingly on the back. The rancid smell of him, so different from the mingled scents of Roger & Gallet shampoo, fresh air, and Tanqueray No. Ten gin that I had known so well, was memorable. I wondered what passersby made of this spectacle of a derelict and a weeping young man locked in an embrace. After a moment, Father disentangled us.

He said, "Awfully good to see you."

And then he turned on his heel and walked away—purposefully, quickly, but not hurriedly. It was not in his genes to hurry.

Soon after this, I moved to Washington and on my lunch hours checked out the Metro stations where he might be begging, but never found him. He never called the cell phone number I had given him.

In early winter on a day after a heavy snowfall, I received a call from the police, who had found my cell phone number in the pocket of a street person who had been stabbed to death as he slept in the doorway of a building not far from the Capitol. I went to the morgue and identified the body. I had never before seen his naked body. When I had imagined him as a corpse, he was always lying in dim light in a coffin, fully dressed, wearing his habitual half-smile. Now, in the bluish fluorescent light, his deeply peaceful face looked quite Christ-like—something like the talismanic photographs of Che Guevara's face after he was slain in Bolivia by friends of Headquarters.

With the help of the staff of a congressman who was a member of Father's Yale society, I arranged for his ashes to be placed in the columbarium in Arlington National Cemetery. The urn was carried to its niche by an honor guard of frozen-faced young soldiers wearing dress-blue uniforms. A chaplain read from scripture. I did not listen to the words. A recording of "Taps" was played.

I was the only mourner. I had bought a funeral notice in the *Washington Post* and informed a silent Mother of his death by telephone. She did not show up, and neither did anyone from Headquarters or his secret society or anywhere else from the lost city of his past. I placed the urn in its niche, and as I did so, my unconscious mind, if that's what the agent of these visions was, provided me with another surprise.

Without warning, rage took possession of me. I shook with the palsy of it. The diffident chaplain looked at me with alarm, so I guess my face was contorted—red, possibly, wet with tears certainly. I could no more control what was happening to me than I could have controlled a fall from the top of the Empire State Building. I uttered a loud sob, then another and another—not because I was grief-stricken, but because I felt uncontrollable anger. I had never experienced anything like this before, but I immediately recognized it for what it was, the internal savage bursting out of the cave.

This time a different being had come up behind me and laid another kind of hands upon me. I wanted revenge. I hungered for it. I cared for nothing else.

This was what those bastards had done to my father to avenge a joke— a fucking *joke*!

In an act that would have been unimaginable to me before I met my real self that day, I swore on Father's ashes that I would make Headquarters pay. I would make it my life's purpose to make it pay.

3

It was exhilarating to have a secret purpose to live by. Until that bone-rattling epiphany in the columbarium at Arlington I had been a stranger to such excitement, just as I was new to hatred. Nevertheless I would have my revenge. It was all I wanted. My intention was irrevocable. The problem was, how to put the plot in motion. Obviously the only way to carry out my plan to wreck the mechanism that had destroyed my father, to put an end to the damned thing, was to get inside it and by doing good work, earn the absolute trust that alone could make my revenge possible.

Given my father's odor among the old guard, this was no small under-taking. Any number of approaches were open to me, most of them unpromising. However, I was not a babe in the woods. I knew how the Headquarters mind worked. I had been around Headquarters people for most of my life, and I was sure that at least some of Father's admirers would wish to help me. Even his enemies would be impelled to give me the benefit of the doubt because one of their delusions about themselves was that they believed in fair play, that the code they lived by mandated fair play. They weren't the sort of fellows, they told themselves, who punished sin unto the third, or even the second, generation. The problem was finding a way in, so as to give them their favorite thing: an opportunity to congratulate themselves.

According to a training manual called *Locks, Picks, Flaps and Seals* that Father liked to quote, there was no lock that could not be picked, no code that could not be broken. What man had devised, man could circumvent. He was fond of quoting his favorite author, W. Somerset Maugham, whom he loved for his clear-eyed cynicism, to the effect that happiness comes only by indirection and can never be achieved by a conscious effort of the will. In other words, don't try to create opportunity. Instead, wait for it to come your way and when it does, manage it. Of course he had done exactly that at the Plantation and in Moscow, and it had cost him dearly. But that didn't mean that the principle was unsound.

Actually I suspected that the opportunity I awaited had already come my way. I assumed that the venture capitalist who had appeared out of the blue was in the employ of Headquarters, or at least did Headquarters favors in return for the favors it could do for him. Further, I suspected that this absurdly easy job with the venture capitalist, for which I was grossly overpaid, was something Father's admirers at Headquarters had arranged as a way of assuaging their guilt for not having had the stones to stand up for him. The bottom line was that I was not sure who I was working for, or what exactly I was doing, or who benefitted from the result-free things I did.

Sometimes days, even weeks, would go by without a word from the venture capitalist. When he did call, he sounded like he had spoken to me ten minutes earlier, in tones normally used when talking to one's best friend. To kill time I read scholarly books on jihadism and postmodern novels dripping with narcissism in which nothing interesting ever happened. I watched movies on the enormous flat television screen that came with the free apartment, had dinner with old friends, looked up women I had known in school who now had power jobs in the administration or on Capitol Hill and were in many cases freshly divorced and adventurous in their sex lives. Few asked questions about my work. Rarely did they imagine it could be as interesting or as important as what they were doing. Washington was full of people who made good money for achieving results that could not be measured and that they couldn't talk about.

It is easier to agree with a theory such as Father's notion about opportunity than it is to live by it. Little by little I grew tired of keeping an ear cocked for opportunity to knock. I liked to go to the National Gallery. Viewing the paintings that great artists had plucked from thin air was an experience as close to spiritual escape as the modern world provides. The negative part was that, thanks to twenty-first-century technology from which there was no escape, you remained in constant touch with anyone who wanted to punch in your cell phone number and yank you back into the world.

One day as I approached Jan de Bray's *Portrait of the Artist's Parents,* a lanky man stepped between me and the painting as if I were invisible. I half recognized him: something about his shoulders, which were high and unnaturally square. I drifted to the next picture and looked him over more carefully. I knew his profile—long straight nose, clean jawline, oddly whorled ear. He was bald now and wore a hearing aid, but I remembered him from my childhood, when he was often at our house. He had been Father's classmate at school and they had both ended up at Headquarters—in those days there was nothing unusual about that in their circle. A quarter century before, he had been Robert Redford handsome, with a full head of thick blond hair and keen blue eyes beneath thick eyebrows. Now he was a cartoon of that person in shades of gray.

Still I remembered him as he had been—in every way. Once during a party in our large overfurnished apartment in Budapest when I was twelve or so, I wandered into the kitchen and found him kissing my mother, who was kissing him back in a way that suggested they had done this many times before.

I said, "Bill Stringfellow?"

Stringfellow hadn't seen me in twenty years.

He looked me up and down and said, "Good grief, you look just like your old man."

The National Gallery of Art was the last place I would have expected to bump into the Bill Stringfellow I used to know. He was no art lover. What I remembered best about him was his hunger for exercise. Back then, he ran miles before breakfast, he played tennis on his lunch hour and handball after work, he swam laps and played water polo in the YMCA pool. On Saturdays he took thirty-mile bicycle rides and sometimes, on Sundays, organized Kennedy-style neighborhood touch football games. The gym fad had not yet come into being, but if that form of exertion had then existed, I have no doubt that Bill would have found time to work out on the apparatuses.

He and his pretty but eerily silent wife lived just down the street from our house in McLean, and he and Father sometimes overlapped in the same foreign capital. I found myself remembering, as the artist's grim parents looked the other way, that Mother had taken up predawn running in the months before we were posted to Hungary, so maybe Bill did find time for another form of exercise. Certainly Mother returned flushed and smiling from her daily workout.

Stringfellow took no time to exchange pleasantries but glanced at his watch and said, "Look, I've got an appointment in two minutes. But let's meet in the café in the underground passage at eleven sharp and talk about old times. Now shoo. You don't want to meet this character."

I understood. Stringfellow was meeting an agent and I was—by inheritance, I guess—still eligible to know this. This was good news. If he was having clandestine meetings, he was still working. Therefore he was a godsend, because his looks and brains and good work had won him high rank, so he knew the combination to the invisible lock on Headquarters.

His invitation to coffee might just mean that he thought he owed Father's memory a favor—that because of those encounters with Mother and the fact that he had in cold blood watched Father drown, he might blackmail himself into lending me a hand. Bill Stringfellow might be a stranger to guilt. But he lived by the code of snobs. If he and Father had not actually been fast friends, they had for most of their lives been members of the same cohort. Sticking together, doing each other favors, was the founding obligation of the code. I was not sure where Bill's screwing my mother fitted into that value system.

At the café, instead of coffee he drank a bottle of water, my treat. He asked what I had been up to. I told him.

He said, "Arabic, Farsi, Hebrew? Anything else?"

"Pashto. I flounder around in a couple of European languages."

"Credentials?"

"Doctorate in Islamic studies."

"What university?"

I told him. He whistled. "You're a recruiter's dream."

Stringfellow leaned toward me, lowered his voice as if sharing a delicate secret, and said, "Look, I'm sorry about your father. Damn shame."

"I agree."

Stringfellow said, "Where was he buried?"

"He wasn't. He was cremated and inurned—that's the official term—in the columbarium, quote-unquote, at Arlington."

Stringfellow snorted. "He would have gotten a kick out of that."

"Out of what?"

"The terminology. He was in the all-time backfield of the politically incorrect. Brilliant, but reckless."

"He was?"

"All his life. He was the same at school, a disruptive influence. The faculty detested him because he made fun of them, joked circles around them in class, made the boys laugh at them. He was constantly in the doghouse, not that it made a particle of difference to him. He was what he was. So are all of us from the moment the sperm penetrates the egg, but your father absolutely insisted on it."

"That was the problem?"

"There were those who thought he was too witty to be lovable. He refused to hide his intelligence or suppress his amusement—just simply refused to accept the principle. Not that he didn't have his successes. He did, the other guys admired him even if they didn't have the guts to emulate him, which didn't cause the people in charge to love him any the more."

All true. I waited to hear more.

Stringfellow filled the silence. "Don't misunderstand me. He got a raw deal. Lots of us were unhappy about that."

"That's good to know. There were no sympathy cards."

"No? I'm not surprised. Nobody writes to a pariah. Who was at the—what's the word?"

"Inurnment," I said. "Me."

"Just you? Not your Mother?"

I maintained my silence. Stringfellow searched my face for an answer, and found it, I guess.

"Damn shame," he said again.

He looked as though he had just begun to talk, but I didn't want him to unload everything at this meeting. If that happened I might never see him again, and I wanted this conversation to go on. Stringfellow was my best chance, my way in.

I said, "Tell me what *you're* up to. Or as much as you can."

"Same old same old," said Stringfellow.

"You must be near retirement."

"I *am* retired."

"But you still meet people at a prearranged time in front of a particular Dutch painting?"

He smiled. "I went back to work on a contract. Lots of formers do that. The money is pretty good—government pensions are not all they're cracked up to be."

"So our war on terror has blown someone some good?"

"Make that terror's war on us. But yes. There are a lot more slots since 9/11 and a lot of the younger fellows don't want to go to places where there are suicide bombers and boredom and very little pussy. That's not what they signed up for. A faint heart is now regarded as acceptable, I can't imagine why."

We talked about the past, about my childhood. He remembered a surprising amount about me—for example, the time he threw me a pass in a touch football game when I was about ten and somehow I caught the ball in the end zone. He had taught me to play backgammon and cribbage. Our families picnicked together at home and abroad, boated on the Danube and, cheering, watched the Germans tear down the Wall in Berlin. When everyone was in Virginia at the same time, Stringfellow had sometimes taken me to Orioles games during the team's great days: Ripken, Mussina, Eddie Murray.

We talked for an hour or more before he got a phone call and had to run. In the process I think I was transformed in his mind from the child he remembered into the grown-up I had become. I came back into focus. This was vital.

I gave him my business card. He told me his phone number, speaking the digits rapidly, as if I were a junior spook required to memorize it. In fact I did remember it long enough to write it down as he rode the moving walkway into the crowd of sightseers.

As we parted—no handshake—he said, "Funny, you do look like your father but you don't remind me of him in any way."

He offered this rude insult to my father's memory as if it were a compliment.

After a fashion, this was encouraging. Although federal law prohibits discrimination on the basis of race, religion, or national origin, and by implication, DNA, and all that jazz about fair play, I was still under no illusion that Headquarters would be eager to hire my father's son. On the other hand, Bill Stringfellow had a point—I was a recruiter's dream, possessed of all the skills and credentials an intelligence service looks for in a candidate for seduction.

Besides that, I was a Headquarters brat who knew the rules, even if my parent had broken nearly all of them. In my case, however, qualifications would not be enough to overcome the distaste of the old guard for anyone related to my father. Knocking on the front door would be futile. Headquarters—or more accurately, someone within Headquarters who had been on Father's side—had to seek me out and let me in the back door. Stringfellow was perfect for the part. The back door to an intelligence service is always open. When an operational purpose exists, the most unbreakable rules can be finessed.

I let a few days go by, then called the cell phone number Stringfellow had given me. I half expected a female computer to answer and tell me the number I had reached was not in service. Instead, after six rings, I heard Bill's preppy drawl repeating the last four digits of the number, as was Headquarters' style.

I identified myself.

A droplet of silence. Then, in a flat tone, he said, "What?"—as in, "what do you want?"

"I'm calling to invite you to lunch."

"You are? Why?"

"Because our last conversation was left unfinished."

"And you think we need to tie up the loose ends?"

More gratuitous rudeness. This was a test.

I said, "Come on, Bill. I'm just inviting you to lunch. A simple yes or no will do."

More silence. Then, "Where? When?"

I named a pricey wheeler-dealers' hangout on K Street.

"Thursday at twelve?"

"Do they know you in this place?"

"I've been there once before. We'll probably get a table next to the kitchen."

"All right. But if I'm more than ten minutes late, it means something has come up and I can't make it."

Click. The scene was set, and I hoped Stringfellow thought he was the one who had set it.

I was in no way sure that Bill Stringfellow would show up, but if he did, it would be for an operational purpose and the ball would be rolling. On Thursday I waited in the restaurant suppressing expectation, and eight minutes after I was seated Stringfellow appeared.

He spotted me at once and made his way to my table. He beckoned a waiter.

"Pellegrino," he said. "Cold. Large bottle, in an ice bucket."

The waiter scurried away. *His Master's Voice.*

To me, Stringfellow said, "So what's edible here?"

"Wild mushroom strudel. The rockfish. I haven't tried anything else."

"You always eat the same thing?"

"As I said, this is the second time I've been here."

"No wonder you got such a good table."

We were, as I had expected, at the worst table in the restaurant. Stringfellow's tone was just short of contemptuous and offered no hint that he was kidding. You might think he was a son of a bitch, but Stringfellow didn't mind that. It didn't matter to him what you thought of him. Playing this role was his stock-in-trade, and it occurred to me as the waiter poured his Italian mineral water that this might be one of the reasons for his success with women. His scorn made them want to make amends for giving offense when none was intended.

Stringfellow ordered the dishes I had recommended—the first step in his imminent transformation into a nice guy. He was a workmanlike eater and gave his food his full attention, picking up the crumbs of the strudel crust with his fingers and popping them into his mouth, demolishing the fish and the four tiny potatoes that came with it. He ordered Gorgonzola and a pear for dessert. I asked for a different kind of cheese and grapes.

He pointed a finger at the grapes: "Little capsules of sugar," he said.

I said, "Then I'm surprised you didn't order them yourself. All that exercise must burn up a lot of sugar. Or are you no longer into that?"

"Shorter distances, slower time, less sweat, creakier joints, but I still work out whenever I can. And you're right, burning up sugar is one of the benefits."

I ordered a double espresso. Stringfellow stuck to Pellegrino. He didn't need caffeine.

He put a slice of pear into his mouth and chewed. "You mentioned the other day that you had a job," he said. "Doing what?"

I described what I did.

He said, "You get paid for this?"

"Yes."

"How much?"

He asked for this information as if he had a natural right to know it. Why should I object? He could keep a secret, he had known me all my life. He was more to me than my father's colleague and my mother's lover.

I gave him a number, less than my actual salary and bonuses but more, I was sure, than he had made in the best year he ever worked at Headquarters.

"Impressive," Stringfellow said. "And who exactly do you work for again?"

I told him the venture capitalist's name.

"Rings no bells," Stringfellow said. "Who is he?"

"He's a venture capitalist."

"Where does the money come from?"

"Capitalistic ventures, I guess."

"You *guess*? You checked him out, of course. What did you find out?"

"I Googled him. Sixty-five entries, all of which confirmed his story."

"What kind of entries?"

"Mentions in the *Wall Street Journal* and the *Financial Times* about deals he was involved in. He says he went to Yale, and sure enough, he's listed on the rolls as an alumnus. Ezra Stiles College, class of '86, economics major with a minor in Japanese."

Stringfellow said, "And he just appeared out of the blue and said he wanted to pay you all that money to run errands?"

"You could say that. He was introduced by a professor we both had. The professor vouched for him."

"Which professor?"

"Maude Fisk, the Arabist."

"Don't know her, either. After my time. You're not worried that you might be working unwittingly for the Saudi intelligence service or the Mossad or that this man of mystery finances terrorist operations?"

I said, "Let me ask *you* a question. Why are you asking me these questions?"

"Professional habit," Stringfellow replied. "Avuncular concern. To postpone talking about your father. Also because I like asking questions better than I like answering them."

"Are we here to talk about my father?"

"Aren't we?"

"There's not much to be said about him I haven't already heard. I know how he was and what he is said to have done and what the consequences were."

"He did it up brown, all right. You think he got what was coming to him?"

"I think he got screwed. But it's over. He's ashes. There aren't twenty people left in the world who would recognize his name if they read it on his niche in the columbarium."

"You're not going to brief your kids, supposing you have any?"

"No, and no."

This was profoundly misleading, but lies are the truth of spies, and in every way that mattered, I was already an operative in the field, laying the groundwork for an operation that might take twenty-five years to bear fruit. By that time, of course, the people on whom I was planning to take my revenge would be gone and forgotten, but it was the institution I wanted to shatter.

This was a new thought. It made me smile to myself.

Stringfellow said, "What's so funny?"

"Just thinking of Father."

"You learned to like him, then?"

"I always did."

"Really? You didn't seem to like him all that much when you were a kid."

As if he had just hooked me up to a polygraph, Headquarters's tool of tools, he watched for a reaction.

When none emerged, Stringfellow said, "He and I had a funny sort of relationship. I liked him well enough, and I think he may have thought I was all right, but that warped sense of humor of his was a problem. You couldn't penetrate it. It was his psychological hiding place. That was true even when he was fourteen."

And until the day he died, I thought.

"Your mother talked about that," Stringfellow said. "She—"

I showed him my palm. "If you don't mind, I'd rather not talk to you about my mother."

This turned the tables. Stringfellow looked as if he had just walked full tilt into a plate glass door. He shut up and gave me a look of surprise.

I *knew.* He had been caught in the act by a child. He hadn't expected this.

The next few minutes were wordless. I paid the check. We made our way outside. The moment we emerged from the refrigerated restaurant into the sweltering Washington day, our clothes began to absorb—*suck*—the humidity.

Stringfellow said, "Are you still an Orioles fan?"

"I guess so, but I can't tell the new players without a scorecard. I lost touch with the team while I was abroad."

"That happens. They'll be in town, playing the Nats in an interleague game on Sunday. I have a couple of tickets behind the third-base dugout. Want to join me?"

"Gladly."

He fished a ticket from his coat pocket and handed it to me. "See you there, game starts at one o'clock. And, oh, we'll be joined by another guy. An admirer of your father's."

The ball was rolling.

4

On the day of the game the venture capitalist phoned at six in the morning and asked me to meet a client at a golf resort in West Virginia.

"Take your clubs," he said. "Tee time is eleven o'clock. Lunch afterward. Shortish, stocky fellow, Mediterranean looks, call him Karim. You won't have to let him win."

"Any particular topic of conversation?"

"He'll fill you in."

It was a four-hour drive from Washington to the resort. I left regrets on Bill Stringfellow's voice mail and was on my way in twenty minutes, golf clubs and spikes in the trunk, cup of coffee in my left hand, NPR's *Morning Edition* on the radio. In the dappled morning light the city, wrapped in a light mist, looked more beautiful than it really was.

Karim turned out to be an unsmiling Iranian with cold brown eyes and a dark blue chin. He wore a white visor and shirt that made the stubble more noticeable. He shook my hand, looked me straight in the eye and nodded, as if my face matched a face he had seen in photographs. For the first five minutes he spoke native American English. After we teed off and were alone, he switched to Farsi and, when I spoke the language, became more genial. He made small talk about the shots we made or didn't make and the magnificent course, which had been designed with people who could afford the heavy greens fees in mind. He paid me no compliments on my fluency, unless simply talking to me as if I were a native speaker could be considered a nod of approval.

We played nine holes. He was a very good golfer. We had bet a dollar a stroke, and after nine holes I paid my debt.

He took the twenty-dollar bill. This was six dollars more than I owed him but he offered no change. Now that we were no longer alone, he switched back to English.

"If you don't mind, we'll have lunch in my room," he said.

A table was already set—cold soup, grilled salmon, and salad. No alcohol, no dessert. Like Bill Stringfellow, Karim was a businesslike eater—no conversation. Evidently he had got the pleasantries out of the way on the fairway.

Karim poured the coffee, thin, bitter, scalding-hot American stuff, and as we drank it he produced a thin canvas briefcase from behind a sofa cushion. He extracted the six one-dollar bills he owed me and handed them to me along with a sheet of paper folded in quarters and a pen. He handed both to me, dollars with one hand, paper and pen with the other.

I unfolded the paper. It was a secrecy agreement. In the lingo, it was sterile—no letterhead, no hint of exactly whose secrets I was, by signing it, promising never to divulge to anyone, under any circumstances, under penalty of perjury and other more punitive federal laws.

Karim said, "If you'll sign that paper, we can get down to the business at hand."

I signed it.

Karim put the document back into the briefcase and withdrew a blue-backed legal document.

He said, "Read this carefully, please. Twice. Take your time. Then we'll talk. Please hold the questions until after you've read it."

He moved to another chair and opened a copy of the *Washington Post*.

The blue-backed document was, as I had surmised, a contract of employment. No one had ever described such a contract to me, but as a little spy at my parents' parties and barbecues I had overheard enough so that its appearance and contents and the manner in which it had been rendered came as no surprise.

The contract was addressed, as if it were a letter, to Mr. Randolph A. Sinclair. That is not my name, but I knew, too, that it was the pseudonym—"funny name"—by which I would be identified in top secret files, and with which I would sign this contract and all official internal documents throughout the career that was being offered to me.

The terms were simple and clear. I would do as I was told, go where I was sent, and keep the secrets I was entrusted with. I could be fired with or without cause at any time without notice or explanation. These were the essentials. There was also a certain amount of boilerplate, but no more than any contract contains. I would be deemed to have reported for duty by signing the contract. My starting salary would be that of a Step 5 GS-13, the civil service grade that corresponds to the military rank of lieutenant-colonel—the same as Father's before he was busted to GS-11. The salary was significantly less than I was now being paid, but there would be allowances, mostly tax free, that would narrow the gap.

I said, "What will I be doing, exactly?"

"It's impossible to predict," Karim said. "As your contract states, whatever is required."

"Where will I be doing this?"

"Wherever you're needed."

"Inside or outside?"

"An insider on the outside for the time being. You'll have too much rank, given your age and experience, to work at Headquarters. We can hardly start you off as a deputy branch chief."

"This says I start immediately. I don't have a security clearance."

"But you do. You'll have to be polygraphed before your employment becomes official, but that's a formality. You'll do that in the next room before you leave here. It's like an electrocardiogram."

"Why are you interested in me? And why are you paying me so much money?"

"Your qualifications, the job you did for Jeffrey."

Jeffrey was the venture capitalist's name.

"But actually for Headquarters?"

No answer.

I said, "You do know who my father was?"

Karim was prepared for this question.

He said, "We're not hiring your father."

"How can his reputation not enter into it?"

Karim looked at me without expression, wordlessly, for a long moment. Why was I arguing against my own interests?

Finally he said, "If you sign this contract, your life starts over on Monday. If you don't, you'll be unemployed. We won't bother you again."

"What exactly will happen on Monday if I sign?"

"You will be collected at seven-thirty A.M. in front of Zorba's Café—you know where it is—by a man in a gray Toyota Corolla with Maryland plates. Take a suitcase—one suit or blazer and dress trousers, a week's worth of casual clothes, a rain jacket, a sweater, walking shoes. The driver will roll down the window and say, 'Top of the mornin', George, climb in.' You will respond, 'You're right on time, Harold, let's hit the highway.'"

Karim got up and knocked on the door that led to the next room. The polygraph operator, a fiftyish fellow in jeans who looked like he had tucked a medicine ball under his T-shirt, opened the door. He hooked me up to his machine and tonelessly asked me the questions you might expect him to ask. Was I a traitor, a thief, did I use illegal drugs, did I ever get drunk, how often did I masturbate and did I watch pornography while I did it? Had I ever committed murder, rape, or sexually molested a child or an animal? Since none of these was the right question—how could it be?—I answered truthfully. The whole process was as painless as Karim had suggested it would be.

Apparently I passed, because I signed the contract moments after I returned to Karim's room.

Karim administered the oath. Before he did so, he said, "This is not an oath to an abstraction. It is a promise, sacred and irrevocable, to human beings who will entrust you with their lives, their families, their reputations. Bear that always in mind."

I had never taken oaths seriously. In the past, I knew, they had led to a lot of mischief. I raised my right hand and repeated the words of the oath. They were simple and written in such a way that they could not possibly be misunderstood. We shook on it.

As I closed the door behind me I was shaking hands with myself. Against all odds I had done what I had set out to do, and it had been a walk in the park, requiring nothing but a straight face and my signature. My father's friends had made this happen. What other explanation could there be? I didn't speculate on their reasons. I was in, as I had wanted to be. That's all I needed to know.

But was it?

After I had driven a hundred miles in a euphoric daze, I felt the body punch of reality. What had I done? I stopped the car and got out. It was a bright midsummer day, so hot that the view of the Blue Ridge Mountains was slightly blurred by the overheated air. A tamed landscape, picture-book fields of crops in the near distance, green forest beyond, lay between the mountains and me.

I was all alone in the rest area, no sound to be heard, no other human being or dwelling to be seen. A wave of anxiety broke over me. For a long moment, as if I were in fact underwater, I could not breathe. I saw myself signing the contract, smelled the ink, heard the scratch of the pen. Good God, what had I done in the grip of exaltation? I didn't really know. Had I signed up with Headquarters, as I had believed, and thereby hammered the first nail into the coffin I planned to build for it, or had I walked into a trap from which I would never escape? Would the gray Toyota Corolla that was going to pick me up in front of Zorba's Café the next morning bright and early carry me a mile closer to my revenge, or render me into the hands of torturers who awaited me at some black site in Turkey or Egypt or Afghanistan?

I told myself to get a grip. If Karim was what I had taken him to be, I was home free. But was he? I had no idea. For all I knew he had murdered and taken the place of the person I was supposed to meet. I had taken it on faith that this total stranger who showed me no credentials was who and what he did not say he was. I had taken the authenticity of the secrecy agreement and the contract on faith. I had signed the documents, I had handed myself over to I knew not what or whom.

True, Jeffrey the venture capitalist, whom I had also taken on blind trust, had put the two of us together. But who and what was Jeffrey? It was not beyond the capability of hackers to create a Google entry for an impostor. Was he real? Who controlled him? My old professor, naive as she was, had vouched for him, but as Bill Stringfellow had asked, what was that worth? Stringfellow, friend of the family, had brusquely been cut out of the game and I had been glad to let this happen because he had cuckolded my father and I didn't like the way he played the snob. I could hardly call him up now and ask him if he knew anyone named Karim.

This was a full-scale fit of paranoia. I understood that, even as fear shook me like a rag doll. I had, as Bill Stringfellow might have phrased it, put a foot wrong. Even if Karim was the genuine Headquarters officer

I had taken him to be, even if I had signed up with the right employer, I had behaved like a credulous fool.

I willed myself to end this one-man wrestling match, but the anxiety would not quit.

Doom held me in its hand.

When in an irrational state, it helps to talk. I had no one to talk to, I never did, so I talked to myself. I gave myself a tongue-lashing. Like a Communist or a Christian gone berserk during a self-criticism session, I put myself on trial not only for the failures of the day, but also for every stupid move I had ever made, and I could remember them all.

After all this venting, I felt somewhat better. The odds were that Karim was exactly what I had taken him to be, that the door of Father's enemies had opened and let me in, and the game really was afoot. If so, I had a problem. I had imagined I could do what I wanted to do alone. Now I saw that this was impossible, because from now on anxiety was going to be my constant companion.

The loner I was going to make of myself needed someone to talk to—someone to whom I could speak truth. Someone who would speak truth to me. I could not live without this—literally. But there were no candidates for the job.

At the time I didn't know that Luz Aguilar existed, let alone that she, too, had a father who had been destroyed by fools and a thirst for revenge that was equal to my own. But that was the moment when, consciously or unconsciously, I started to look for her.

5

The gray Toyota Corolla, gleaming with wax and neat as a pin inside, picked me up in front of Zorba's at 7:29 A.M. This was a noteworthy feat of timing, considering how heavy traffic was at that hour of the morning. It was a bright day. The driver, a ruddy, gray-haired fellow who wore a blazer of Master's Cup green, repeated the recognition phrase Karim had given me. I supplied the response.

"Hop in," he said. I hopped in anyway.

Offering a meaty hand, he said, "I'm Sam. Please let me have your wallet and your cell phone."

I handed them over. Sam gave me a receipt, typed on plain paper and already signed with an illegible scrawl.

He said, "Thanks. This stuff will be returned to you when you finish your mission. Meanwhile it'll be sealed in a bag and locked in a safe. No one will have access to it. No photographs, no uploads. As the saying goes, your privacy is important to us. Do you have any other ID on your person or in your luggage? Luggage tag? Checkbook, anything?"

"No."

I had very little cash in my pocket, and no way of getting any without an ATM card unless I wanted to beg for quarters outside a Metro station. For a moment I was tempted to repeat my earlier tantrum and accuse myself of being stupid, naive, docile, contemptible. I shoved the impulse back into the primitive brain. Sam put my belongings into a plastic bag, sealed it, and tossed it into the glove compartment.

He said, "Don't reveal your true name to anyone you meet while this lasts. Okay?"

While what lasts?

I said, "What alias should I use?"

"Your choice, but something you're sure you can remember, like the name of your best buddy in third grade. Or your worst enemy, as long as he's not somebody we know."

He took his eyes off the road for an instant and flashed another white smile.

He said, "Ridiculous, this mumbo jumbo, but it's de rigueur. Before you know it, it'll be second nature to you. Rigmarole is important in this business. So is trust. One reinforces the other. They're just forms of reassurance, really. Recite the jabberwocky, get the answer you expect, and you know you're talking to the right person. Unless, of course, the contact is an imposter who kidnapped the right person and assumed his identity after torturing the password and countersign out of him. Have you snatched anyone who looks just like you and waterboarded them lately?"

I didn't respond. He ran on.

"You'd think that an organization that wants to be impenetrable would also want to be unpredictable, mix up the procedures, keep outsiders guessing, but that's not the way it works," he said. "You'll live according to black etiquette from now on. It's not complicated, but you have to stick to the formula. The alternative is pandemonium. The Brits taught us the drill, as they call tradecraft, when we were babes in the woods, back during the Second World War, and I guess the Romans trained the Brits and the Greeks the Romans, and the gods trained the Greeks, so we're reading from a rule book written on clay tablets in cuneiform."

Sam went on with this banter, never silent for a moment, during the drive to a farmhouse in the mountains of western Maryland. It was his way, I supposed, of fending off questions. I was under no illusion that he was making it all up as he went along. Probably he had tried out these same quips on every novice he ever collected in his Corolla. The house came into view at last.

Sam said, *"Nous sommes arrivés."*

The house was a puritanically plain two-story structure, square and painted white, maybe a hundred years old, with a big front porch. Rocking chairs on the stoop. Flowering shrubs. Hollyhocks and daisies in the flower beds. A swing hung from the branch of an oak, a basketball hoop missing the webbing was nailed to the barn. An old mud-splashed pickup truck was parked in the driveway. There were other outbuildings, a chicken coop, a corncrib, a barn of unpainted lumber weathered gray. Corn and potatoes and other crops grew in nearby fields. It didn't quite have the feel of a working farm. It looked like what it was, a stage set. Whether it would have seemed that way if I hadn't known it was a safe house was another question.

Sam used his smart phone to turn off the alarm system and unlock the door—two dead bolts. We went inside.

"Nobody home yet," Sam said, as if in my untrained state I wouldn't have noticed this without help.

He showed me around, as if teaching me how to case a joint: decent, worn furniture, rag rugs and samplers (LET ME LIVE IN A HOUSE BY THE SIDE OF THE ROAD AND BE A FRIEND TO MAN.) in the living and dining rooms, linoleum in the kitchen, varnished woodwork and flowered wallpaper throughout. Two bedrooms and one bath with tub but no shower upstairs, faded, mended Walmart clothes in the closets and drawers, a spare room fitted out like a home office: old desk, outdated computer with no Internet connection. No printer. A rotary dial black telephone.

Sam said, "Don't use the phone. Store nothing on the computer's hard drive. The CD and flash drives are disabled. Can you cook?"

"I can use a microwave."

"Good. The nearest McDonald's is ten miles down the road, and you'll have no wheels after the other guys go home at the end of the day, so it's heat up this stuff or go hungry."

Tires crunched in the gravel drive. Sam held out a hand.

"So long," he said. "Have fun."

As the front door opened and another total stranger entered, Sam went out the back door. The newcomer, tall and lean, wore jeans and an old shirt and brand-new Converse sneakers. He, too, held out his hand. I wondered if there was a secret Headquarters grip and if I would learn it as part of my training. The newcomer was totally bald, with bushy eyebrows and an incongruous postage stamp of beard on his lower lip.

In a hard-edged midwestern voice he said, "I'm Fred. What do you want me to call you?"

"Suit yourself."

"You have no preference?"

"No."

He said, "OK. I'll call you 'You.'"

"Fine."

"While you're here I'll be your acting case officer. You know that term?"

I didn't answer the question.

Eyebrows raised, Fred said, "That's a yes?"

"I've been to the movies."

He said, "Look, relax. I know all this must seem odd and you're wondering if we are what we say we are and why or whether you should trust us, but we mean you no harm. Pretty soon you'll be able to tell the difference between our ways and insanity. My function is to be with you throughout this process. While it lasts, I am your best and only friend. My function is to answer your questions, protect you from discovery and harm, vouch for the other people who come through the door, make sure you have what you need and, prime objective, make sure you have absorbed the Knowledge, capital *K*."

"Like a London cabdriver?"

"More like Mark Twain's riverboat captain. The practice of espionage is like the Mississippi. You want to have the whole river in your mind, know where the channel is, where it's shallow, where the hidden sandbars are located, where and how to find the safe landings and send a message in a bottle if the need arises. But the river changes with time and the weather—sometimes very suddenly. It isn't like a city where the streets have names and always take you to a certain destination and nowhere else. So you have to keep your eyes peeled and your wits about you every minute."

He sounded just as rehearsed as Sam. No doubt Fred had spoken these words to many neophytes before me, but his fluency, his command of the language, his confident manner and tone, impressed me all the same. Their lines might be memorized, but so were Shakespeare's, and like Shakespeare they made you want to hear what was coming next. They had a belonger's kind of humor that was all their own. This came to me as no surprise. Headquarters people, all of them, were smart—amusing when they wanted to be. Father never brought a dullard home.

Fred said, "Any questions?"

"Yes. What can I expect, and how long is this phase going to last?"

"You can expect interesting stuff and a certain amount of what will seem silly stuff. Keep an open mind about both. The course will last a month, maybe six weeks, depending on what we're instructed to teach you. You were sprung on us out of nowhere and at short notice. The syllabus is still under construction."

"I thought you trained people in groups."

"Usually we do. You're a special case."

"Why?"

Fred said, "There are quite a few becauses. You're coming in with much more rank than is usual for a beginner. You're going to be working on the outside, undercover, as what is called an Undoc or undocumented operative, so no one in Headquarters is supposed to know you under your true name except the people who will eventually handle you directly. That category doesn't include me or anyone else you'll meet in this house, so don't tell us who you really are. The director and the rest of management don't *want* to know about people like you, so they can truthfully say they've never heard of you should the need arise. We work in compartments in this business. Nobody outside your compartment will ever know everything about you and most will know nothing."

Oh. So that's how Father's sympathizers were managing this—by hiding me in plain sight. I was a penetration agent already and wonder of wonders, my target had made this happen. How amused, how unsurprised Father would have been.

I said, "Are you in my compartment?"

"For the time being, for the purpose at hand, we are together in a temporary compartment. When we're done with the job we came to do, the compartment will cease to exist and for all intents and purposes, so will I. I have a job to do, cluing you in, and when I have done the job, that's the end of our relationship. Forgetting faces and names is my specialty, and anyway I don't know your true name or even your crypt and never want to know, so as a matter of self-discipline you should never let it slip. You did exactly the right thing by not telling me who you are, and you should never tell me or anyone else you meet in this house. This is the place where you learn to trust no one under any circumstances. When this is over, you'll walk out of the house and out of my mind and never come back to visit at either place. If we meet on the street in Islamabad or hiking all alone across the Sahara Desert in opposite directions, and such things do happen, we'll be mutually invisible. No eye contact, no smile, no nothing. Thus endeth the lesson."

"So now what?"

"Now we make some coffee—espresso, I understand you prefer it. We converse. Apart from your duty to remain anonymous, you have unconditional freedom of speech, and you're expected to speak your mind no matter what the subject. This is a bedrock principle. Otherwise you're not much good to us. I'll show you training films and talk shop. Other people, specialists in the skills of the craft, some of which may seem laughable to you. I assure you they are anything but. Mostly, we wait for the others to show up. That may be the most useful part of the process—learning to wait, getting used to uncertainty, living with frustration. You'll be doing a lot of all three in this business. That's what field operatives do—wait for someone to show up, wait for someone to tell them something they want to know or ask them to do something Headquarters wants to get done. It's important to know how to endure the ennui, how to recognize the right moment when it comes, how not to look to others like you're desperate to take a leak, and all this without going crazy."

Fred had just told me a deep secret I already knew, having absorbed it by osmosis in the company of spies: secret work had its rewarding moments, but most of the time it was a drag. Fred studied my face as he spoke. He saw, I thought, that I already understood that simple fact and smiled a cynic's half-hidden smile of approval. I liked that. I liked him. I liked my prospects. I told myself to shut off the warm feelings and remember why I was here.

Nevertheless, despite my best efforts, a funny thing happened in the weeks that followed. Emotionally, I joined the club. I told myself this was essential to my cover. In a way I was already an honorary member. In the six weeks I spent at Moonshine Manor, as the instructors called the farmhouse, I underwent something like a homecoming. Nearly everyone

I met reminded me in some way of my father and his friends. This came as no surprise. Father's sympathizers had, after all, sent the people I met, and though they kept up the pretense of my anonymity, I detected signs that they knew exactly who I was and where I came from. A sense of belonging gradually awakened within me.

Even if early memories had not been rekindled I would have taken pleasure in the company I was keeping. The people who came to teach me were brighter by several IQ points, or so it seemed to me, than any other group I had known before. After years in academia in the company of people whose minds were closed to everything their code forbade them to believe, these men and women were open-minded as a matter of professional necessity. They were good company—their humor, their refusal to be judgmental, the unswerving, even instinctive way in which they chose reality over delusion. The atmosphere was intoxicating— especially knowing, as I did after years and years of higher education, that no scholar I had ever encountered would believe for a nanosecond what I just got through telling you.

Not that I wasn't cautioned to think twice. Fred was there to confiscate the rose-colored glasses.

"Don't get carried away," he said. "Everyone who comes here is on his best behavior. There's a reason for that. They're expected to make a good impression on newcomers and stimulate exactly the reaction you seem to be having. Plus, you're no run-of-the-mill recruit. Personages on high are interested in you. These guys are not supposed to know that, but they do. In time—who knows?—you yourself may become a personage on high. They want to please such personages. But remember where you are and what we do in this profession, and what *you're* going to be doing. Espionage is not religion or politics, whose appeal derives from the contradiction of reality. In theory, at least, it is the enemy of moral certitude, the defender of proof. Proof is almost always just beyond reach, but it's useful to know as much as it is possible to know. An intelligence service is authorized under the unspoken law to carry out its responsibilities by any means necessary. The fact is, intelligence services *exist* to commit crimes on foreign soil for the benefit of a government. That is their charter, their reason for being. Espionage is a criminal activity, and in every country but their own, spies are felons and worse than felons. Never forget that. What we do, what we are, deserve at least some of the skepticism this activity inspires."

Now he studied my face, eyes alert, smile repressed. Apparently he gleaned some fragment of my thoughts—or wanted me to think that he did. He released the smile.

Again he said, "Thus endeth the lesson."

In the short time we remained together, Fred never again strayed into philosophy. My time at Moonshine Manor flew. I went forth into the world. Firearms instruction excepted, few of the clandestine techniques I learned from my teachers were of much use to me in the years that followed. They just sprayed paint on the invisible man that I was supposed to be. In time the sense of camaraderie was cooled by experience as I discovered that not everyone I met inside the Inside was all that different, after all was said and done, from the folks I knew in academia and politics.

Mammals are mammals. They like to stay close to one another, to walk as one in a perpetual circle, mentally in step, to be the same color and size, to munch the same grass, to go back the next year to the same starting point and do it all over again, to see the genetic and other benefits of having mavericks like my father who left the herd eaten by predators.

Headquarters was not a breed apart, just another herd.

I never truly belonged to the herd or wanted to belong. But I got better and better at impersonation. Little by little, my doppelgänger came into being, and then became me as I, in turn, gradually became my doppelgänger. In the end I was the role and the role was me. Even the polygraph could not tell the difference.

At times, it is true, I longed to be myself, to be free to be myself in the presence of a witness—just one. And so I waited for Luz—pictured her, searched for her, talked to her in my mind. Knew I would know her when I found her.

6

For five years after I left Moonshine Manor I never set foot in Headquarters—or for that matter, in the United States. Unlike Father, I was sent immediately into the heart of darkness, which in my time was Islam. It was a superb hiding place. My targets were terrorism and terrorists. I lived like a terrorist, under many aliases. I operated alone and reported directly to a single person at Headquarters. I was constantly on the move, sometimes visiting half a dozen countries and speaking as many languages and dialects in twice as many days. I liked the work and to my surprise discovered that I had a knack for it. Despite Fred's warnings about boredom, I found it unfailingly interesting. True, it involved a lot of wasted time, but what line of human endeavor does not? I liked the danger, which was real and constant. I liked keeping my eyes open and my wits about me during every waking moment.

Every month, usually in some out-of-the-way retreat in the European countryside, I met my handler, Bill Stringfellow. I had always liked him within limits. Over time my misgivings about him dissipated and I began to regard him with something like affection. As a handler Bill—a former chief of the division I now worked for—was competence itself, never a wrong move or a foolish word. From the beginning of our new relationship he dropped his avuncular manner and treated me as an equal. When we were together, he gave me his full attention. When we were apart I had the sense, even though I knew this was in no way justified or even possible, that he was looking out for me.

In operational matters Bill made sure I had what I needed and on the whole, gave me my head. He kept his word without fail and to the letter telling me what to do but never how to do it. He knew the craft of espionage inside out, and he was good company—a tonic, actually, because on the surface at least, he was so completely himself. Bill liked to meet at taxpayer expense in Europe at isolated châteaux and *schlosses* that had been converted into hotels with restaurants that were listed in the Michelin guides. We would arrive at some converted castle separately, meet as if by chance in the bar and for the benefit of the staff and the other guests, mimic taking a liking to each other, then bond like the only two English speakers on a Chinese ship, eat dinner together, drink together, play golf or tennis after breakfast and backgammon after dinner—passions of Bill's that I could take or leave alone.

Business—what I had done since last we met and how I had done it, what Headquarters thought I should do next—was conducted on long hikes well out of the range of listening devices. Bill was in his sixties, but his appetite for vigorous exercise was as keen as ever.

The shop within Headquarters that Bill now worked for part-time, and in his heyday had practically reinvented in its post–Cold War form, was only marginally interested in gathering information. Its mission was covert action—in Bill's words, its purpose was to make things happen. If interesting information came my way, as it often did in the ordinary course of things, I tossed it into the pot by sending a coded but inane text to a cell phone with a Chicago number. I would never hear whether the information was useful or whether, like most of the millions of snowflakes of fact and gossip that fell on Headquarters every day, it melted as soon as it was touched.

We did what we did, in Bill Stringfellow's words, by finding people who wanted to do something that was somehow, even if only barely, in the American interest, and making it possible (money, information, advice) for them to do it. What I mostly did, or tried to do, was find ways to hunt down terrorists like vermin and capture them, or arrange for them to be killed if capture proved to be impractical, as it often did. This involved making friends with their friends, then watching or bribing the friends, and hoping they would lead us to the cell composed of two brothers and a cousin that was thought by its members to be impenetrable.

Many of these helpers were women. Terrorists tend to regard themselves as monks in the business of providing burnt offerings to the one God, but most are horny young men who can hardly wait for the seventy-two virgins that service martyrs in paradise. This led to disillusion among some of the girls who had simply wanted the thrill of screwing a man who might blow himself up or be shot dead by an American assassin. When they discovered that their boyfriends just wanted to get laid before they died and true love was not part of the bargain, they wanted out and in some cases were willing to pay for a visa and an airline ticket to America by betraying the lovers who had tricked them into meaningless sex.

For the obvious reason that I could not be identified as the nemesis of jihadists and go on living, others did the wet work. Our shop managed a corps of special op types whose specialties were assassination and abduction. When I had identified a target, I asked Bill Stringfellow to call in the troops, and they did the job, almost always in dead of night. They arrived out of darkness and did their work in darkness and then vanished into a deeper darkness, leaving corpses behind and taking drugged captives with them in shackles. I had no problem with this. The martyrs we made were the enemy. In war the objective is to kill the enemy before he kills you. Doing so within largely undefined limits is sanctioned by international law and ancient tradition. I thought that terrorism, in reality, was more a bloody nuisance to my country than an existential threat, but even so, why should it get away with mindless murder and mayhem as if it had a moral right to do such things without consequences?

Whatever precautions I might take, I knew I could not go on doing what I did forever and live long enough to exact the vengeance that was my purpose in life and in this job. I lived defensively. I kept moving, never remaining for long in any one place. I had no home apart from hotels along my circuit. I never went near an American embassy or a safe house. Usually I indentified the specific targets. No one, after all, told American infantrymen which Germans to kill in World War II.

Because of my need to travel incognito, Bill Stringfellow supplied me with the necessary genuine-false passports stamped with the necessary visas, along with driver's licenses and other ID in many names and nationalities. Because many of the passports were issued by minor Latin countries whose obliging intelligence services supplied Headquarters with blanks, I studied Spanish, learning from recordings at first, then working with the Honduran tutor. No one ever questioned my credentials, let alone tested my Spanish, and eventually I knew the language well enough to read *Don Quixote* and Lorca or answer the questions I was likely to be asked by passport inspectors.

I never used disguises because they did not work for me, as they invariably did for Sherlock Holmes, and because I saw no benefit in having a false beard ripped off my face by a terrorist or a policeman. Stringfellow, also a skeptic about wigs and fake teeth, told me the story of a Headquarters type who surprised his wife, who had just arrived in the hotel room in a foreign city where they were meeting after a long separation, by walking out of the bathroom naked, with an erection, wearing a full disguise—wig, mustache, eyebrows, false nose, glasses. She shot him dead with the ladies model .32-caliber pistol, a present from her doting father, that she always carried in her purse. Luckily, her husband had a large life insurance policy.

In the fifth year of our time together, Stringfellow was hit by a hit-and-run driver while bicycling in the predawn darkness on a country road a few miles from McLean. This news was delivered to me in a castle in Bavaria by Father's enemy Amzi Strange, whom I had never met before and was the last man on Earth I would have chosen to bring me such tidings.

"Broke damned near every bone in Bill's body," Amzi said, as if shouting this detail out the window. "Fractured skull, broken spine, broken legs. Died instantly, they said for the benefit of his wife and kids, but no one ever dies instantly. If you've ever broken a bone, you can imagine what having a dozen broken all at once must have felt like in his last moments."

After delivering this summary Amzi said, "I stand in need of orientation, so I've got some questions for you. Stringfellow kept you to himself and went around me to get the director to sign off on your many promotions and citations. What's your rank now, three-star general?"

I said, "Let me ask you a question. Who exactly are you?"

He said, "My name is Amzi Strange. Does that help?"

"It provides a point of reference."

Amzi was the deputy director for operations. In other words, he ran the show. Yet he had come himself to give me the news. Why hadn't he just sent a lackey? The answer to that question had to be Father. Amzi must have wanted to take a look at the imbecile's kid.

I said, "I'm flattered that you took the time to come all this way."

"Glad to do it. Let me flatter you some more. You're a fucking legend. How much of your reputation is smoke and mirrors remains to be determined, but that glowing record is in the files for posterity to wonder over."

Watching my face intently, he waited for a reaction, a reply, and when he didn't get one, rose from his chair, walked to the window, and looked out at the manicured gardens. If I had been carrying a gun I could have shot him in the back of the neck, Lubyanka style.

He said, "This joint sure is Stringfellow's kind of place. Old Bill had aristocratic tastes."

Then, without taking another breath, he looked at his watch and said, "Get room service on the horn. Order lunch. Light. Tell them to deliver everything all at once."

Amzi was another very fast eater. While I was still working on the appetizer he chewed and gulped down everything before him as if he were a machine. He put down his cutlery with a clatter.

When I looked up from my plate, he waved a hand and, as if I were asking his approval to finish my lunch, said, "Take your time. We've got all day."

Amzi Strange was a solid, muscular type with a flat belly rare in a large fifty-something man who worked all day at a desk and had no time to exercise beyond hurrying to the men's room. This was not the only difference between him and Bill Stringfellow. After lunch Bill and I would have hiked for miles in the mountain air, maybe even climbed a little—the Zugspitze and other peaks of the Wetterstein Alps were visible from the castle. Amzi chose to remain indoors in an easy chair.

As soon as I ate the last bite on my plate and wiped my lips with the napkin, he came straight to the point.

"I omitted a detail about Stringfellow's death," Amzi said. "Have you finished your lunch?"

"Yes."

Amzi said, "He was decapitated. After the car hit him."

The picture that flashed in my mind when I heard this was Bill Stringfellow kissing my mother in our kitchen in Budapest. Amzi watched my reaction with open curiosity. What he saw in my face could probably have been mistaken for shock and grief.

I said, "This is public knowledge? It was in the papers?"

"No. We had a little luck. A local sheriff's deputy found him. Why I don't know, but Bill had his Headquarters credentials on him. The sheriff called us. He doesn't like reporters."

I said, "Did they cut off his head while he was still alive?"

"The county coroner thought so. Also that he had been kicked around after he was hit by the car, so they must have been seeking information, like where you were."

I asked no more questions.

Amzi said, "You're looking a little peaked. Take a minute if you need it."

I waved a hand: *go on.*

Amzi said, "We're bringing you home."

I said, "You are? Why?"

"It's pretty fucking obvious. They thought Stringfellow knew where to find you. That's why they were kicking his broken bones. He left you out in the open for too long. A lot of people including me are surprised you're still among the living, and I don't want to upset you, but that may not continue much longer unless we get you out of sight."

Virginia didn't seem to be a safe haven. But what was?

I said, "What do you know beyond what you just told me?"

"That's all we need to know," Amzi said. "But the stations—more than one—and the French and the Mossad have all picked up whispers that you're the talk of the jihad. There's a fatwa out on you. You're the target of the year. If the bad guys find you, they'll saw off *your* head with a dull knife and send the video to Al Jazeera and FedEx the head to us. The whole fucking Islamist movement is looking for you. They could find you tomorrow."

There was nothing implausible about this. I had been exposed for half a decade, I had left a trail of dead jihadists behind me, and it was a wonder, really, that I was still in one piece.

Amzi said, "Speak only good of the dead and all that, but Stringfellow overexposed you because you made him look good, so don't think you have to hunt down his murderers and any of that crap."

I said, "If they know so much about me, why haven't they done something about me before this?"

"Because nobody including us knows where you are from one day to the next, and maybe they don't really know who you really are or what you look like. Where *do* you live?"

"Wherever I happen to be."

"No fixed abode?"

"No."

"So you live on the expense account?"

It's a short distance from the tragic to the trivial. The answer to Amzi's question was yes, because I was constantly on the move. I waited for whatever he was going to say next.

He said, "You must have a pile of back pay in the bank."

"Assuming my salary and allowances are deposited every month, probably."

"You don't check your balance?"

"I have no mailing address and I don't use the Internet and as you know, I haven't been to the U.S. for a while."

"No wonder you're an object of superstitious awe."

I said, "You insist on my coming home?"

"You bet your ass I do."

He groped in a shopping bag and handed me a brand-new, presumably genuine-genuine, blue U.S. passport in my true name. Then he gave me a manila envelope stuffed with brand-new hundreds and fifties, just as Bill used to do. I signed a receipt.

"You can turn in a final expense account when you get back," he said.

"When will that be?"

"Today, if we wanted to lose your assets, but you'll have to say goodbye to the boys and girls and hand them over to the next guys."

"'Guys,' plural?"

"We'll split your caseload up among the stations as soon as you tell us what's going on and who the assets really are. Stringfellow took your secrets to the grave with him. We don't want them shutting down the whole fucking network because only one guy knows who everyone is."

"I'll be surprised if any of them will want to be handed over."

"If they want to keep on getting the money, they'll cope. All promises made by you will be kept."

"Am I supposed to introduce them to the new guys?"

"It's customary. They've all got your cell phone number—Stringfellow actually shared that with us. They'll call. When you answer they'll say, 'Matt Tannenbaum gave me your number.' Response: 'Matt the bookworm? What's he reading these days?' Response: 'Harlequins.' Any questions?"

"What am I going to be doing from now on?"

"Your guess is as good as mine. You're the original round peg and all we've got back home is square holes."

"So what are the possibilities?"

"I guess you could impart your wisdom to the rest of us. Sooner or later, we'll find or invent something that takes advantage of your experience and talent. You should cool off for a while. You'd make an outstanding instructor in the training division."

"The Plantation? No thanks."

"There's no such thing as no thanks in this business."

"Then this is good-bye, because the Plantation is out."

These words came from the depths. I wanted to advance my plan, to penetrate, to spoil, to humiliate. I couldn't do that by running a classroom at the Plantation and sending dewy-eyed recruits to their capture and death in the abattoir that was the Middle East. Or being reminded daily of the horseplay that had sealed Father's fate.

Amzi said, "Simmer down. Obviously you'll be working in anti-terrorism. It just takes a while to figure out where and how. Islamist nutcases are not the only terrorists in the world. New ones crawl out from under rocks every day all over the planet. You've got a gift for finding and killing the fuckers. So that's what you'll be doing. But you can't do it in Arabia anymore."

He looked at his watch, yawned, and rose to his feet.

"We're done," he said. "I've got to get some sleep. I leave right after breakfast. Stay out of sight. Eat in your room. You've got a month to clean up behind the elephant before you get on a plane. We'll talk again when you get home, work something out. I know it's bad taste to tell a professional like you to watch his ass, but watch your ass."

The next morning I checked out of the hotel at six. There in the lobby, waiting and watching for who knew what, was Amzi, sprawled in an easy chair, white skin showing between his ankle socks and the cuffs of his trousers, tiny spectacles perched on his nose. He was reading, or pretending to read, the *Süddeutsche Zeitung* and did not look up.

7

Two weeks after my meeting with Amzi in the Bavarian Alps I found myself walking in blistering midday heat down a narrow street in Sana'a as the *dhuhr* prayer was being called from the minarets. The sun was a blister on a pallid sky. The street was crowded, but no one paid any particular attention to me. My coloring is dark, made darker by the sun, and my face, thanks to the nose, could be mistaken for one of the many typical ones seen in the Near East. I had lived in Islam long enough to have acquired the local gestures and walk, and I spoke Arabic well enough to be mistaken for someone who had learned it at his mother's knee.

I was being followed by a tall Arab in Western clothes. His reflection, which I glimpsed in shop windows, was unthreatening. The man's posture was not the usual one for this part of the world. He carried himself like an American, so I decided to consider the possibility that he probably was the station type I had come to Yemen to meet and introduce to a local asset. This was a risky supposition. He could just as well have been an assassin who had traveled all the way from Dearborn or Los Angeles or New Jersey to wage jihad and had been ordered to demonstrate his sincerity by murdering an American on his lunch hour along with twenty other good Muslim souls who had never done anyone harm and just happened to be in the wrong place at the wrong time.

In the next shop window—there weren't many of those in this neighborhood—I watched my shadow take a cell phone out of his pocket and punch a single key. My own phone rang. This wasn't part of the contact plan I had made with the Headquarters man who set up this meeting, but the American voice on the line was the same.

He said, "Hey, how'd the game come out last night?"

I replied, "Five–four Yankees. Walk-off double by Texeira."

The voice said, "Great. So let's get together."

This was shoddy tradecraft. Foreigner places call. Second foreigner, who is fifty feet away, answers on the first ring. Both speak English into their phones. At the next corner I crossed the street and plunged into a knot of jostling Yemenis. As a centipede in dishdasha they plunged into the seething traffic. I went with them. Horns blared, curses were shouted, fists were shaken. The tall Arab elbowed his way to me and passed me a canvas shopping bag containing, among other items, the carbon-black, one-of-a-kind snub-nosed .45-caliber revolver I pouched from station to station.

My firearms instructor at Moonshine Manor had sworn by the good old reliable .45: "*Shoot a man five times in the chest with a nine-millimeter popgun and the bullet goes right through him and he keeps on coming. Fire one .45 slug into his big toe and he's immobilized by pain and shock.*" He had recommended the master gunsmith in Tennessee who built my .45 to order.

In the shopping bag were other essentials: spare loads of ammunition, a first aid kit, and aerosol cans of pepper spray and wasp and hornet killer that could project a stream of poison that would blind and suffocate a human being at a distance of fifteen feet. Also an envelope stuffed with euros for the asset I was on my way to meet.

The asset, who was barely old enough to shave, awaited me in a darkened house at the end of a blind alley. The alley was the only way in—and more importantly, the only way out. We had met here before, a foolhardy risk I countenanced because the asset was an exceptionally good source, and because he said he felt safe here as nowhere else. The empty house had belonged to his late grandparents. No one in his cell but he knew it existed. As a child he had spent happy hours playing in the streets. He knew the neighborhood's secret shortcuts, its good hiding places.

He opened the door when I knocked in a certain sequence known only to him and me and shouted in Arabic, *It's me, Aashiq Muhammad*, which means "adorer of the Prophet." The single room was small and shadowy. It had no windows. A weak lightbulb hung on a frayed wire from the ceiling. On the floor lay a rumpled sleeping pallet and two cushions to sit upon, and between them a low table with a bottle of water. On a shelf stood a small-screen television set tuned at maximum volume to Al Jazeera. The usual anti-U.S. slogans were painted in Arabic script on one of the whitewashed walls. Against the opposite wall stood an electric hot plate for cooking, a sink with a dripping cold-water tap and beneath it, the necessary bucket, covered with a towel.

My host was a young man I called Faraj. He was a member of a terrorist cell composed of two other postadolescents and a slightly older man. Though in theory everyone in the cell was equal, the grown-up was actually in charge. Until a few months before, when I found Faraj through his ex-girlfriend, he had had three cousins in the cell. Now there were only two. The third and youngest one had been turned into a suicide bomber by a stern jihadist introduced by the older terrorist.

The jihadist had assured him that he would be made whole again by an angel after he blew himself up and would be awakened from death by houris he could pleasure without interruption for eternity, one after another or all at once. They would turn back into innocent virgins, hymens mended, ready for a new deflowering, each time he used them. The absurdity, the blasphemous cynicism of it, broke the spell of jihad for Faraj.

After greetings that involved the usual references to Allah and his Prophet—for the purposes of our relationship Faraj thought or pretended to think I was a Muslim, though I had never told him any such thing—we sat down on the cushions. As I had been advised to do at Moonshine Manor, I took the cushion that put my back to the wall. Faraj didn't like having his back to the door, but I was the one with the euros, so he sat where I asked him to sit. He leaned closer and because the television was blaring, delivered his report into my ear. His hot breath, heavy with moisture, was unpleasant.

He had something important to tell me: Faraj and his surviving cousins and another boy who had just joined the cell had been ordered to carry out simultaneous suicide bombing attacks on the American ambassador and the chief of station. They would pull up beside their cars on motorbikes and blow themselves and the Americans up. Special, very powerful suicide vests were being prepared. There would be nothing left of the Americans or of the boys, either, except in the case of the Muslims, their immortal souls, but the angels would know the boys and the houris would be waiting for them, wet between their legs.

When was this going to happen?

Faraj told me the date and hour and location.

As he uttered the last syllable of the last word of his report, the door was blown open. I had been watching the door while I listened to Faraj, and I was still listening when I saw it expand slightly and for a tiny fraction of a second become plumper, as if it were being pumped full of liquid. Then it leaped off its hinges as if weightless, flew across the tiny room, and smashed into the wall inches from my head. Had I been a little taller, it would have killed me.

A large man with a curved butcher knife in his hand rushed out of the flash and the dust made by the explosion and cut Faraj's throat. The knife was sharp, the man was strong. The cut was deep, halfway to the bone, severing the jugular and the carotid artery. Faraj's strong, young heart pumped out plumes of blood that splashed on the wall and soaked the assassin and me.

All the time I had been listening to Faraj I had been holding the .45 in my hand inside the shopping bag. Now I lifted it, shopping bag and all, and because the man with the knife was no threat to me for the moment, shot the first man who followed him through the space where the door used to be. The .45-caliber hollow-point round hit this fellow in the center of the forehead. His skull exploded. Blood and brains splashed into the face of the man behind him, who was pointing an AK-47 at me and screaming curses. He looked a little like Faraj and I thought, *That must be one of the cousins* and shot him twice in the chest. The impact knocked him over backward.

By now the man with the knife had cut Faraj's neck all the way to the spine and was trying to twist off the head. The sound of the shots—a .45 makes a lot of noise when it goes off in a confined space—woke this psychopath from the ecstasy in which he appeared to be lost. His eyes fastened onto me. He let go of Faraj's head, which fell onto the dead man's chest where, attached by a length of neck bone and a strip of skin, it dangled upside down, mouth agape and tongue hanging out, eyes staring, as if taking one last look at the world. Could it be that Faraj's brain might not yet be dead and he could still see me? In my state of shock, I thought this was possible.

His murderer uttered a roar and lifted his knife. I shot him in the left eye—I could hardly miss because it was no more than twelve inches away. Through all this I had remained sitting on the floor. He fell on top of me. His dead weight pinned me against the wall. The Arabic graffiti, like everything else in the room, were splashed with gore. I wriggled free, subduing panic but only just. I reloaded the .45 without knowing I was doing this. I did not fear for my life. There are worse things than sudden death. Whoever came through the door, and there would be more than one attacker, would not kill me. Instead, if I didn't kill them first, they would capture me and torture me until I told them lies they were willing to believe and the time came to decapitate me on camera.

No one came through the door. I didn't expect this state of things to endure. I could not go into the alley covered in blood. With my cell phone, as robotically as I had reloaded the .45, I took photographs of myself, of the shopping bag and its contents, of the corpses, of the knife used by Faraj's executioner, of the terrorists' weapons, of the blood-splashed walls, of the jagged hole in the wall where the door used to be. I washed the blood off my face and rinsed my hair under the tap and soaked and wrung out the black T-shirt I had been wearing until the rinse water was no longer pink, then put it back on.

I walked out into the teeming street. No one followed me. No one gave me a second look. I was breathing as if I had just run the mile, and as I walked I fought to control this. Within minutes my hair and the T-shirt were dried by the sun. It seemed unwise to return to my hotel. I had cash in my pocket and in the shopping bag along with genuine-false credit cards and the Venezuelan passport I was using for this trip. I found a taxi and went to the airport, and with Faraj's euros bought the last business-class ticket to Zurich and a new shirt with a replica of Andy Warhol's Marilyn Monroe silk-screened on it. In the men's room I sat in a stall and, using the app supplied by Headquarters, composed and encrypted a text message describing the day's events. I wiped the .45 clean of blood and my fingerprints, and put it back into the shopping bag with everything else except the euros, then dropped it into the trash can and covered it with used paper towels.

At the gate, hoping that it would be read in time to warn the ambassador and the chief of station to stay home on the date Faraj had supplied with his final breath, I texted the encrypted message to the number in Chicago.

Through all this I fought back nausea. As the wheels of the Swissair airbus lifted, I grabbed a vomit bag, but though I heaved and choked, I brought up nothing but the sour taste of what I couldn't get rid of.

8

Amzi Strange said, "You've got five years' worth of unused vacation time and money in the bank, and considering what you've been up to, you've gotta want to recharge the battery, so why don't you take some time off? Two months, say."

"Why would I want to do that?"

"To get away from it all."

"I've been away from it all for five years."

"So?"

"I'm tired of being alone."

"You don't have to be alone. Take a woman along."

"I don't know any women."

"Find one when you get where you're going. You can hire a good-looking hooker in the prime of life anywhere in the world for maybe three hundred a pop, so if you get laid every other day, sixty days would cost you ten grand, max."

It was hard not to be amused by this brute.

I said, "That's not a low estimate?"

"Double it. It's still the price of two months of marriage with five times as much sex, more variety, and a lot less grief."

"So what do you and Headquarters get out of that?"

"Time to think. Like I told you, nobody knows what to do with you."

I said, "It's obvious what to do with me. You know what I can do. Find a way for me to do more of it."

"Send you back to the Land of Nod? You'd be dead in a week."

"To quote you, Islamists are not the only terrorists in the world. If I can penetrate the jihad, I can penetrate other things."

"Like what?"

"Like Russians. Or whoever except maybe North Koreans. Name it. But as part of the whole. Inside. Not as a singleton."

"Why not? Working alone with your ass hanging out is what you're good at. You just said so yourself."

"It's too limiting. I belong inside and you know it. You'd be remiss if you let me go to waste, and I won't stand in the corner because you guys are too insular to see what you've got and make use of it."

Amzi mimed a smile.

He said, "I'm fucking stunned. Such modesty."

I said, "Let me ask you a question. Is the problem that you don't have a slot for me and can't invent one, or that somebody doesn't want the competition?"

No reply, but I had expected none.

Amzi said, "Do you speak Russian?"

"Not yet."

"But next week you will?"

The answer to Amzi's question was no. I'd have to study and listen a little longer than that. Amzi spoke Russian, and I guessed from the way he spoke English that learning it hadn't been easy for him. But actually it was easy for me to learn languages. I soaked up strange tongues and remembered them the way other people memorize a Gershwin tune after hearing it once. This ear for gibberish was my only natural aptitude.

I said, "You're interested in Russia?"

"You could say that," Amzi replied. "Everybody's interested in the Russians. Fuckers just won't quit."

Amzi's demeanor changed. He had kidded around long enough. He said, "Are you serious about Russia?"

"Yes."

Amzi glanced at the row of clocks on his office wall that told him what time it was in half a dozen foreign capitals. He waved his hand, as if shooing a fly, and perched his reading glasses on his nose. He picked up a file, put his feet on his desk, and began to read. He paid no further attention to me. I left.

Despite Amzi's history with my father, despite his foul mouth and his insulting manner, I found it difficult to dislike this man. His was one of the first names on the short list of people I intended to destroy if he gave me the start I needed, and I felt no guilt or regret about that. However, I could like him in spite of myself and still not forget what he was and what he had done and what he deserved.

Hate the sin, love the sinner.

I was given an office whose size befitted my rank, a telephone, a computer, a safe, a burn basket, but no assistant or guide who knew the ropes, so my contact with my fellow spooks was limited. I was as isolated and as different in this hive of spies as I had been in the crowds of shouting Muslims in which I had lately lived. In a way this was an affirmation—you have to be noticed to be ignored. Once in a while someone nodded to me in the cafeteria or gazed at me through the glass walls of my office as if I were a tropical fish. Few ventured to speak to me. I did not hunger for company but I wondered what it all meant. Was this an organized shunning? Was I reliving Father's last days in this building? I saw him in my mind as I had seen him in our final moment together: the rags, the backpack, the jaunty wave good-bye, the wry half smile on his dirty face.

I asked Amzi for an explanation.

He said, "Relax. There's no fucking conspiracy. You're a legend, I already told you that, so the troops don't know whether to genuflect or wash your feet when they run into you in the hallways. Sooner or later they'll realize what a wonderful person you really are and you'll have more friends than you need. It would spoil everything if I ordered everybody to be nice to you. Give it time. They'll work up their courage and make the moves."

I would have felt better if it *had* been a conspiracy. Apart from Amzi, who was too busy hoodwinking the rest of mankind to spend much time manipulating me, I had no superior between me and Amzi and no subordinates. Therefore I had nothing to do.

I bought a home study course in Russian and spent most of my days listening to stilted conversations over earphones and repeating what I heard or listening to audiobooks in Russian. At night I watched Russian movies from Netflix. After a month or so I understood about half the dialogue unless there was a lot of slang.

One day while I was listening to a Chekhov short story with my eyes closed, my telephone rang. When I picked up, a female voice, lifting half an octave as she spoke her name, said, "This is *Rose*mary?"

From me, silence. I didn't remember anybody named Rosemary.

The voice said, "In Mr. *Strange*'s office?"

"Yes?"

"You are to report to the director's reception room at zero eight-fifteen tomorrow morning. Mr. Strange will meet you five minutes earlier, outside the door."

"Why?"

"Zero eight-ten, outside the door," Rosemary said, and hung up.

I called her back. "Where is the director's reception room?"

She gave me directions.

At 8:10 Amzi appeared and ushered me into the sanctum sanctorum. Half a dozen self-confident men and women including, inevitably, a couple of faces I vaguely remembered from childhood, were bunched up on the large Persian carpet. A bottle of champagne stood in an ice bucket on a side table. Conversation was muted.

At precisely 8:15, a second door was opened by a short man, not quite a midget. The Director, who looked like the high-powered Wall Street lawyer he used to be and would be again, and then some, after he had served his hitch as a not-so-public servant, strode briskly into the room. He took up a position in front of the flags, and while a photographer took pictures, read a citation in a mellifluous baritone. The short man produced a leather box embossed in gold with the Headquarters seal. The Director removed a medal from the box, shook out the ribbon, and hung it around my neck.

He shook my hand firmly, looked me straight in the eyes for a count of five, and said, "Congratulations. Brilliant work. The president of the United States has been made aware of your outstanding service to your country."

He looked at me as if to let me know that these ritualistic words carried more than their usual weight because, as the media never tired of repeating, he was a friend of the president's, a kingmaker. He had known him When.

A champagne cork popped. A waiter in a white jacket materialized. He poured a tablespoon of California champagne into glasses and passed them around. The Director lifted his glass. Everyone else followed suit.

From his diaphragm the Director said, "To good deeds in the service of this country that we love. And to you, sir."

That was all he had time for. The short man opened the door and held it. The Director walked through it. Some but not all of the others shook hands with me and then, like the Director, they had to dash.

A tall man whom I vaguely remembered from the old days was the last to shake hands.

He said, "Tom Terhune. Your father would be proud."

Terhune was a murmurer, so I had to listen hard to hear him.

"More likely amused."

"Don't be too sure. He expected great things from you."

This was news to me. But a wave of emotion ran through me. Not for the first or the last time, I wondered where this overwhelming love for a man I hardly knew until our last hour together had come from and how it had become the driving force in my life.

Terhune, a watchful fellow, noticed that his words had had an effect on me.

He said, "I'd like to renew acquaintances. Are you free for dinner a week from Wednesday?"

I said, "Yes."

I was always free for dinner, and I wanted to find out more about this man whom I was not quite sure I remembered.

"Seven o'clock then, at Kazan's in McLean. It's in a shopping center. Do you remember it?"

I did. Turkish food. The place had been one of Father's hangouts. He had taken me there for my birthday a couple of times.

I said, "It's still there? Fine."

Terhune nodded, glanced at his watch, and left. Like the others, he stepped lively, not a second to waste.

Outside the door, Amzi was waiting for me.

He said, "You know Terhune?"

"Not really."

"Good man, but only his dog can hear him. Nice medal. People have killed for it. Just like you did. Or died for it. How come you're still wearing it?"

"What else would I do with it?"

"It's customary to give it back so they can lock it up in the Director's safe. They give it to your widow when you die. She can hang it around her neck while she bangs her second husband or melt it down for the next hero."

As Amzi spoke the Director's private door opened and the short man reentered, carrying the empty medal box in his hand. He gave me an expectant look. I took off the medal and handed it to him. I hadn't had a chance to examine it, so I never did find out what motto, if any, was stamped on the obverse.

Terhune was known in Kazan's restaurant. He didn't have to order because the waiter already knew what he wanted. I ordered the same, lamb stew cooked in yogurt. Terhune ordered a brand of vodka I had never heard of—chilled, no ice. When the waiter asked me what I wanted, I asked for spring water.

Terhune said, "You don't drink alcohol?"

"I gave it up so the Muslims wouldn't smell it on me."

He asked me how my mother was. I didn't know. While I was in the Middle East, she had sold the house in which I had grown up. She wrote, tersely, that she could not go on living in the wreckage of her old life, meeting people who knew all about her husband's shame and turned away their faces every time she ran into them in Safeway. She was moving far away to be with her lover. She didn't specify where. This parting was not so very different from my father's good-bye to me.

I said, "My mother and I are not in touch."

Terhune, showing no unseemly surprise, dropped the subject.

He said, "Fill me in. What does Amzi have you doing?"

"Nothing."

"Literally?"

"Yes."

"No busywork while he finds the right slot for you?"

"So far, no."

"The days must go by slowly."

CHARLES McCARRY

"Not really."

"No? How do you pass the time?"

"I study Russian. One of those home study courses."

"Why?"

"In case it comes in handy. And I like learning languages."

"Is it any good at this point?"

"Hard to tell when I have no one to talk to but myself."

In Russian, Terhune said, "Can you read it, write it, understand it over the telephone, recognize the words in a song?"

In the same language I replied, "About half."

"How long have you been at this?"

"About a month."

"And already you halfway understand? You must be a quick study."

"I watch a lot of Russian movies and listen to audiobooks."

"Which books?"

"So far, Pushkin's poetry and Chekhov's short stories."

"Good choices. Pure pleasure in the original. Why, really, are you doing this?"

"I want to run operations against the Russians."

"Not the Chinese, the target of the moment?"

"No."

"Why not?"

"Because it's beyond us, because it's pointless, because it has no alphabet. Because no outside power has ever destroyed China, but if you hang around long enough, it always destroys itself."

Terhune said, "You should write an op-ed. In English."

The waiter reappeared. Terhune ordered two Turkish coffees. Switching to English he asked me how long it had taken me to learn Arabic and Farsi to the point of fluency. I told him the truth: not very long. He looked like he believed me, but given the life he had led, how would you know?

86

He said, speaking English again, "What you need now is someone to speak Russian to. I know a native speaker who might help if you're interested."

"I'm interested if he or she is up-to-date on slang."

"This fellow is up-to-date on pretty much everything. A Jesuit priest. He was born in Russia of Russian parents and left when he was twelve and emigrated to the States when his mother married an American citizen. His father had been shot for the usual Soviet reasons, which is to say no sane reason. He and his mother always spoke Russian to each other and she had Russian friends, so he kept up on the language. Because he spoke it like a native and knew the culture as if he had never left Moscow, he was sent into the Soviet Union by the Jesuit order and lived there as a hidden priest for twenty years. He worked in mines and factories during the day and at night baptized babies, heard confessions, said mass in secret. And wrote intelligence reports in Aramaic to his father provincial in the USA that the Moscow station transmitted for him."

"The Jesuits shared his reports with you?"

"Sometimes, on their own initiative. Otherwise no, and we didn't peek."

"You must have been tempted."

"We were somewhat short of Aramaic speakers. And besides, the Aramaic was encrypted."

"I didn't know there were Roman Catholics in Russia."

"There are Roman Catholics everywhere, thanks in good part to the Jesuits, and there were a lot more of them in the USSR after twenty years of Father Yuri."

"How do you know him?"

"When I was chief of station in Moscow, the KGB sniffed him out. Before they could grab him we documented him and helped get him out of the country. When I got back to Washington he looked me up to say thank you. We became friends."

"What does he do now?"

"What Jesuits do. If you want to meet him, I can introduce you."

"I'd appreciate it."

"What's your cell phone number?"

I told him. Tom didn't need to write it down.

He said, "You'll get a call in a day or two."

I said, "I have a question."

"Ask it."

"How did a son of my father get by the dragons and get recruited?"

Judging by the look in Terhune's eyes, this was a question he had expected.

He said, "It wasn't complicated. You were qualified."

"That hardly seems like enough, given the backstory."

"Quiet words were spoken by your good friend Bill Stringfellow, and others followed suit."

"Why?"

"Because Bill was respected and because, believe it or not, your father still has admirers. Some of them thought he paid too high a price for a youthful prank that told Headquarters more about itself than it wanted to know. With his brains and aptitude, he should have made it to the top. A lot of people thought he would. He was prevented from doing so by the fuddy-duddies. Half the organization thought that he had been robbed of his destiny and as a by-product of that, the organization had been robbed of what he might have done for it."

"So it happened for sentimental reasons?"

"There was no cabal, if that's what you mean. But as far as I know, nobody told the people upstairs whose son you are, but that's as far as it went. You have a common last name."

"Does Amzi know?"

"Who knows what Amzi knows? But it's more likely than not. All he has to do is look at you."

"Given the history, why would he let such a thing happen?"

"You'd have to ask Amzi that question, but I wouldn't necessarily advise you to ask it."

There was little left to say. Terhune paid the check. I tried to split it, but he said, "You can leave the tip. Two twenties will do. When you can understand every word Father Yuri speaks or that Pushkin and Chekhov wrote plus the lyrics of 'Dark Eyes,' give me a call."

In the parking lot he said, "Listen. Whatever you might think you owe anybody because of the past, you don't. And even if you did, you would have already paid off the principal and interest. You're even."

Not quite yet.

9

Father Yuri was a plain man with a brilliant mind. He seldom spoke a word a small child could not have understood or expressed a thought that didn't turn out to be a Matryoshka doll. On our first day together, we met in the early morning—the mist had not yet burned off—at the twenty-sixth president's statue on Theodore Roosevelt Island in the Potomac. As we walked the island's trails, deer, herds of them, watched us. Father Yuri could not have been less than seventy and looked older—a consequence, perhaps, of two decades on the famously nutritious Soviet diet. He was a sturdy broad-shouldered man with the legs of a fullback. His thick gray hair was cut short. Ruddy complexion, Slavic cheekbones, pug nose. Like Chekhov he was a descendant of serfs and looked it. Clearly his face had been his fortune as he stayed alive and unimprisoned for half a lifetime under the nose of the Soviet apparatus. He walked purposefully, like a pilgrim on his way to Jerusalem, all the while speaking Russian and listening to my lame attempts to speak it in return. When the hike ended he was as fresh as he had been at the beginning.

In English he said, "You've got a quick ear. Your Russian got better in the last ninety minutes. How often do you want to do this?"

"Every morning. Is that possible?"

He thought for a moment, then said, "Sundays excepted, yes. Let's meet by the president's statue at six-fifteen. Get rid of the home study records, the diction is weak. Stop listening to Chekhov and Pushkin on your iPod or you'll end up sounding like a prerevolutionary aristocrat. Read contemporary authors, magazines, newspapers. The library where you work has them all. Keep going with the movies but only ones made in the last ten years."

I took his advice as gospel. I grew fond of him very quickly. To the degree permitted by his vocation, this seemed to be reciprocated. Father Yuri took pleasure in my progress, and as my capacity improved, we gradually began to exchange small confidences. Although this made me wary, I pushed paranoia aside. What difference did it make if the Jesuits knew all my secrets? They weren't going to tell anybody but other Jesuits. Father Yuri never mentioned God, but if he had, I would have listened.

This doesn't mean I was sidling toward conversion. I did not believe in gods as man has so far imagined them. I could not believe unless the mind of the creator turned out to be the invisible, invincible, omnipresent, immortal bacteria and viruses that collectively drove the evolution of our species over billions of years with the objective of producing an organism intelligent enough to transport the microbes to other planets so they could begin the process all over again. Concomitantly this infinite mind programmed humanity to despoil the planet, so it would have an incentive to leave. In an imaginary deity this would be called God's plan and be regarded by believers as unquestionable. In the case of bacteria, which are known to have existed on Earth for at least 3.4 billion years and live in and profoundly affect the bodies of every organism on the planet, denial would be automatic.

This hypothesis made sense to me, but I decided not to discuss it with a Jesuit.

We encountered almost no one on our early walks apart from the occasional earnest runner, usually a military type, but one morning we came upon a Latino family lost in the woods. They were frantic, but the sight of Father Yuri's clerical collar calmed them down.

"God has sent us the good father," the mother told her children.

In Spanish—the mother and the children spoke no English—Father Yuri invited them to follow us to the parking lot. On the way he conversed happily with the children. I talked to the parents. They were from Paraguay (the husband, a diplomat, had just been posted to Washington), and in the few minutes we were together they told me what they said was the most interesting thing about their country, that in the late nineteenth century all but about 40,000 Paraguayan males—the few survivors of the gender were mostly old men and small boys—had been killed in a hopeless war with Argentina, Uruguay, and Brazil. This slaughter turned the country into a land of widows, orphans, and girls who had no one to marry. A carnival of polygyny was the result, so if you fell in love you never knew if you and the object of your affection had the same grandfather. It was not polite to ask.

After the Paraguayans drove away, Father Yuri asked me where I had learned Spanish and why. I told him and asked him the same questions.

He said, "I ministered to some Spanish Catholics—the children of Spanish Communists, now grown up, who had been kidnapped by the NKVD, as the Cheka then called itself, during the Spanish Civil War and taken to the Soviet Union. By chance—if anything is by chance—I met a man who wanted to return to God, so I revealed myself. He led me to others and they led me to more, and eventually to secret Catholics from other Spanish-speaking countries. There were a surprising number of them. Some were the half-Russian children of the kidnapped children. They didn't want to pray in Russian, the language of atheism, so I learned Spanish. They were my teachers."

"Dangerous work."

"For them, yes, because most of them were married to Russians who didn't know they prayed in secret and were so terrified of the secret police that they might have denounced them. But they believed that Jesus would protect them. They survived, so who knows, maybe he did."

Father Yuri's references to the Trinity were rare. Nevertheless, or maybe therefore, our conversations became more interesting. After a few days we stopped discussing the day's news and the weather and baseball and instead talked about living a fictitious life among exotic peoples and speaking their languages as if they were your own. I never learned where exactly Father Yuri had lived and operated in Russia and never asked. Nor did I name the countries in which I had worked or even the other languages I spoke. I assumed Tom Terhune, who seemed to trust him absolutely, had already supplied him with this information, and maybe more.

The differences between the life of a Jesuit and that of a spy are not so very great. Each trades in souls. Each belongs to a secret community united by belief and ritual to which, except for rare mutations like me, they are committed heart, mind, and soul. Both play a role designed to blur their reality, both are entrusted by strangers with secrets they have sworn an oath never to reveal, both work against a defined enemy (the same one under different funny names, Father Yuri might have thought) for a clear but unachievable purpose, and derive from their work roughly the same amalgam of guilt and satisfaction, disillusion and moral satisfaction, self-loathing and flagellation. The priest saves souls, the spy preserves illusions.

We quickly became friends of a sort, and in a limited sense each other's confessors—what sort of people we had handled, what we had seen, how that affects the mind and the way the world looks. Interest is the key to learning, and as anyone who has ever been in love knows, few things are more interesting than looking into another mind and discovering a simulacrum of oneself.

At heart, Father Yuri was as much the skeptic as I was, and in my own way I was as much of a believer as he was. As he might have put it if he had been an ordinary teacher, you cannot be a doubter if you didn't begin as a believer, and vice versa. I learned more from him in a short time than from anyone else I had ever known, yet at the end of the course I could not have described what exactly I had learned any more than I could have recited the details of the process by which my body manufactured new cells.

I may have been a fast learner by nature, but I had never learned a language so quickly as this. Usually it takes years to be able to see into a foreign language and to hear its echoes. After ten weeks with Father Yuri I could do this, up to a point, with Russian, in which I had not until recently been able to put two words together.

Then, abruptly, the tutorial came to an end. There was no ceremonial good-bye.

On a misty morning very like the one on which we met, Father Yuri said, "I think we're finished. Keep working on vocabulary, not because you'll need to use more words than you already know, but so you'll understand what's being said to you."

I said, "I'm very grateful."

Father Yuri, on the brink of a smile, nodded and without offering to shake hands, departed.

On the way to Headquarters I called Tom Terhune, also in his car from the sound of the background noise, and gave him the news.

Tom said, "Same restaurant, same time, tomorrow."

When I arrived on the stroke of seven, he was waiting at his table, the same one as the last time, which made me wonder if it might be the one bugged by Turkish intelligence or the Bureau, or Headquarters, or all three.

We spoke Russian. Between the appetizer and the entrée, Tom said, still talking Russian, "I was told by our friend that you were an above-average student, and you certainly don't sound like someone who didn't speak a word a couple of months ago."

"Thanks to you, I had a good teacher."

"We must arrange more exposure to the language. I've talked to Amzi about this."

"Why?"

"Because that's the way we do things. Also, it's unwise to try to keep secrets from Amzi."

"What was his reaction?"

"None, essentially. I asked if I could have you. He said yes. He seemed pleased to get you off his hands."

Tom was the chief of the division that included Russia and the rest of the former Soviet Union.

I said, "So what are you going to do with me?"

"Send you out into the world and hope that you'll be loved and understood. You can't hang around Headquarters much longer. You're a born singleton. Please accept this. Working alone in the field is your natural role, therefore your professional destiny, and there's no escape from it any more than John Wayne could avoid being typecast as a gunfighter with a heart of gold."

I liked plain talk, but this was a blow. I had to know the essential secrets in order to do what I wanted to do, and Headquarters was their only repository. After I knew these things, I would go into the field, yes. That was the plan. But first, penetration.

I said, "What exactly do you have in mind?"

Tom said, "I'm open to suggestions."

"Good. I have the bare bones of an idea, but I can't write you a detailed outline. Not yet."

"Then give me the bare bones."

This took a few minutes. One of Father Yuri's stories—parables, really, in which no one was ever identified, so I never knew whether they were reportages or addenda to Matthew, Mark, Luke and John—revealed to me an unlocked door into the Russian connections with terrorism. It was a feeling rather than a well-reasoned plan. I didn't quite know how to convey this to Tom Terhune, who, I thought, was not the kind of man to trust leaps of intuition.

After Russia, Father Yuri was sent to South America—or so I deduced because he didn't name the continent, let alone the specific country where he worked. At the time, leftist youth in many countries were waging revolution with Chairman Mao's *Little Red Book* as their field manual. During the counterculture there were probably as many copies of Mao's scripture in the hands of activists and dilettantes as there now are copies of the Holy Koran. Father Yuri or his superiors reasoned, or more likely took it for granted, that what had been true about the children of Spanish Communists in Russia must be true about Communists in Latin America. All were fugitives from the Church. The subconscious longing for a reunion with Jesus must be the same in both places. Father Yuri had saved captive souls in Russia, why should he not rescue lost souls in Uruguay or Colombia or Argentina?

Everything—this is me talking, not Father Yuri, though he certainly knew it as well as I did—begins with 1. Find a single person who wants something you have the power to give him and you're in business. Often, even usually, this single person will find *you*. After that it is just a matter of reading the signs and establishing, as lovers do, how much alike you and the target are, and turning down the bed.

One person who found Father Yuri, a handsome young man with an incandescent personality and the smile, as Father Yuri put it, of an angel, approached the Jesuit very early one spring morning in a city park in a grove of lush rosewood trees and giant jacarandas in full purple bloom. Father Yuri had noticed him before. This was the first time their eyes had met. The young man looked behind him, looked down the path behind Father Yuri, then stopped in his tracks and waited.

When Father Yuri was close enough, the young man whispered, "Father, will you hear my confession?"

"Certainly."

"Here, now."

"As you wish."

"Thank you. Keep walking, please. I will follow and confess as we walk."

"No. You can't walk and worry about discovery and make a proper confession at the same time. Under that tree." Father Yuri nodded at the large trunk of a rosewood, a few meters ahead. "We can stand on either side of the tree if you like."

The young man looked behind him again. He was not trembling, he was in command of himself. But he was afraid. What had he done to be in such a state? Whom did he fear?

He said, "This will take a long time, Father."

Beneath the great trees the light was dim, as in a confessional. After the young man uttered—detonated—his first sentence, Father Yuri knew why he needed a priest. This was an anguished soul. More than that, it was the soul he had come here to find—or, as the Jesuit had it, the one soul God had sent him here to help.

This boy was a murderer many times over. He had killed or ordered the killing of many men (he did not murder women or children except by accident). He didn't know exactly how many because he had licensed others to kill in his name and he did not always know about all their homicides. He was a terrorist and not only a terrorist but the leader of a terrorist group whose objective was to destroy the Establishment, the very history of his country, to raze its institutions, to liquidate as many of the bourgeoisie as necessary to force them to submit to the power of the people. He was a kidnapper, too: He and his group routinely abducted bankers, politicians, lawyers, and rich men and other capitalist exploiters and held them in "people's prisons," such as a closet or a makeshift tent in a slum apartment, before trying them and in most cases executing them for crimes against the people. Some of the zealots betrayed their own fathers to the avengers of the people, because the destruction of the family, the basic unit of this corrupt society and the only thing stronger than politics, was the first imperative of the revolution.

Now this man had seen the other side of vengeance. Military intelligence had arrested his wife. He showed Father Yuri a picture of a breathtakingly beautiful woman, as if seeing her perfect face would help the priest understand his desperation. If he had married a plain girl, would his loss have been smaller? The young man's estranged father, a member of parliament, had confirmed that she was being interrogated at a military base. This meant beatings, electric shock, repeated near-drowning, broken bones, torn flesh. It meant rape and every form of sodomy by many rapists. Because she was guilty—she was a devoted comrade and had killed to prove it—it meant, in the end, painful death. The young man, though he was an atheist, thought it possible that God had punished her in order to punish him, and that He wasn't done yet. The couple had a daughter, now twelve years old. Was she next?

God had come back to this young man in wrath, showing him that He existed. He had made him understand how he deserved the punishment meted out to him. The young man felt that Jesus was waiting for him to make amends, that some great penance was expected of him, that perhaps his wife would be spared further suffering if he understood what was expected of him. He wanted to be told what that was, what he had to do to end this nightmare.

Father Yuri, who knew that everything he was hearing might well be a lie this supplicant was telling himself but also that it might not be, asked what he thought his wife's torturers wanted.

"They want names," the young man said. "She will never tell them."

"Will you tell them?"

"Never. It would betray her and everything she is."

"God understands that. That doesn't mean He will forgive your rejecting the penance you think He is demanding. Do you pray?"

"Not since I was a child. But since she was taken, yes."

"Has your daughter been raised in the faith?"

"No. Just the opposite."

"Then you have put a child's soul in peril. Have you considered the possibility that this is the reason for His anger?"

"No. The idea terrifies me."

"Your penance is this: a hundred Our Fathers every day you remain alive. A hundred thoughts each day about how to give God what He wants. You know what it is. You must find a way to give it to Him. You cannot keep the faith with evil and with Him, too. You must pray for a Good Samaritan to raise you up and make you see the way. There *is* a way. Begin to believe by believing that."

"What is that way, Father?"

"I am not the Good Samaritan," said Father Yuri. "God will send him to you. But you must recognize him, accept him, do as he asks."

At this point I had asked Father Yuri if this had in fact happened. Father Yuri said, "Only God knows that."

In the restaurant, Tom Terhune listened to Father Yuri's story without interrupting. He was amused.

"Actually," he said, "Amzi was the Good Samaritan."

10

Terhune advised me to read the Headquarters file on Father Yuri's young man in torment. After that we'd talk to Amzi.

After all my scheming, it was as simple as that. It was a thick file. It confirmed what Father Yuri had already told me and a good deal more besides—names, photographs, details. Father Yuri's supplicant was named Alejandro Aguilar. In photographs his wife, Felicia, was indeed beautiful—a Madonna with the fierce eyes of a hater.

Both had genteel parents, distinguished ancestors. The difference between them was at the same time trivial and profound: Felicia was penniless, Alejandro had a trust fund. They named their daughter Luz because communism had shown them the light when she was still a fetus. There were pictures of her as a child and as the striking twenty-nine-year-old woman she was now. She was not as photogenic as her parents, how could anyone be? I wondered how much of this information was fiction or guesswork or wishful thinking—not least because Alejandro Aguilar himself was the source for most of it and he was a zealot who subscribed to a belief system in which virtuous lies were authentic truth because any evil act or intention ascribed to the class enemy was almost certainly true and even if it was not, served the purposes of the revolution.

At the time in question, almost twenty years in the past, Amzi had been chief of the Latin America division. He had seen in Alejandros's distress an opportunity to take possession of a terrorist commander. Because Amzi wanted the chief of station in Buenos Aires to stay out of this for the sake of future relations with the locals, whose toes would be stepped upon by the operation he had in mind, he had flown down from Virginia to handle it himself.

"It wasn't rocket science," Amzi said. "We knew the military had taken this guy's wife. We knew this was driving him crazy. We overheard him saying so over and over again on wiretaps. His wife must have been one hell of a piece of ass, because he just lost it when they took her away. We were listening to him. He had some nutty idea he could rescue her, storm the military base or something. This guy thought he was a pimpernel. He never spent two nights running in any one of the hidey-holes he used. We knew this because one of our techs sneaked into one of his dumps while he slept— Alejandro didn't believe in lookouts. He knew the military's goon squad, if it found him, would just shoot the guards and blow the door and grab him. The only defense was to make it impossible for the enemy to find him.

"He had this rucksack he carried at all times. Some people thought it had a bomb in it so he could blow up himself and anyone who tried to capture him, but the tech said it was just an overnight bag with a couple of guns inside. The tech bugged the rucksack. Also one of Alejandro's shoes—he only had one pair because he lived in poverty like the downtrodden masses. So we knew where he was every minute and most of the time we could hear him talking if we stayed close enough to pick up the transmission. Which we did. I took a whole surveillance team with me, faces the locals didn't know. Very costly. But we had to get there first.

"Alejandro was right: The army would just grab him and torture everything he knew out of him," Amzi said. "They had faith in their methods, but there was no possibility he'd tell them anything but lies. He'd die with Felicia and the two of them wouldn't even tell Saint Peter or the devil, depending on which one was handling the interrogation of their immortal souls. What we wanted was people we could turn and work with in the future. The military just wanted to exterminate the bastards. They weren't stupid enough to think we'd ever tell them everything if we got our hands on Aguilar, but something was better than nothing and they might find him before we turned him and made him untouchable because he belonged to us."

One night when Alejandro was returning from interrogating an enemy of the people, Amzi stepped out of the shadows.

In Spanish he said, "Hello, Alejandro. I mean you no harm. I think you know where I come from and what I do for a living. If you want your wife back, you'll listen to me."

Aguilar moved his hand toward his belt. Amzi stabbed him hard on the chest with a blunt forefinger. "Don't even think about it. Guns are pointed at you from every direction by men who can see in the dark. If you make a move on me, you're a dead man. Ask yourself how that would help your wife."

At these words, four of Amzi's men, standing within ten feet of him and Aguilar, whistled the first four notes of "Yankee Doodle." An Amzi touch—a night without ridicule was a night wasted.

To me Amzi said, "My guys were wearing night-vision goggles, but there were no guns pointed at him. In a situation like this, the sound of gunfire is the sound of failure. But he thought he was in the presence of the Big Bad Wolf, so he believed me."

Amzi told Aguilar the deal. Aguilar would give him the names of his fighters. Amzi would trade some of the names to the military in return for the release of the wife. Headquarters, which Aguilar, like a lot of other brainwashed nutcases, thought was omnipresent and omniscient and possessed unlimited power and wealth, would get him and his wife and daughter out of the country and give them a new identity with genuine-false credentials and an introduction to a world-class plastic surgeon, and pay all the bills. They would be protected, and paid, for the rest of their lives.

Aguilar said, in English, "Never, you son of a bitch."

"OK," Amzi said. "Then what's happening to your wife will go on happening and in the end, trust me, they'll beat her and gang-bang her until she tells them everything. They won't let her die until she does that, even if it takes years. Then the same thing will happen to you and you will break, too."

"So you say."

Amzi said, "Has your daughter reached puberty?"

"*WHAT?*"

"It's something to consider, my friend, knowing what you know about your enemy's interrogation techniques. If your wife won't break and you won't use your head, what do you think they'll do next to encourage you to change your minds?"

The night sky was overcast. It was pitch-dark—no moon, no stars, no glimmer of streetlight in the blighted neighborhood where they stood. The two men had not seen each other's faces, only heard voices. Now Amzi pointed a small flashlight at his own face and turned it on. Aguilar he left in the dark, because he already knew what he looked like.

He said, "That's so's you'll know who I am the next time we get together. Think it over when you calm down, Alejandro. I'll find you again. Soon, in daylight, because one way or another, you may not have much time left. You can tell me then what your decision is and we'll go from there."

Three mornings later, in a different part of the city, Amzi was waiting for Alejandro when he emerged from a different lair he thought only he knew existed. When he caught sight of the North American he looked, Amzi said, like his heart had squirted out of his asshole. He brushed past Amzi, ignoring him, and walked rapidly down the street. Amzi followed. Two of his men shadowed them on the opposite sidewalk. Alejandro didn't seem to pick up on them.

Amzi said, "I was surprised he didn't see them, this guy supposedly being such a Moriarty, but I thought maybe he figured he was safe with us—not because he realized what pussies we really were, but because we wanted something from him and wouldn't whack him until he gave it to us. Or even then, but how could he believe that? He thought he was swimming in the sea of the noble workers he was always talking about and they would protect him. The fact is they would have taken one look at him and known he was a rich kid in disguise, so they would have just stood back and let him be grabbed, hoping he'd get what was coming to him."

After ten minutes or so during which Amzi determined that no one was following *him*, he closed the gap between him and Alejandro and in his shittiest Spanish (Amzi's phrase) he said, "Yes or no or don't know?"

Alejandro, eyes front, trudged on in silence.

Amzi said, "OK. I'm going to go around you and lead on. Don't shoot me in the back unless you think this is a good day to die. If you stay with me, I'll know you want to talk business."

Alejandro stayed with him. A couple of blocks ahead, a van was parked at the curb. As they approached, the rear door slid open. Amzi got in. Alejandro followed him.

I said, "What if he hadn't done that?"

Amzi glowered at the interruption.

He said, "There was no Plan B because Plan B is a fucking cop-out."

Amzi didn't search Alejandro. He was a guest, a possible colleague and future friend, not a prisoner. They drove in silence to the countryside. Alejandro showed no fear but he refused to speak inside the van.

"He thought the vehicle was bugged," Amzi said. "How right he was, for a change."

It was a long ride and for all Alejandro knew he was being kidnapped. His behavior was stoic. Amzi gave him no credit for this. He figured Alejandro was just another college-educated, which was to say *indoctrinated,* upper-class brat who thought he was untouchable.

"To eliminate any idea that I was wired," Amzi said, "I suggested we both take off all our clothes and go for a walk bare ass. He nodded and stripped, and off we went into the woods like the odd couple. He took his *pistola* with him—a Makarov, naturally. Don't ask me why. There were four of my guys within earshot. He must have known he wouldn't live long if he fixed his weapon. Maybe he planned to shoot himself if I led him into an ambush. I didn't say a word about it."

When they were out of earshot of the van, Alejandro said, "Tell me exactly how this would work."

Amzi repeated what he had said in the dark.

Alejandro said, "*All* the names?"

"That's right. If you're as smart as I think you are, you've kept your troops in a state of ignorance so they can't do you much harm if they break. For this thing to work, though, I'll need two who can tell them everything or almost everything."

"Why two?"

"In case one of them dies while refusing to answer questions. The military has to get the information it wants or they'll never let your wife go."

"Why would they let her go?"

"Because they'll get zip from us if they don't promise to let her go."

"They'll lie."

"Not to us."

Alejandro said, "What happens to the people you don't hand over?"

Amzi knew Alejandro would save his friends, men and women of his own class, and born commissar that he was, put the peasants and workers on the death list with godlike indifference. That was why he was interested in the survivors. They would be welcomed home by their families. All they had to do when playtime was over was get a haircut and show up, put on suits and ties, and accept their elders' blessing. They would go back to respectability as if nothing had ever happened.

Amzi said, "We'll take care of them. Your friends will be our friends."

"Good luck. You can't buy them."

Amzi, whose experience had taught him you could buy anyone if you made the right offer, let that pass. He knew Alejandro's crowd didn't need the money. But they had other needs.

He said, "You'll be long gone before they can figure everything out. They'll think you're dead and your wife, too, if that's what you're worried about."

"What I'm worried about," Alejandro said, "is trusting you."

"There's no eleventh commandment that says you have to trust anybody except the Almighty, and like the Bible tells us, that's usually a mistake. But what other choice have you got? If you do nothing, your wife will die and so will you. Same thing happens if I screw you over. But if I don't screw you over, and I won't, you get her back, you live to a ripe old age in a country of your choice where nobody knows who you are, and after a while nobody in Argentina will remember who you were anyway. So what have you got to lose?"

"Except my honor."

Amzi said, "I wanted to ask this shithead what the fuck he thought *that* was and how much it would bring at auction, but I just smiled sympathetically, like I understood all too well how hard it was for an idealist like him to sell out his principles."

Amzi drank coffee from the mug on his desk.

"Coffee's cold, goddam it," he said.

He picked up the phone and told Rosemary to bring him another cup.

When the new, steaming coffee arrived he gulped half a cup of it as if it were ice water.

Then he said, "Meanwhile, back at the nudist camp, Alejandro walked away into the woods to think things over in solitude. I stayed where I was. Where was he going to go with no clothes on? After half an hour or so he came back.

He said, "All right. But if I don't get her back, I'll kill you, and if you kill me first, somebody else will kill you and your entire family if it takes twenty years."

Amzi said, "You've got a deal. Let's get back to the vehicle where you can make out the list."

At this point, Amzi stopped talking. He drank the rest of his coffee in two or three swallows, his cold eyes on me all the while—honest Amzi, tough as nails, gruff as Zeus, all-business.

He said, "Questions?"

"Only one," I said. "Then what happened?"

"He gave me the names. I gave the military the ones I had no reason to keep for myself. The military arrested the whole bunch in one big raid. After they pumped them out, they let Alejandro's wife go as agreed. She led them straight to Alejandro. Before the happy couple could kiss, they arrested him and rearrested her."

"They broke their word to you?"

"They hadn't promised not to rearrest her or to let him go."

"You stood aside and let them take them?"

Amzi answered this question by not answering it.

"They disappeared," he said. "In those days that was like saying the military threw them out of an airplane over the Atlantic Ocean—from a mile up, so they'd have time to think on the way down."

"Is that what happened?"

Again, no answer. He drank the rest of his coffee.

I said, "The daughter?"

"Nothing happened to her except orphanhood. Her grandparents raised her. If it's OK by you, I want to ask *you* a question. What exactly makes you need to know all this?"

I told him. Of course Tom Terhune had already told him what I had in mind or Amzi wouldn't have wasted this fifteen minutes on me. Even if Amzi skipped lunch there were only thirty-two such chunks of time in an eight-hour working day and he had many applicants for them. My idea was a simple one, so making my pitch didn't take long.

I wasn't quite finished when he looked at the clocks again and said, "Pretty good idea. Slim fucking chance of it working out. But go ahead. Go slow, step carefully. This girl is just as smart as her mother, which means she's just as crazy, too, so watch your ass. If you get thrown out of an airplane we don't know you."

Something resembling a flicker of benevolence crossed Amzi's face. While it lasted I almost thought he might wish me well. He saw the point: Alejandro Aguilar's daughter was the key to his old idea that the freedom fighters he had saved for future use, her secret family, might come in handy after all.

What he didn't know was, there was something about Luz Aguilar that came to me off the glossy prints like a pheromone.

11

For a couple of months after our first meeting on that summer morning in Los Bosques de Palermo, my relationship with Luz was a model of decorum. We met monthly under strict rules of tradecraft. She played the game and behaved with a solemnity that suggested she was handing over nuclear secrets. This wasn't entirely a charade. No matter how much times had changed, military intelligence and the secret police had not forgotten whose blood ran in her veins, and I had to assume they kept an eye on her.

So did I, and through my contact reports, so did Tom Terhune and Amzi. I was no more certain of what he was up to—why he was letting me do what I was doing—than I knew about intelligent life in another galaxy, but it was best to step carefully.

Luz never stepped out of character—cool, careful, dressed like a *Vogue* model, yet sexually aloof in a don't-even-think-about-it way. But I did think about it. I had no sex life, and had had none for some time. In the Near East it would have been suicidal to mess around with the women I handled, almost all of whom were devout Muslims who didn't dally with unclean unbelievers, and anyway they were usually dressed in hijab so it was impossible even to imagine the body that lurked inside the chador or the burka. For five years I had never been in any one place long enough to get to know a Western woman well enough even to speak the word *bed*. Prostitutes were too perfunctory to be worth the risk and expense.

The truth was, I hadn't gotten laid on a regular basis since college. Therefore I was as horny as a fifteen-year-old. Luz rendered this condition infinitely worse. I hadn't expected this when I made my plans for her. But I was susceptible and I knew I wasn't going to get over it. She was a woman after all, so occasionally she tossed me the bone of a sidelong glance, even a smile, or when making a point, touched the back of my hand with a fingertip. But usually she was all-business. She submitted to the puppetry of tradecraft as if it were a testimonial to my importance.

Our stilted behavior in public was an advertisement of espionage to anyone who knew what tradecraft looked like. I mean to say, why would a man and a woman in the prime of life keep on meeting at odd hours in out-of-the-way places and never smile at each other or touch? By every rule of espionage, Luz could never be trusted. She was the child of a man and woman whose ghosts, unhinged by politics as they had been in life, cried out for revenge.

We met on weekdays in the early morning when the streets were deserted, or nearly so. After a couple of months, she suggested meeting, instead, on a Sunday afternoon. Why didn't I come to her place for lunch? This would give us privacy, shield us from inquisitive eyes.

"On the street, when men look at me, they see you, too," she said. "Women look at you and do the same. It makes me nervous."

Her building, she said, usually was quiet on weekends—people slept late or went to the country, to the parks, to Grandmother's house. Amzi would have said I was out of my fucking mind to agree to ignore procedure like an amateur and walk into a place I had to assume was bugged, but I had testosterone running out of my ears, so I ignored the rules and agreed.

When I rang the doorbell Luz greeted me with a polite smile and a handshake. I thought the pressure lingered ever so briefly. If so, this was the most intimate physical contact we had ever had, but she gave me no reason to hope for more. She was as modestly dressed as a nun—black trousers, crisp white shirt buttoned to the throat, no jewelry except her little gold cross, no perfume, hair pulled back. The apartment was flooded with sunlight: good furniture, abstract paintings, flowers, a large photograph of her parents with a small child that was unmistakably Luz. Even at five or six she had looked like a preliminary sketch of the woman she became. She gave me a glass of orange juice mixed with Argentinean sparkling wine. We chatted as we drank—neutral subjects only. She could not have been more ladylike or sent me a plainer message that I should get no ungentlemanly ideas.

Incongruously, romantic music played on the stereo—Bruch's "Second Violin Concerto." Did I like Bruch? She thought the music, clearly composed in a sexual daze, was ravishing.

We ate a cold lunch, drank rosé wine from small glasses. We said nothing worth remembering. After dessert she shooed me into the living room. I heard her clearing away the dishes and putting them in the sink. I smelled coffee, and she brought two large cups of it. Standing over me, she took a sip. This slight movement caused her slim body to move inside her clothes: the lift of a hip, the curve of a breast.

In English, speaking it to me for the first time, she said, "I've been reading your mind."

"In Spanish or English?"

"No words. Just pictures."

"And what do you see?"

"Mostly you're fucking me."

She was watching me. Would my cup rattle in its saucer? Was I going to deny the fantasy or admit my furtive guilt? Her face, still as a picture, told me nothing about which she might prefer.

Smiling pleasantly, as if we were just passing the time of day, I said, "ESP lives."

"So what I see is the reality?"

"Sadly, no. Daydreams."

"You daydream a lot?"

I told her the truth. "Where you are concerned, I do hardly anything else."

No smile, no frown, no lifting of the eyebrows, nothing in the unreadable brown eyes. Luz finished her coffee. She smiled her tiny smile. She turned her back and walked out of the room and disappeared into a hallway.

I finished the teaspoon of espresso left in my cup, cleaned out her cup with my tongue, and then followed her down the hall past arty photographs of Alejandro and his sad-faced, breathtaking Felicia. The door at the end of the hall was ajar. I pushed it open all the way and walked in. Luz stood in front of a full-length mirror.

She was naked. I saw all of her, every pore, front and back, at the same time and realized what a poor thing imagination is. I took off my clothes and dropped them where I stood. She had done the same.

She looked downward and said, "My, you *do* think forbidden thoughts."

She took the part of my body in which all the rest of me, body and switched-off mind, was concentrated, and as if it were a tiller, turned me ninety degrees to the left so she could see herself in the mirror, and then fell to her knees.

In the next half hour Luz got the full benefit of my five years of sexual deprivation and filled the room with loud, seemingly involuntary shouts of pleasure in a throaty voice I had never heard before. She knew *The Joy of Sex* forward and backward and every time we changed positions I felt I was inside a different woman.

After a while we fell asleep, or at least I did. I smelled her in my sleep, felt her skin, felt the warm, sticky moisture of her drying on myself. I had an erection. I wanted to wake up and wake Luz by sliding it into her. I swam upward toward this wondrous reality.

Before I could open my eyes, a shrill male voice screamed, "*Wake up, you son of a bitch!*"

Luz sat bolt upright—I felt this rather than saw it—and uttered a theatrical scream. In a theatrical voice she cried, "Pedro!"

I opened my eyes. Pedro, a very young, skinny, wild-eyed person showering spit as he shouted, needed a shave. In his trembling hand he held an open switchblade knife to my throat. He wore a heavy gold signet ring on his knife hand. He smelled of whiskey and sweat and of something I had often smelled before in the course of duty—madness. As I had been taught at Moonshine Manor, I grabbed his wrist with my left hand and slammed the heel of my right hand into his chin. His eyes rolled back in his head. He was catapulted from the bed as if weightless. The knife spun in the air—all this happening in slow motion. Pedro's nerveless body hit the floor with a soft thump. He was unconscious, or dead, I couldn't tell which.

Neither could Luz. She screamed again, this time as if she meant it.

In English, as if it were the language of murder, she cried, "You've killed him!"

She leaped out of bed and knelt beside Pedro. He looked like a child that had been hit by a car. She pinched his lower lip, hard. His eyes fluttered. She slapped his face. He groaned. She slapped him again, harder. His eyes opened. He saw me standing over him, switchblade in hand, and tried to scream. He croaked instead. Naked Luz helped him gently to his feet and murmuring words of encouragement, helped him stagger out the door. I heard the front door close and the snick of the lock.

Luz came back into the room, her hair wild, her eyes shining. She had curly pubic hair. One tendril hung from the point of the delta, like a little goatee. I had not noticed this charming detail before. It had an immediate physical effect. I was still standing, the glittering knife in my hand.

I said, "What was that supposed to be?"

"Pedro's a cousin, doing me a favor."

"He's crazy?"

"A little, in a nice way. He's gay. He's done it before. It was a game. The knife was supposed to expose the real you. Would you jump out the window or see the joke, have an erection, and jump on me?"

She looked down, checking my condition, and for the first time ever, smiled a real, a delighted smile.

She said, "So what's it going to be, the window or me?"

12

After that Sunday afternoon, sex became our medium of communication. Neither of us could get enough of it and though in the beginning each suspected that the other was faking it—how could this state of constant arousal be real, how could it last?—doubts weakened with each hour in bed. Lust turned incrementally into love. Against my nature and my will, I began to understand that the absurd phrase "grand passion" was, like most clichés, shorthand for an ancient and undeniable truth.

I had no choice but to tell Headquarters what was going on—not the deep truth I have just told you, but the bare fact that my agent and I were having sex. This was risky. Case officers are not supposed to fall into bed with their assets.

Moonshine Manor wisdom: *Steer clear of temptation and she is ours, put a hand on her breast and you are hers.*

Like every other intelligence service, Headquarters had people under contract to do whatever fucking might be necessary. The forbidden does occur, however, and when it does, the officer who has cuckolded Headquarters is expected to report the violation, introduce his replacement—ideally a member of the same sex as the tumbled agent—with the least possible delay, and break the connection forever. Usually they do just that because they know that the guilty secret will make the needle skid at the next polygraph session. Marrying the agent is an option, but Headquarters (think Amzi) would assume that this meant that the agent had, so to speak, run a successful penetration op and screwed her way into the inner circle of trust in the service of whatever dark force was running him or her. I don't know what the procedure is in the case of gay lovers.

However, the rules were more flexible in my case. Soon after I realized that I would not be able to resist the flesh-and-blood Luz, I told Tom Terhune that I planned to do anything necessary, up to and including marriage, to gain full control of Luz. Tom had reservations, but he understood that Luz was the indispensable element in the operation. Through Luz and only through Luz would I reach the disciples of her father who could identify the Russians whom Headquarters hoped to beguile, bewilder, and betray. I had to put her into my pocket by any means necessary.

Tom passed my intention on to Amzi, who continued to behave like my ultimate case officer even though in theory I was Tom's agent. Amzi gave his approval with the proviso that I should fucking well keep Headquarters informed of every in- and outstroke.

"Direct quote," said Tom.

Needless to say I had no intention of following this instruction. But this was an opportunity to build cover for my hidden purposes, so I did submit largely fictitious details of a measured and cold-blooded seduction. In the end, as we know, Luz grabbed the tiller, and the plan for disinterested seduction flew into the wastebasket.

From the start she and I abandoned tradecraft—or more accurately, substituted a higher form of tradecraft, namely reality. We were lovers. We behaved like lovers. We spent every free hour with each other, including lunch hours, during which we remained on our feet only long enough to gulp something at a fast-food counter on our way back to our offices. We groped each other in the back row at the movies, we dined and nuzzled in restaurants, we kissed on the street. If there was a more demonstrative couple in Buenos Aires, we never ran into them.

The local station chief thought, as he was meant to do, that all this was good if unconventional cover. He also thought it was unseemly, but he had had little or no authority over me. I was Amzi's boy, attached to the station for office space and communications support. I reported directly to Headquarters. Besides that, there was my reputation as a lone wolf, my premature rank (I had been promoted twice and was now the same pay grade as a brigadier general even though I had no troops to command), along with my bizarre position as an outsider who was actually an insider who had powerful champions. For appearances' sake, I asked the COS to give me things to do for the benefit of the locals. This would help them to look upon Luz and me as a genuine case of a crazy love. That happened to be the truth, the advantages of which tend to escape those who live within a culture of deceit. I couldn't have stopped making unprotected love to Luz if she had told me she had AIDS. She seemed to feel the same. Given the choice by Satan between dominion over heaven and earth and her vagina, I would have chosen her vagina.

Luz wasn't interested in foreplay. She rarely had a sexual impulse or any other kind of impulse she did not act upon without hesitation. What she wanted to do, she did. She had no caution. In this as in practically every other way, she was unlike any other woman I had ever known. It wasn't as though she didn't look before she leaped, but no matter what, she always leaped, never hesitated.

This recklessness spoke a language I understood. In my own life, almost everything I had ever done on impulse had turned out well, whereas nearly everything I had done by calculation, such as treating my father like a dog, had ended badly. This did not bode well in terms of finding happiness in the life of calculation I had chosen on impulse. Lost in that contradiction? So was I.

I understood on the day I saw Luz shimmering in that mirror that there was no point in telling her the truth on the installment plan. Out with it! was the only way to deliver the message. However, given Luz's almost pathological decisiveness, there were only two possible reactions: Yes or Get Lost. If the answer was Get Lost, her next decision would be to walk out of my life. I would never fuck her again. The thought was unbearable. It intensified my need for her, so we fucked even more, fucked ourselves to sleep. When at home we lived without clothes so that we wouldn't lose a minute before acting on desire. This was Luz's idea. We cooked, ate, read, watched movies naked so as not to waste a second in acting on the controlling, the irresistible impulse that drove our lives. Even if we were five steps away from the bed, we did not stagger toward it but coupled where we found ourselves.

One Sunday I woke from a nap and found Luz in the kitchen, grinding coffee. She was fully dressed, trousers and turtleneck, every centimeter of skin but her hands and face covered up. What did this mean?

She said, "Get dressed. I want to talk to you."

She gave me a large bowl of café con leche, as if it were breakfast time instead of ten o'clock in the evening. We sat opposite each other, the kitchen table between us, and drank the whole bowlful of coffee. Too much sugar as usual.

Luz said, "I've been reading your mind again."

"Has the movie changed?"

"In a way."

No smile. Overnight she had once again become the cool and collected stranger I had met in Los Bosques de Palermo. *What was this?* Would the Luz I loved ever come back to me?

As it turned out, she was just having an intuitive moment.

She said, "You want to tell me something. I can feel it. Get it out of the way. Tell me."

I was only too glad to do as she asked. I said, "I want you to help me burn down Headquarters."

"That's a figure of speech?"

I nodded.

She said, "For what purpose would we do this? Say what you mean, no metaphors, no similes."

She gestured for more.

I dumped the whole demented operational plan on her. She listened intently. Gradually her thoughts began to show on her face. Watching her as this happened was something like watching a reader who is becoming interested in a book and is entering a different world: tiny smiles, quick pursing of the lips, forefinger lifting the corner of a page so as to turn it without losing a moment.

Any other woman would have thought I was crazy and changed the subject. Luz was unfazed. I might as well have been talking about the weather. I couldn't tell whether this reaction signified disinterest or was a sign that she was just as crazy as I was.

I told her more—far more. I told her what I knew about Amzi and her parents. I didn't want to give her false hope that her parents might be alive. I was a fool to do this, but I wanted to leave nothing unsaid between us.

When I was done, Luz burst into tears. She was wracked by sobs. She was the very picture of heartbreak. It was beautiful, in some incomprehensible way, to be present at the moment that such a thing happened to another human being, let alone to someone you loved with every cell in your body. You might think that what I was doing was a greater cruelty than what Amzi had done. But if I left anything out, she would sooner or later have discovered that I had deceived her, and this would kill the absolute trust that was the essential element of our partnership in vengeance.

And then what would we have had left?

I knew better than to touch her or even speak. This lasted for a long time. When it was over, and this happened abruptly, she let the tears dry on her face before she spoke.

When she did, she said in a steady voice, "I think we had better get married if we're going to do this thing together."

I thought so, too.

13

Luz took me home to meet her grandparents, who looked like royalty that had walked out of a Velázquez on the day it was painted and had been aging gracefully ever since.

Alejandro, their only child, was born just before his mother entered menopause. Joy had gone out of their lives when he renounced them and everything they had taught him. A quarter of a century later they were very sad people still. But they were a pleasure to be with because of their transparent love for Luz, their exquisite manners, and their beautiful Spanish. Both had been educated in Spain. By now I understood the language well enough—even spoke it well enough so that *porteños* did not cringe at the sound of my voice—to know that I was hearing from them a kind of Castilian that was on the point of extinction.

How, I wondered, had they felt while listening to Marx torturing Cervantes in the coarsened speech of their deluded son and his joyless wife? If they were surprised that Luz had brought a Yanqui home with her—she hardly paused for breath after the introductions before informing them that we intended to marry—nothing showed on their faces apart from a very brief widening of the eyes.

We drank aged Argentinean Manzanilla, ate a five-course, three-wine dinner served by a butler in frayed livery that was almost as old as he was. We lingered over coffee in front of a wood fire. The *abuelos,* as Luz always called her grandparents no matter which language she was speaking, never asked me a question about myself. There was no need: Luz itemized the essentials. They listened as if they had somehow known all about me before they knew I existed. Luz loved them deeply, and we went back to their house often, but their manner never changed. The *abuelos* were proper in every way. They offered hospitality, not quite the same thing as acceptance, but more than I deserved. After all, I was inflicting upon them the loss of the only descendant they had left to love. I was going to make her disappear, transport her to my barbarous country.

Luz also introduced me, one by one, to her honorary uncles and aunts, the former terrorists Alejandro had handed over to Amzi instead of giving them to the military. Few of them had accepted Amzi's offers of secret employment, but most must have given him information and other kinds of help or they wouldn't have been where they were today—or even alive if he had chosen to tell the military who they were. Some of them could barely contain the loathing they felt for me and would have felt for any North American who worked inside the U.S. embassy. Even if I was not a baddy personally, I was still an agent of capitalist imperialism and deserved death even if it was merely social death, the only sort of assassination still available to them. Others were more mannerly, if only to preserve the illusion that they had left the folly of their youth behind them. They were respectable now, and because the respectability was a disguise, they took care not to let the masks slip. One and all behaved as if they were at all times gazing into invisible mirrors.

None of this meant they had foresworn the true faith. The catechism of the radical left still trumped reality. In the United States they would have gone on shouting out the vocabulary of slogans that was the Esperanto of their youth. For them, such behavior remained unwise. They were in hiding for life. They never knew whom they might be talking to or what that fellow down the table who didn't sing with the choir might really be—or worse, what he *used* to be. Or whom he knew.

I did not regard their hostility as a problem. From an operational viewpoint, it was a good thing that they had never changed. The important thing was, they hated the same Headquarters I had targeted. When offered the chance to carry out one last revolutionary act, perhaps with luck to slay the vile monster, they would not refuse, as long as they didn't have to be suicide bombers, which was a job best left to persons of less value than themselves.

Luz shared this analysis. This surprised me. Politically speaking, these people had raised her. They had baptized and confirmed her. They had shown themselves to her as they really were because it was her birthright to be trusted. They were her political tutors. They had taught her to be undyingly proud of her father and mother. They had told her stories of their heroism, told her secrets, painted in her mind a picture of Alejandro as paladin of the people, slayer of fascist dragons, the very definition of righteousness, and of Felicia as his Joan of Ark.

Alejandro, they believed, had saved every one of their lives. They knew he had done this by sacrificing everyone else, but by the time Luz was old enough to be told the legend, they had buried the memory of the price he had paid. They assumed he had done what he had done to save the revolution, namely themselves. He had not, after all, sacrificed anyone who mattered. They knew what they knew because they had been what they had been, and in their minds they had never changed even if capitalism had made some of them very rich.

Money and respectability were their impenetrable cover. Alejandro's pragmatism, learned from Marx and Mao and his own intestines, had taught them this. They owed him too much, he had sacrificed too much, for them ever to change their ideas.

Luz was the living credential I had needed to enter this fun house. She was the only credential I needed, because I had no plan to ask these people personally for help or information. I knew they would refuse me out of hand. They would not, could not refuse Luz. They would assume that the political education they had given her meant that whatever she did for the rest of her life, she would do for the cause, which lived on in her like a transmission of genes. They never doubted that they were right about her. By nature and nurture she was the enemy of the enemies of mankind. If she was marrying one of those enemies, it had to be for correct reasons. They would help her carry out whatever secret purpose she might have. It was their duty to help—their penance for living on after Alejandro had died for what they told themselves they themselves had been willing to die for.

By wink, nudge, and tone, Luz made silent excuses for me: After all, they could hardly expect me, as a serving officer of the U.S. government, to join openly in their Orwellian hour of hate. The fact that I was in love with the daughter of two of the greatest haters of America who ever lived must mean that there might, just possibly, be hope for me after all.

One of the regulars at these affairs was a quiet man named Diego Aguilar Ordoñez. He was a distant cousin of Alejandro's and looked a little like him, though less tall, less handsome, less charismatic. Diego had salt-and-pepper hair, quiet eyes, an arched nose out of a cinquecento painting, a look of perpetually amused, benevolent intelligence. He stood out for his modest manner, his plain dress. Sometimes I tried to visualize the rest of this crowd, now wearing bespoke suits and designer dresses, as they must have looked in their terrorist days—both genders wearing *descamisados* clothing, though they had never in their lives performed an hour of manual labor. Unwashed, braless, bearded, long-haired, in need of a bath. Solemn in their narcissism.

Oddly, Diego was the only one who still wore a beard—a well-kept spade but a beard just the same. He was a surgeon. During the revolution he had somehow completed his residency at the Hospital Británico in Buenos Aires while acting as Alejandro's chief of operations. It was he who had planned the bombings and the assassinations and assigned others to carry them out. He was, Luz said, Alejandro's oldest and closest friend. The way the others treated him, as if he had inherited custody of Alejandro's aura, set him apart. If anyone in this crowd had been a primary target for recruitment by the Russians, Diego was the likeliest candidate. He had been the administrator of the revolution—in bourgeois terminology, prime minister to Alejandro's president for eternity. Through him the KGB could manipulate Alejandro. With his help, they could nurse the revolution. By helping him they could befriend and eventually control Alejandro, who might become Argentina's Lenin. There was small chance of this actually happening, but if conditions were right, stranger things had come to pass: Consider the improbable Fidel Castro. Everything begins with 1.

At these parties, Luz invariably had private moments with the aunts and uncles. One or another of them would put an arm around her and lead her into another room. I would see the two of them talking intently, looking deeply into each other's smiling eyes, the aunts and uncles touching Luz's hands or cheeks as if they had wandered out of the moment and into a memory.

This behavior seemed more intense in Diego's case, the conversations lasted longer, Luz usually came back from their encounters with shining eyes. Clearly he was special, closer to her than the rest. She had almost never spoken about him. I felt something like jealousy.

One evening I asked her on the way home what was going on.

She said, "After the worst happened, Diego saved me. He was the one who loved me the most, actually loved me for myself, not just because I was my father's child. I could feel that. I still do. He knew my father and mother better than anyone in the world, better than a child ever could know them, and he made them real in my mind. When I look at Diego I see Alejandro standing beside him. If the others are like aunts and uncles, Diego is like the father. He has always looked after me as a father looks after a daughter. Sometimes I think Alejandro willed me to him."

In bed after her visits with Diego, Luz seemed more tender, less aggressive than usual—shy, even, as if her hour with him had subtracted some of her love for me. Had the shade of Alejandro followed us home from the party and now stood guard over our bed? Was that what she imagined? Luz murmured in her sleep, so I could only be sure she was awake when she was silent. I seldom caught words but detected changes in her tone of voice. Often she sounded as if she were arguing with some figment in her dream, stridently demanding that something that belonged to her be given back.

On Diego nights her voice was soft. She sounded like a child wheedling for something she wanted. She smiled and laughed softly. This kept me awake for hours.

The next morning as we ate our bread and jam and drank our café con leche, she still had a faraway look in her eye. After breakfast she brushed her teeth, a lengthy process in Luz's case, while I scanned the newspapers.

When she came back to the kitchen there was something different about her. She gave me a searching look, as if in the night she had learned something about me she had not known before.

I asked her the question that had kept me awake most of the night. "You think Diego is the one we can trust?"

She immediately knew what I was talking about, as though she had picked up the scent of my intentions.

She said, "The only one. But he knows who you work for, so that's a problem."

"How does he know?"

"My love, *everyone* knows."

"You told them?"

"You think I would reveal such a thing? It wasn't necessary. They can tell."

We began to see Diego alone, just the three of us together, always in out-of-the-way places outside the city—small country restaurants, day sails aboard Diego's ketch among the picture puzzle islands of the Paraná River Delta, days on horseback on the pampas, picnics. Diego was good at everything—sailor, rider, cook, you name it. He was always the host, and like a man who is wary of being poisoned, he would not allow us to provide a crumb or a bottle of wine for the picnic basket or pay for so much as a cup of coffee.

All the while he was assessing me, of course, but he always treated me as if I had stepped off an airplane that same morning. The talk was always general. He didn't discuss his work because, Luz said, doing so might compromise doctor-patient confidentiality, and besides, he had already heard, many times over, every question a layman could possibly ask about medical matters.

He didn't talk about himself or about the past. Nor did he ever ask me about my work or pose a personal question. Knowing the one all-encompassing thing he knew about me seemed to be enough for him. I did not believe this was true or that it would last, but I accepted the pretense. To all appearances Diego was a gentle man, kindness itself—an angel, Luz said.

He was the best surgeon in Argentina. He operated on the poor without charge. He had saved many lives. Perhaps, in his mind, he was paying a debt. If he was haunted by the innumerable murders and mutilations he had arranged in his youth—agonizing deaths and wounds designed to horrify and to show that the revolution and its justice would stop at nothing—he showed no sign of it. I had never before met a person who seemed so at peace with himself, and few who were half as likeable.

This weird detachment, this deft separation of the Siamese twins that were the old ruthless Diego and the new saintly Diego, could only mean one thing: He was capable of anything. He could suture the two Diegos together again whenever he liked.

Diego had a beach house on the Atlantic at Las Grutas in Patagonia, a thousand kilometers south of Buenos Aires. In early February, during Carnival, he invited us to spend a long weekend with him there. We flew down in his twin-engine Beechcraft. Diego was a pilot, mainly because the airplane made it easier for him to fly to remote parts of the country on weekends to perform pro bono surgery on the poor.

His house, which overlooked a broad and sandy beach, was a stark-white Rubik's puzzle of concrete cubes designed by one of the honorary uncles who was an avant-garde architect. There was no telephone, no television, no radio, but he did own a Clearaudio sound system with JBL speakers that had cost not less than fifty thousand dollars. Luz played the Brandenburg concertos the whole weekend because Diego liked Bach's mathematical filigree. The water, like the weather, was a few degrees warmer here than in Buenos Aires. At night you could hear the surf, smell the sea. Summer was at its height, so there were a lot of people on the beach. We stayed away from them. We swam in the sea in the early morning and played tennis afterward on Diego's court. Diego was an excellent player. So was Luz. I was rusty—the desert countries are not good places to chase a bouncing ball in the sun. Diego was the same person—one personality visible, the other hidden, a twinning I felt more and more strongly the longer, I cannot truthfully say "the better," I knew him.

There were no servants. Diego did the cooking, Luz the housekeeping. She knew the house, knew the routine, knew where everything was. On the morning of the final day, he went back to Buenos Aires and his practice. Luz and I stayed behind.

"Stay the week," he said. "I'll come back on Friday, I have an operation in San Antonio Oeste, and we'll fly home late Sunday."

We accepted. There was no reason not to. Fortuitously, Luz had taken the whole week off, and I could take whatever operational time was needed.

Diego said, "One small thing. A friend of mine will be stopping by sometime this week, I'm not sure which day, if you don't mind giving him dinner and putting him up overnight. He's a Russian. You'll enjoy him."

Ah, a Russian.

Arkady Barburin, as he called himself, turned up at about five the following afternoon, bearing two chilled bottles of Cristal Champagne and a flat can of Beluga caviar. I wondered if he knew that Roederer had created this wine for Tsar Alexander II. Probably he did. He was a lover of minutiae, one of the new Russians, or maybe a re-creation of the old type we knew from nineteenth-century novels. He was interested in everything, a man of the world—well barbered, well dressed, smiling, a good talker, mannerly. A sort of Slavic Diego, you might say, including the inner twin that listened but never spoke. His *porteño* Spanish was flawless. He was in the import-export business, the South American representative of a Russian conglomerate whose Roman alphabet acronym he pronounced slowly in case Luz and I might have heard of it. I hadn't. This was far more sophisticated cover than the Soviet intelligence services could ever have provided. Caviar, Arkady said, was his favorite import. He hoped we liked it. We did. Luz made the usual accompaniments, and we ate it all with one bottle of the Cristal and drank the other with the sea bass she cooked.

Even before we drank the second bottle of Roederer, Arkady was entirely open to questions. That was his shtick. He was good at it. I asked him how he happened to know Diego.

"He saved my life—bypass surgery," Arkady said. "I was feeling a bit dizzy, shortness of breath, inexplicable pain in my left thigh. Diego was recommended by my doctor as the best surgeon in Buenos Aires. He saw me on fifteen minutes' notice, listened to my heart, put me on a treadmill, and two hours later put me on the operating table. I said, 'Can't this wait?' He said, 'If you want to die in the elevator, yes.' Quadruple bypass surgery. I've felt like a billion rubles ever since."

As usual, Diego had been right. We enjoyed Arkady. He could talk about anything and give every impression that he knew what he was talking about. His sentences moved on an undercurrent of humor.

How had he become Diego's friend instead of just another ex-patient? How did anyone become a friend? They just hit it off, they were a lot alike despite having grown up in entirely different cultures half a world apart. In far different circumstances, too, Diego being an aristocrat, Arkady the descendant of serfs and peasants and workers. Arkady recited his autobiography, a fundamental giveaway: Only spies and others with something to hide act as if they want you to know everything about them on first meeting. In their case, the legend usually is pure fiction.

His grandfather, he said, was on Old Bolshevik who had actually known Lenin even before he came to power. After Lenin died, the old man made a joke about Stalin while drunk and was exiled to Siberia. He never came back. When this happened Arkady's father was already in university and a candidate for Party membership. He thought his life was over, but Stalin died in timely fashion, so he was allowed back in the fold. Arkady was born into the fold. He went to good schools and was accepted at a good university, which of course he named—Lomonosov, in Moscow.

"I studied economics but I was a capitalist by nature and instinct, also religious though I got over that, God knows where all that came from," Arkady told us, "so when Gorbachev came and the Soviet Union fell into pieces there was a market for my ambitions, and here I am."

Did he have a wife? Luz asked.

"Alas, no. There was a woman I loved when I was young, gorgeous and good, but at heart a Komsomol who never grew up, a Stalinist Peter Pan. She longed for a Communist world, wanted to work for an ideal instead of profit, so it was impossible."

"What happened to her?"

"What usually happens. One day we were together never to part, and then we had an extra drink and a quarrel and the next day she disappeared. I kept looking for her and sometimes like Dr. Zhivago on his trolley car I saw a girl on the street and thought it was her and hurried to catch up. But it was always the wrong girl. It took me twenty years to have the heart attack."

Arkady left the following afternoon. Before he got into his Mercedes he hugged Luz and warmly shook my hand.

"This was fun," he said in English. "Let's stay in touch. I'm having a little anniversary party Saturday after next for my open-heart surgery. Diego will be the guest of honor. Please come—eight o'clock, dinner, tango, casual dress."

He handed each of us a calling card. "No gifts," he said, touching his chest. "Diego has taken care of that."

Arkady was following the script.

14

At Arkady's party, a handful of aunts and uncles mingled with a new-rich crowd of several nationalities, including a knot of expatriate Russians wearing ten-thousand-dollar wristwatches and displaying lissome young wives in couturier dresses that probably cost about the same. As usual, the aunts and uncles embraced Luz as if she had just gotten home from her sophomore year abroad and greeted me with perfunctory smiles before whisking her away and leaving me standing all by myself.

My isolation didn't last long. Arkady appeared in a matter of minutes with a fellow Russian in tow.

He said, in English, "Say hello to Boris Gusarov. He works in our embassy, one of the higher-ups, so you two should have a lot in common."

I said, "I wonder about that. I'm pretty lowly."

Boris, watching my eyes to see if I understood, said something to me in Russian: "I, too, am lowly. But I think you are modest and are not so lowly."

In Russian I said, "I am just as capable of being lowly as you are, Dmitri."

"My name is Boris."

"I know. I was joking."

"Joking?" Boris said. "Explain to me what is funny."

I said, "Have you ever seen the movie *Dr. Strangelove?*"

"No."

"In it, Peter Sellers, the actor playing a prissy American president, tells the drunken Soviet prime minister over the hotline just before the Russian blows up the world with his Doomsday Machine, 'I am capable of being just as sorry as you are, Dmitri.'"

Boris laughed—two barks. "Very amusing. The American president is sober?"

"In every way. He's a liberal."

"You speak our language very well," Boris said. "Let's talk Russian, do you mind?"

"No, but why?"

"I've been speaking Spanish all day. I'm tired of it. Speaking Russian doesn't seem to be much of an effort for you. Did you have a Russian mother? Wife? Girlfriend? Friend of the same sex?"

Was he trying to be offensive? When I didn't answer these rude questions immediately, Boris beckoned words from my mouth with a crooked forefinger. Obviously it was Boris's habit to let people know from the first moment who the alpha male in this conversation was going to be.

Diego arrived. Arkady exclaimed, "Ah, the guest of honor!"

He hurried across the room, smiling happily, arms outspread in welcome.

Boris said, "Doctors are always late. It is required by the Hippocratic oath."

Maybe he was just trying to be funny. I didn't answer. Boris, his face close to mine, asked me ten rapid personal questions, all the while searching my face, as if like a living polygraph he could tell whether I was answering with the truth.

On the eleventh question I said, "Good to meet you, Boris."

And walked away.

Boris gasped, recoiling from this insult.

On the fringe of the party I found a plainly dressed Argentinean couple standing alone in silence. We chatted. They were polite but puzzled. Who was I? They had never seen me before. I looked like a Yanqui but didn't sound like one.

Finally I introduced myself.

"Ah, Luz's friend from the north," the husband said. "We've heard about you. Diego speaks highly of you."

Really?

I said, "You and Diego are friends?"

"Since childhood. He and Violeta, here, are medical colleagues."

Violeta, he said, was a surgical nurse. She assisted at some of Diego's operations, especially the ones he performed on weekends for the poor.

"Diego has saved many, many lives. In his airplane he will go anywhere at a moment's notice to save the life of a worker," Violeta said, eyes ashine. "He always says that if you save one life, you save many—a wife or a husband, children, a mother, even children of the children that the saved person has not yet conceived and their children."

Of course the opposite was true when you exploded a bomb in a crowded room—but why mention that?

I said, "Then you must have known Luz's father."

Silence, then a reluctant nod from the husband, as if he was afraid he might utter an unmanly sob if he gave me his answer out loud. Violeta squeezed his hand, smiled up at him.

She said, "For many years Firmin's mother was his family's cook. My own father also worked for the Ordoñezes. Diego was like a cousin. The children were a commune in our neighborhood. You are lucky to know Diego, to have his good opinion. He doesn't make new friends easily."

I wanted this conversation to go on, but before I could think of something to say in return, Violeta nodded brusquely, having said all she wanted to say, and then took her husband by the hand and led him away. I watched them greet Diego and embrace him—the woman kissed him three times on the cheeks. Diego put an arm around the man's shoulders.

While all this was happening Arkady, a tall man, was gazing at me over the heads of the crowd. Boris was standing where I had left him, glaring at me. Arkady lifted his eyebrows: *What was going on?*

Abruptly, Boris departed without saying good night. I didn't think I had seen the last of him. Rejection is a motivator for the Borises of this world. He would find a way to have his way. He would come at me from a different direction and balance my insult with a worse insult of his own. I was content to wait for him to make the next move.

A week or so later, out of the blue, Arkady invited me to lunch at Chan Chan, a so-called closed-door restaurant near Palacio Barolo. The chef specialized in creative fish dishes—no meat on the menu.

"It's a nice change from steak, steak, steak and chimichurri, chimichurri, chimichurri," said Arkady.

So it was. During the appetizer, lobster salad, and the entrée, grilled sea bass, we talked about football—soccer in American English—in Russian. Arkady played in the park on Sundays with a team composed of expat Russians. It was called Gospoda—"the Lords," or "the Gentlemen." Under Stalin, this counterrevolutionary name would have been more than enough to land the whole team in the gulag.

Did I play football? I told him I had played in school. Was I any good? Within my limits, I said, I had been adequate. I had a knack for scoring but was no great shakes at anything else. As a fifteen-year-old, by sheer luck, I had, in practice, got the ball past a friend of my school's coach, a world-class goalkeeper who had played in the Olympics for, I think, Cameroon.

"What luck!" Arkady said, impressed. "We desperately need a striker. Ours was transferred by his company to Paris, the lucky dog. With your Russian, you could impersonate someone from Omsk or Tomsk and no one would be the wiser except Boris, amazing fellow, who figures absolutely everything out. And he'd never tell."

Arkady studied my reaction when he mentioned Boris's name.

I said, "What position does Boris play?"

"Goalkeeper, what else?" Arkady said. "I'm serious. Will you try out for us?"

"I don't think that would be good for my career, but thanks."

Arkady mimed deep disappointment.

The waiter brought flan for me. Arkady skipped dessert. While I ate mine, he revealed the purpose of this luncheon.

"Speaking of Boris," he said, "he's puzzled by what happened at the party. A little hurt, too."

"'Hurt'? What does he think happened?"

"You left him on the dance floor."

Arkady's tone was light, but the look on his face was dead serious. "He wonders what he did to offend you. What *did* happen?"

"He put his hand on my ass."

"Boris? You're joking."

"Of course I am. But he comes on strong."

"In what way?"

"Being interrogated as if I had just been arrested on suspicion of counterrevolutionary thought is not my idea of conversation."

Arkady said, "Oh, that. I should have warned you. That's because Boris is shy, so he rattles off questions so he won't have to answer questions. It's just the old 'the best defense is a good offense.' After the first fifteen minutes, he relaxes and becomes good company. He's a good guy, really."

I worked on my flan and made no reply.

Arkady broke the silence.

"I knew Boris in university days," he said. "Football again. My weekend team sometimes played his team. We'd drink together, both teams, afterward. Boris may look like a gorilla, but he's got a deep and open mind. Smart. Trustworthy, loyal, friendly. Photographic memory. Good chess player. I never won a game he didn't let me win. Do you play chess?"

"Maybe not at Boris's level."

Arkady said, "Look—really, no kidding, Boris is OK. Do yourself and me a favor. Give him a second chance."

I said, "You're the buddy broker?"

He flushed: *And I thought* Boris *was rude?*

The waiter brought coffee. Arkady sipped his and recovered.

With a smile, he said, "I just think you and Boris would get along just fine once the bad moment was behind you. I'd ask you and Luz to have dinner with me with Boris as the extra man, but somehow I don't think that would work out."

I didn't contradict him on that point. I didn't want to kill all possibility of seeing Boris when I was in control, so I said, "I understand, Arkady. He's your friend. He has hidden qualities. But what's the point?"

"I think the two of you would get along if you gave him the benefit of the doubt."

I tried to look skeptical.

After a moment of thought, as if he had not invited me to Chan Chan in order to make the exact suggestion he was about to make, Arkady said, "How about this? We meet at the soccer ground in the park—seemingly by chance if that's the way you want to do it—and you kick a few while Boris keeps goal. He's good at it. He won't let you get one by him if he can help it, I promise."

I expelled a heavy OK-I-give-up breath and said, "All right, Arkady. Saturday?"

"Perfect," Arkady said. "Before it gets hot? Seven o'clock?"

"Fine."

At this, Arkady smiled as if it had just stopped snowing in Moscow.

Keeping my date with Boris cost me a hundred dollars for soccer cleats. I wore my running clothes and to warm up, ran the mile to the park in running shoes with the cleats hanging around my neck and bouncing on my chest.

When I arrived on the stroke of seven, having taken a detour to kill time, Arkady and Boris were already at the football pitch. Boris, who wore his Gospoda goalkeeper's uniform, stood in the goal. Arkady was kicking the ball to him. The Russians saw me immediately but went on with their drill while I took a drink of water.

Arkady had a strong leg but was a wild kicker. This made Boris's job somewhat more challenging, but he was remarkably nimble for a man who looked more like a weight lifter than a whippet.

I studied him. He moved to his left less quickly than he moved to his right. He had a tendency to twitch right, wasting a fraction of a second before plunging left.

Finally, Arkady launched his final kick and in Russian shouted, "Fifty!" Boris made a nice save.

Arkady, smiling, walked toward me with hand outstretched; Boris stayed where he was.

"You made it," Arkady said, squeezing my hand. He was as sweaty as I was. "Welcome," he said. "We were getting ready for the masked striker. You remember Boris."

I nodded to Boris, who nodded back. He made an attempt to invest the gesture with cordiality, but his true intention was written all over him: His plan was to beat me, badly, and reestablish chimpanzee rank. I thought the first part was possible. I hadn't kicked a soccer ball into a net for twenty years. I mentioned this. Boris stared at me unsmiling, as if he would soon get the truth out of me.

I hoped so. Boris had a weakness in his play, and I thought I knew what that weakness was and how to take advantage of it. I knew, too, that it was possible to get lucky, because every goal I had ever scored owed more to good luck than to skill. Because of the daily runs my legs were strong enough. Also, I supposed my body would awaken its own memory of how to play the game. It all depended on my brain. If it would consent to stop giving my muscles orders for a while and let my muscles do the thinking, I might have a chance.

Arkady said, "Do you want to warm up or are you loose enough already?"

"I'm good."

Boris, still wordless—not trusting himself to talk without firing questions, maybe—trotted back to the cage, doing some sort of calisthenics as he went.

Arkady said, "OK. Ten practice kicks, then fifty kicks that count. Agreed?"

"Whatever you say."

"Just like in a match, you only need one goal to win."

I said, "How many penalty kicks?"

"Five at the end, if you need them. Is that agreeable?"

"Generous. Are you going to pass me the ball?"

"With pleasure."

I said, "Let's skip the practice kicks."

"Really?"

"Don't want to wear myself out."

Arkady made a gesture. Boris flung the ball into play. At first, because of my long layoff from the game, I didn't quite know where I was or what I was trying to do. After the first few kicks, however, I began to enjoy myself. I had never taken soccer very seriously, but it had its moments: I did like to score. The rest of it I could take or leave alone, and as a bored kid in a suburb I mostly just counted the minutes until the clock ran out.

Arkady was far and away the best passer I had ever played with. He was quick, instinctive, agile. It didn't take the two of us long to find a rhythm. I made some bad shots—a few of them deliberate—and some good shots, the latter mostly to Boris's strong side. He gobbled them up. I'm left-footed by nature, so naturally he began to concentrate on his right side. I flubbed a shot, then gave him a couple of saves to his right, then flubbed one over the goal. You might have thought all these mistakes would have aroused Boris's suspicions that I was up to no good, but maybe because I was an American (so what could I know about soccer?), this didn't seem to be the case.

On the twenty-eighth try, I used my right foot for the first time to drive a shot to his left. He couldn't reach it: 1–0 USA.

Boris glared at me with a suspicion that verged on loathing: How had I done that?

Arkady said, "Game over."

I said, "Let's go to fifty as agreed, if that's OK with Boris."

Boris said, "Do a hundred if you want."

These were the first words he had uttered all morning.

I made no further effort to humiliate Boris, but by now luck was fully awake and on my side. I made two more goals, one of them to Boris's right, his strong side, because by that time he was concentrating almost all of his attention on his left.

When the contest was over, Boris managed to smile. He shook my hand with a warmth that was intended to be believable.

He said, "Very enjoyable. You should play for America in the World Cup. Arkady, you're the captain, invite him to practice with Gospoda. It would be good for us to go up against this American. For me especially."

"Good idea, but I don't think we can convince him."

Arkady threw an arm around my shoulders.

"Congratulations," he said in a hearty voice. "It was a pleasure to play with you. Have you really not played for twenty years or is what just happened the famous American tricky Dicky?"

I said, "I enjoyed it, too."

Arkady looked up at the sun.

"Time for coffee," he said. "There's a good place not far away. Boris pays."

Boris skipped the coffee and ordered a large dish of vanilla ice cream. Did he always eat ice cream for breakfast?

"Only on certain days," Boris said. "Do you play chess?"

"Sort of."

Boris smiled—broadly, seemingly without rancor. This changed the look of him for the better.

He said, "You mean it's been twenty years since you moved a chess piece? Let's have a game soon. This time I will be on my guard."

He was still smiling.

I said, "Sure. Why not?"

15

I had done what I could do to encourage the Russians. Now I waited for them to make the next move. A week passed, then two. I kept up my routine, assuming they already knew it in detail, and sure enough, one morning early as I ran in the same park where we had had our football shootout, I spotted Boris lumbering toward me from the opposite direction.

Even at a distance he was unmistakable, a squat figure wearing a white sweatband, a dark blue singlet and red shorts—the colors of the latest and in all probability, temporary Russian flag. When we drew closer, he did not bother to register surprise. He just stopped in his tracks and ran in place, thick legs pumping, until I reached him. Then he turned around and fell into step with me, eyes front. I offered no comment, and for the rest of the run, maybe half an hour, neither of us spoke. We were running on a dirt path. His heavy footfall caused little tremors in the earth. I could feel it, or imagined I could, through the soles of my running shoes.

We came to the end of the running path and pulled up. Boris, half smiling, offered his hand. We shook. His grip was painful. He probably could have fractured the bones if he wished.

He said, in English, "Fancy meeting you here."

"Indeed. I didn't know you were a runner, Boris."

Another small smile: He was not at ease. He said, "Goalkeepers need strong legs. Feel like a coffee?"

"Why not?"

He led me to a different coffee bar that looked pretty much the same as the last one—same frowsy woman at the cash register, same painfully bored kid at the machine. Both were watching U.S. reality television dubbed in Spanish. The volume was high. This made understanding Boris a challenge. His bulk notwithstanding, he spoke softly. After the first sip of espresso, he switched from English to Russian. He was still sweating, the cabbage scent of it was noticeable, and he wiped his face with the paper napkin.

He said, "Gospoda plays a team of Italians, the Alpini, this Sunday. They are very good. It will be an uphill battle. Why don't you come?"

He told me when and where the game would be played.

He said, "We can give you a uniform and run you out onto the field if we need a last-minute goal. The Mystery Striker. What is the American slang word for *impostor*?"

"Ringer."

"Even if you won't be a ringer, come anyway."

"I'll try."

"That would be good. We'll be without Arkady, our best player."

"Oh?"

"One of his trips."

Evidently Arkady had spoken his lines in Act One, Scene Two of this comedy, and moved offstage. I wondered how well he really knew Diego—or Boris, for that matter. Watching him dash around the football pitch I had wondered about the quadruple bypass. Now I wondered again.

Boris watched my face. Maybe my skepticism showed. He got up and went to the counter and returned with two more cups of coffee and two dishes of vanilla ice cream.

"That's breakfast?" I said.

"Try it. You'll like it. Ice cream is the best thing after exercise—the sugar, the taste, the reward for punishing your body."

We were seated by the front window, so we could watch the girls as they went by. Boris was appreciative but kept his thoughts to himself. We might as well have been a couple of jocks who had met by chance and had no plans ever to see each other again.

As we parted, shaking hands again, Boris said, "Try to come Sunday. Maybe we can have that game of chess afterward."

He slapped my biceps and grinned. "Maybe you can ambush me again."

Thus began a beautiful friendship.

On Sunday Luz and I went to the football match. The Alpini won 2–1 on a header in extra time. The partisan crowd screamed: There are lots of Argentineans of Italian ancestry.

I didn't see Boris again for a while. I was in no hurry to get together. Then one day I ran into him in a restaurant. He mentioned the chess game again. Although I now lived with Luz, I still had an apartment of my own. That seemed the best and most private meeting place. We agreed to meet there the next Saturday.

Boris wrote down the address, though he probably had long since memorized it. I duly informed the station chief and Headquarters of this arrangement. Amzi and Tom Terhune dispatched a tech to Buenos Aires to make sure that no bugs had been installed in my flat while I was disporting myself with Luz.

The tech found nothing, but of course the possibility existed that he had bugged the apartment as long as he was there. I was fine with that. It could only validate my "loyalty." It would be beneficial to have a record of who was recruiting whom. If I did it right, it might come in handy at the Plantation as a training film. Father would have appreciated that: After all those years of not thinking about him if

I could possibly help it, I was now, unexpectedly, reminded of him almost daily.

In an antiques shop I found a nice chessboard with a set of ivory chessmen. I set it up on the small distressed card table that had come with the apartment. Boris arrived on the dot of nine, an early hour for chess. Luz was still asleep in her own apartment. So was most of the rest of the city. The streets and stairways were deserted. An occasional police siren pierced the weekend quiet. In another apartment someone practiced the first few bars of a Mozart piano concerto over and over again. Boris, apparently a music lover, kept time with his head.

Once again memories awakened. Father taught me to play chess. It was his style to play against the clock like a chess hustler in a park—*move-bang-DING*—and I emulated him. As I got better at the game I beat him once in a while, and he was not one to cheapen the thrill by letting his opponent win. After he left home I played with friends, even joined a chess club at school, but I gave it up when I was posted to the Middle East because, as with everything else, I was never in one place long enough to find an opponent I knew well enough to be confident that he or his friends didn't intend to capture me instead of my queen.

I was rusty, not that it mattered. I realized very quickly that I wasn't in Boris's class. He skunked me in the first game, showing no mercy. Because I was such a hapless opponent, he played even faster than Father, so we had several games before it was time for lunch. I lost them all. But as we went along I began to see the pattern in Boris's method and thought that in time, as my own game came back to me, I might be able to win every once in a while. Boris seemed to have some inkling of what I was thinking. Maybe losing the shootout had planted a seed of doubt in his mind. I hoped so.

For an early lunch I gave him pinot grigio and soup and cold chicken and salad, all straight from the supermarket. We talked about football. He was almost genial.

Boris and I agreed to play chess again the following Saturday. He asked if we could start earlier, say six in the morning. He worked on Saturdays and it was better if he reported for duty on time. We made the change.

I began to enjoy the games. I liked playing with a fresh morning mind, liked feeling that I was recovering lost skills and dim memories of Father's mock glee when he outsmarted me.

After a month or so I was beating Boris maybe half the time—or if he was as good as I thought he was, maybe he was letting me win. Once in a while I made a wrong move just to give him an advantage. Sometimes when this happened he looked up from the board with a flicker of suspicion—was I really that stupid?—but he always took what I offered.

Within boundaries I learned to enjoy Boris's company. This ran counter to my expectations, but Arkady had been right: Once he relaxed, Boris was a likable enough fellow. We didn't talk much, but chess is not a game associated with good conversation. Concentration and silence are the attractions, along with stealth and the potential humiliation of the opponent. No wonder the game is a flattering synonym for underhanded pursuits, especially the craft Boris and I practiced.

After a while, in hopes that this would encourage franker conversation, I shortened the sessions by a game and served coffee. Boris signaled his approval of this time-out by bringing a sack of *medialunas,* as the local version of croissants are called. This gave us half an hour or so to relax, if that's the word for two wary dogs engaged in a sniffing contest. The talk was harmless—football, of course, but also the peculiarities of the Argentineans, who might have been surprised that an American and a Russian found them at least as amusing as they found us.

We avoided world affairs, personal history, politics. I assumed that Boris took it for granted, because he had been educated to think in this way, that all Headquarters types were Nazis. If I did not behave like one, it was because I was foxily concealing the real me. On the other hand I assumed that he was at heart a stalwart Communist who went about spying on the class enemy with the same aggression with which he played goalie and chess. I looked in vain for the fault that would let me get one past him when he leaned the wrong way. He was very professional.

Meanwhile Luz and I continued to see a lot of Diego. She had a birthday coming up in late September, the first month of spring in the Southern Hemisphere, and he invited us to stay at his place in Patagonia for a week or for as long as we chose. He'd fly us down. We could use the old car he kept at the airport. The beaches would be empty—it was too early to swim, but we could take walks and be quite alone. He might come down on weekends but otherwise we'd be alone. We accepted. Luz was tired of the city, tired of not copulating on Saturday mornings—a day without orgasms was a day lost. On her birthday, the *abuelos* hosted a dinner party of old friends of the family: Godmothers and godfathers certified by the Holy Roman Catholic Church, real aunts and uncles and cousins. No honorary aunts and uncles were invited.

"The *abuelos* hate the sight of them because Alejandro died for them and in their opinion all of them together were not worth one of him," Luz said. "*Los descuidados,* the *abuelos* call them, the careless ones."

The *abuelos'* party was on a Saturday. On Sunday the honorary aunts and uncles hired a restaurant and a rock band and threw a birthday party themselves. It was an all-Alejandroista affair—themselves, their kids, and a few uncomfortable foot soldiers of the revolution who looked like street people who had just been given a bath and new clothes by the Argentinean version of the Salvation Army. As usual no one took any interest in the Yanqui interloper. If Luz was in love with me, fine. They were all in favor of sexual experimentation. She was a big girl now, and I must do something for her that she liked having done. Let her enjoy whatever the something was while it lasted. They hoped she'd get over it soon and plug herself into the mother brain again.

The next morning, Diego flew us south. In Patagonia the weather was wonderful, and as Diego had promised, the beaches were deserted and the weekend houses owned by doctors and lawyers and minor tycoons were shuttered. As soon as he left, Luz and I went back to living without clothes. At night we swam naked in the frigid water—the moon waxed the whole time we were there—and made love in the water or on a beach towel or with quivering knees while standing up in the surf. We were alone, all alone, Mr. and Mrs. R. Caruso.

Luz never closed her eyes during sex, so that when I opened mine, there she was, always, concealing nothing. I had never been so happy in my life and I knew I never would be again.

One afternoon, late, we came back from the beach and saw a shiny rental car parked beside the battered Toyota Corolla Diego was letting us use. The stereo was playing guitar music—Bach again. Diego had all of Andrés Segovia's CDs. We went inside and found Diego stretched out on the sofa, sound asleep. Or dead. He was so still, his skin was so gray, that we couldn't tell which until he uttered a sudden loud snore. Luz, who had grasped my forearm for fear that he might be a corpse, giggled.

In a whisper she said, "It must be Friday."

Diego subsided. Luz tiptoed across the room and picked up the books we had been reading, the usual magic realism novel in her case, the poems of the great Russian manic-depressive Anna Akhmatova in mine. We went outside, lay down together in the hammock, and read ourselves to sleep.

When we woke it was almost dark. Lights burned in the house. Different music, American pop sung in Spanish came over the speakers. We heard the clatter of dishes. The thermometer had fallen. Luz, who was wearing a bikini, shivered and hugged herself. As we got closer to the house we smelled something cooking.

We went inside. Boris was setting the table. He was not very good at it. The forks, knives, and spoons were all on one side of the plates, the glasses were plastic tumblers instead of wineglasses. He held a bouquet of checkered napkins in his hand as if trying to figure out what to do with them.

Luz, struck dumb by the uncouth sight of him, scuttled into the bedroom.

I said, "Hello, Boris."

He said, "Hello. Sorry about the surprise—Diego's idea. He tried to call but there was no answer."

"We spend a lot of time on the beach."

Boris said, "Is your wife all right?"

He knew perfectly well that Luz and I weren't married.

I said, "Let me check," and followed Luz into the bedroom

She now wore, to sweet effect, one of my sweaters over her bikini.

She jerked a thumb toward the kitchen and said, "Who's that?"

I told her. She was already fully briefed on my friendship with Boris, but she had never before been in the same room with him.

She said, "That's what I thought. Is Diego out of his mind? This is not supposed to happen."

Luz hated to be left out of the loop. She was in no mood to make allowances. She was agitated, accusation in her eyes, as though Boris's intrusion was my fault. It was against her rules to blame Diego for anything. True, she and I had agreed that she would never meet our targets. Her job was to get the aunts and uncles to identify old Russian acquaintances who had been friends of the revolution. But now the protocol had been broken.

The look on Luz's face asked what was I going to do about this. What was I supposed to do—throw him out of another man's house?

I said, "It's too late to worry about it. I'm going to take a shower before dinner. Want to join me?"

In English Luz said, "I don't fuck when there's a gorilla in the next room."

For dinner Diego made thick spaghetti with a peppery red sauce that had chunks of pancetta in it. Boris knew what it was and named it in Italian: *Bucatini all'Amatriciana*. He scarfed it down.

Italian food was his favorite, he said. Did he get much of it in Moscow? I asked.

"Not like this, but you can get what Russians call Italian food," Boris said. "Now, not before."

I took a plate of pasta and a glass of Argentinian Primitivo to Luz, who was still hiding out in the bedroom. She didn't say thank you. Diego had brought Italian pastries. Would she want some later, and coffee? No reply. She was seething. Her silence was scolding. It was *my* responsibility that Boris had walked in on our happiness. I should have protected her from becoming an entry in a file in Moscow. The fact that she had been in a Russian file all her life simply because she was her father's daughter seemed not to have occurred to her.

At the table, neither Diego nor Boris mentioned her absence. Boris was somewhat gloomy but kept up his end of the conversation. His Spanish was better than I had thought, heavily accented but nimble. We talked about—you guessed it—football. Diego was a great fan. He loved AC Milano. If Italy and Argentina played in the World Cup, he wouldn't know which team to root for. At around nine, after the second grappa, Boris said a perfunctory good night.

Before disappearing he said, "Chess in the morning, the usual time?"

Taking Luz's mood into account, there was no reason to say no.

Just after dawn we played a couple of games—one win apiece. Because Boris was also in a mood, there wasn't much joy in it.

Skidding into English (anything but Spanish), he said, "Let's skip the rubber and run on the beach."

He was already dressed in his running clothes. When I went into the bedroom to change into mine, Luz pretended that she wasn't awake.

Boris and I, all alone on the beach, ran for about an hour on the hard wet sand. After taking his last stride, Boris kicked off his shoes and peeled off his socks and plunged into the surf. He was a strong swimmer. He swam out through the crashing waves until his head was a dot, then tread water for a while before backstroking to shore.

Boris put on his shoes before he got sand on his feet. While he did this I started back to the house, which was still a long way off.

He caught up and said, "Wait. I want to ask you a question."

I stopped and turned around and waited for him to speak. We were maybe ten steps apart. There was a brisk wind, so Boris had to raise his voice in order to be heard.

He said, in Russian, "What are we really up to, you and I?

I said, "I don't follow your meaning."

But I was pretty sure I did.

16

Boris stood between me and the sun. He could see my face, but his was a blur. For a full minute, perhaps longer, the only sounds were wind, gulls, and surf.

He said, "You don't understand? Then let me simplify. I am not trying to recruit you."

"You're not? Then what *are* you doing, volunteering to be recruited?"

"That is not possible. I am offering an arrangement that will permit me to go on working for my country by helping yours."

I said, "A novel idea. How exactly would that work?"

Boris's face changed, as if he had peeled off his gorilla mask because he wanted me to see the real him.

He said, "I will first tell you why. I fear the future—not personally, what does one man matter? But I fear for my country."

He was using a voice that was stronger than the one I was used to.

I said, "Go on."

Boris said, "It is quite simple, a matter of personalities, a difference of opinion about what is Russia."

"And?"

"Listen and I will tell you," Boris said. "I knew our current president when we were both young officers posted to Berlin just before the collapse of the Soviet Union. He hated Gorbachev. A lot of people in our organization hated him because they knew that perestroika was a virus that had infected the Soviet apparatus and for which maybe there was no cure. They were worried about their futures. They knew what had happened in Russia under Bolshevism—men like themselves had helped make it happen—and they knew what could happen to them if reform got out of control. Some seriously thought Gorbachev was working for the Americans, that he had been turned long ago, that he had received his final marching orders when he met with Reagan in Reykjavik and came home covered with shame."

He paused. He stared at me, making sure I was hearing what he was saying to me.

He said, "Our future president was always saying what a great leader Comrade Stalin had been, how admirable his style of leadership was, how he had transformed the Motherland from a backward medieval kingdom into a modern state, a new kind of power that was the only rationale, the only possible model for the future of the world. He was so enthusiastic about the good old days of Bolshevism with its forty million murders of our own people and the suffering it imposed on everybody of every nationality except Stalin's murderers and torturers, mostly Georgians like himself who hated Russians, that at first I thought he was making a sick joke."

I tried not to blink. Boris's reckless words couldn't have been more astonishing if he had suddenly lapsed into fluent Sanskrit. The transformation did not awaken in me an eagerness to believe. Had he really known Vladimir Putin as an equal? This had to be a trap. How could it be anything else? Unless, of course, it was genuine. But how to tell the difference? Maybe his specialty was pouring out his heart to gullible targets. He was good at it. Practice really does make perfect.

No one can spend half a lifetime as an intelligence officer without acquiring the skills of an actor. If Boris was faking this outburst, he was a Barrymore.

I said, "Boris, I already know all about that. So does everybody else who reads the newspapers."

Boris said, "Please. Of course you know. I am trying to make you understand. I want to prevent, or at least make it harder, for this lunatic to re-create the Soviet Union, to push Russia back into the dark closet of history. The United States of America, although it is also led by a corrupt *nomenklatura* that pretends to love the common people in order to repress them and pick their pockets, is still the only force in the world that is strong enough to stand in the way. Therefore I want its help. And to buy that help I must help the United States."

I said, "Isn't that treason under Russian law?"

"To the people in power, perhaps. Not to eternal Russia."

I said, "If you are so loyal to your country, it's your country, right or wrong, yes?"

"Naturally, but it has been wrong long enough. Treason does not interest me. Patriotism does."

That's what they all say. The most eager turncoats generally insist—believe—that they are acting as patriots. The real reason for their actions might lie elsewhere—money, resentment, guilt—but they didn't always realize that, and if that was the case, they would endure torture, even death, to keep their illusion alive.

Boris said, "So this is what I am saying to you: I will help your country if it will help mine."

"I heard you the first time. Tell me, how, precisely, would you go about helping America?"

"By telling it much it does not know and will never know if it lets this opportunity pass. By making things happen it cannot make happen."

"And in return you, Boris not Holy Russia, wants exactly what?"

"We'll get to that. First, my conditions. I will swear no oath, sign no agreement, accept no discipline. You and only you must be my contact."

"Until death do us part?"

Boris brushed that off.

"I do not wish to meet anyone else in your organization under any circumstance whatsoever," he said. "I do not wish to see the faces of your colleagues, ever, or know their names. I will accept no money or other benefit. If I break contact you will not attempt to reestablish it. If I get into trouble and you hear about it you will not attempt to—what a word!—exfiltrate me. You will have nothing in your files that could be used to identify me even a hundred years after you and I are dead—not my true name or any other name by which I may be called, not a photograph, not my physical description, not my personal history. Nothing."

These were not onerous conditions. It would be easy enough to find a way around them, because how would he know? Boris's birth name was certainly not Boris Gusarov, and there was little or no prospect of ever knowing who he really was, because like the rest of our breed he had been many different people according to the situations in which he found himself, and also because neither Headquarters nor I had the means to control what he did or where he went or to catalog the contents of his memory. What he proposed was unusual. But the usual isn't the currency of the parallel universe in which spies operate under different laws of moral physics. He had, after all, just changed into somebody else right in front of my eyes.

I couldn't believe my luck. His idea fitted perfectly into my design for the perfect, the complete revenge I sought.

I said, "Are there others in your service who feel as you do?"

"I suppose so," Boris said. "How could there not be? But we don't get together and drink vodka and sing songs about it."

"But if you were asked to make a suggestion to the others, would you agree?"

"Perhaps. It would depend on the suggestion and who made it. No more questions."

"Just one. What is your rank?"

"I am the resident here. I am like a colonel. When I go back to Moscow, which will happen quite soon, I will be promoted or not promoted, but if I am not promoted I will still be a colonel in the Russian foreign intelligence service and I will still be trusted."

"And if you are promoted, you will be like a general."

"Yes. Like you."

I understood the message: He knew more about me than I thought, that quite possibly he had someone inside Headquarters who was senior enough to know all about me.

I said, "You understand I have no authority to say yes or no to this bolt from the blue."

"I know that, despite your high position. You will need a green light and the switch is in Virginia. Diego and I will go back to the city this afternoon. Before we go I will give you a package. Your people can examine the contents of the package, which must be returned to me in its original condition because I must return it to the registry. Do not attempt to photocopy it. If you do, invisible but indelible security markings will be created. Your superiors have three Saturdays, beginning on the next Saturday after they receive the package, to make up their minds. On the final Saturday, when we play chess, you can tell me what is their decision. They must accept these conditions in their entirety and make no conditions of their own."

Fat chance. But Boris already knew that.

I said, "One final question. Your present posting doesn't seem appropriate to your rank and experience."

"Another similarity in our situations."

"How long have you been in Buenos Aires?"

"Somewhat longer than you."

Full stop.

This time Boris was the one who abruptly turned his back and stepped out of the conversation. I followed, making no attempt to catch up. He had made his pitch. I had thoughts of my own to think.

Boris said nothing more about the package before he and Diego left, but after Luz had gone to sleep—she reinstated our usual sexual routine as soon as the gorilla had departed—I found it in the car. It consisted of about fifty cables and other top secret documents from the files of the Sluzhba Vneshney Razvedki, hence "SVR" in the Roman alphabet. SVR was the Russian equivalent of Headquarters—or if you were a creative thinker, vice versa.

It took me much of the night to make my way through the gobbledygook. Boris had not handed over the crown jewels of the latest version of the Cheka, but what he had provided was tantalizing enough.

There was no point in showing this to Luz, since she didn't read Russian and I had no time to translate, so at breakfast I told her the bare facts. It took a moment for her to realize what I was telling her and what it meant. Her sleepy brown gaze, which had been swimming because I had awakened her with an orgasm, suddenly changed. I saw no sign of rejection, but neither did I behold the glee I had expected. She didn't clap her hands or dance around the room, but she understood as well as I did that from the point of view of our plot or prank or purposes or whatever, we now possessed the keys to the kingdom.

This wasn't an unmixed blessing, and Luz was not the only one to realize that. What I thought I saw in her eyes was uncertainty, anxiety, the realization that danger had just sat down at the table with us.

She and I took the first commercial flight to Buenos Aires. I went straight to the embassy and sent a flash cable to Headquarters. Within the hour I received a reply signed by Tom Terhune ordering me to pouch the material by special courier and take the next available flight to Washington.

That flight left in less than three hours. Luz met me at the airport. In her demeanor I detected not one single point of light. It was raining all over the world.

She said, "Will you ever come back?"

What possible answer could I make to that question? I had not expected what I now saw in her face and heard in her voice. All of a sudden Luz was consumed by apprehension. Did she think the devils I worked for were going to assassinate me, as if I were a second Alejandro?

I should have felt sympathy and I should have found a way to reassure her, but there was no time and what I felt, unforgivably, was exasperation.

I said, "Luz, get a grip."

She gasped like a woman wronged. How could I say such a cruel thing to the woman I loved at such a moment? Did I really love her? Looking into her face was like reading these words in headline type.

The final call for my flight came over the loudspeakers. When I reached for Luz, she stepped back, out of my reach. She walked away, heels clicking, not quite running. I had no time to watch her go out of sight. I cleared security and ran for the flight. I hadn't slept a wink the night before.

I was unconscious before the plane rose into the air.

17

Amzi was on the telephone when Tom Terhune and I entered his office. He was listening in silence to the voice at the other end of the line with a total lack of expression on his face. The call went on far longer than Amzi's usual ten-word limit, so the Director—the one person he couldn't hang up on—must have been the person at the other end. Amzi gestured to the two chairs in front of his desk.

After another five minutes by the clocks on the wall, he said, "It shall be done, sir."

He hung up with a clatter, pointed a finger at me, and said, "Congratulations. Good shooting. Cool head. The Director's esteem is fucking boundless. Now tell me about Boris the Great."

I described the conversation on the beach. I repeated everything I had already reported: The meeting at the party, the shootout on the football pitch, the chance encounter while running in the park, the chess games— everything I thought Headquarters needed to know.

Amzi said, "What do you make of all this?"

I said, "The obvious. Either this guy is on the level or it's a dangle."

"Which possibility do you like better?"

"I waver. He's very good."

"Make a guess. Is the material fake or genuine?"

"Genuine, but there's nothing very useful in it. He's trying to establish trust. Why would he give us stuff we'd know was crap?"

Amzi said, "That's the best you can do? What I need is guidance. Is this the real thing or not? We're done. Think, remember, read this pile of junk again, slower. Think some more. Then we'll talk."

The second and third readings of the documents in Boris's package were no more enlightening than the first. I found nothing new, formed no fresh insights. In the bowels of Headquarters, I assumed, roomfuls of analysts were deconstructing the same papers.

So much for the drama, the excitement, the hairsbreadth thrill of spinning tangled webs.

Amzi called Tom and me back into his office exactly, to the minute, one week after our initial meeting.

The first words out of his mouth were, "Are we any the wiser?"

He pointed at me. "You first."

I said, "Not me."

"Any change in your gut?"

"No. But I say again, Boris isn't stupid enough to give us reason to doubt his good faith at the very outset of this operation. It's not gold, but it's genuine dross."

Amzi said, "I'm staggered by your eloquence. Tom?"

"I second the eloquence."

"So what to do?"

Tom remained silent. I followed his example. Amzi looked from face to face. He said, "You're here to help with the thinking. So help."

Tom said, "There's really not much to add, Amzi. We all know the pluses and minuses. They won't change. In cases like this it's always a question of taking the chance or not taking the chance."

"No shit?"

"The decision is yours. Whatever you decide we'll support unless it's so off the wall we feel the need for a footnote."

To me Amzi said, "How about you, O wizard? Do you also vote for eeny meeny miny mo?"

"If you're asking what I'd do in your place, my decision would be to take it but also take precautions. It's the only way to find out if the offer really is genuine."

"Better to get your fingers burned than not light a fire?"

Tom said, "You might light a fuse."

Amzi said, "What's that supposed to mean?"

Tom said, "Sometimes doing nothing is the right thing to do."

"So I've heard, but not lately," Amzi said. "Doing zip's safer, that's for sure. In years gone by we had a chief of counterintelligence in this building who voted no on every Russian who ever wanted to defect. Fought tooth and nail against letting them walk in and tell us what they had to tell us. They were all dangles, he said, no exceptions. They would mind-fuck us. So, do nothing."

Amzi drank coffee and studied me as if I were Boris and he was admiring the plastic surgery.

"The funny thing was that almost everybody took this nutcase seriously," he said. "It never occurred to anybody that he might not want us talking to KGB defectors because sooner or later a walk-in who knew that he, the nutcase, was the actual sleeper, would show up and blow his cover."

Tom said, "But he wasn't the sleeper."

Amzi said, "He wasn't? You're absolutely sure about that? This guy was the asshole buddy of the worst and most destructive traitor the Brits ever uncovered, and supposedly this broke his heart instead of making him a suspect. That figures. Why? He was above suspicion because he *managed* suspicion for this outfit. But I wondered back then and I wonder now whether he was John the Baptist or the Manchurian candidate. And so should you, because someday the fucker will be reincarnated and you may run into him on some road to Emmaus and walk right by."

Wonders never ceased: Amzi knew his Bible. Tom studied the ceiling. After a time he shifted his gaze back to Amzi and said, "So what do you want us to do?"

"Let me repeat. Number one, I want you to *not* tell me what you think I want to hear or cover your asses by not telling me what you really think. Second, within twenty-four hours I want a balance sheet of the positives and negatives and a rough estimate of the bottom line for a yes and for a no. The Director will make the decision, not me. But he pays you to speak the truth that makes men free, so get to it."

The gnarled finger jabbed the air. "You first."

I said, "Accentuate the positive. Give it a try. It's the only way to find out if Boris is on the level. If he isn't, we can withdraw."

"How do we do that?"

"We disappear without saying good-bye. If he refuses to give up, tell the Cheka what he's been up to."

"They might cremate poor Boris alive."

"That would solve our problem."

Amzi bared his teeth. They were the color of ivory, large, even, and square. I had never before seen him smile.

He said, "Stout lad." He pointed at Tom. "How about you, Tommy Tune?"

Tom Terhune said, "He's got a point. But if we want this apparatchik to have a little respect, we should negotiate his list of conditions. First principle: We control."

"OK. Which demands do we deny?"

"He has to thumbprint something. The ritual is psychologically important. So is money. We should open a bank account for him somewhere in Scandinavia and set up dead drops inside Russia with foreign passports and cash in case he has to get out of the country in a hurry."

"What else?"

"He shouldn't have the power to choose his own handler. This fellow"—he meant me—"is too valuable to devote himself to any one target. Any experienced case officer can do the honors."

I said, "Excuse me, but so far I'm the only one of us he's made contact with and he wants to keep it that way, so what's the profit in introducing him to others and risk losing him?"

"I'll let you know what the Director decides," Amzi said. "Meantime, think about this: Boris recruits his chess partner . . ."

Tom, plainly horrified by what he knew was coming next, started to rise from his chair.

He said, "I don't want to hear the rest of this."

Amzi said, "Sit down. Listen."

Tom stopped while half erect, his knees bent.

Amzi said, "What's the problem? It would be a fake recruitment. It would give Boris an ironclad reason to go anywhere in the world to meet this valuable agent who hobnobs with the big boys at Headquarters. If he tells Moscow up front what he's doing they can't catch him at it, now can they?"

Tom, seething, finished standing up.

He said, "Amzi, you're too clever by half."

Amzi said, "Jolly good of you to say so, old chap. We're done."

So was I, in Tom's plainly visible opinion. I myself thought I was halfway home.

18

The Director, covering his behind by expressing strong reservations for the record, gave us an amber light to put the ball in play. But what if I was unmasked, kidnapped, forced to confess, and put on video for all the world to see while gasping at the dirty tricks Headquarters played on the good people of the SVR who only wanted to do their bit to put an end to American deviltry?

Tom Terhune was uneasy about this possibility. To Amzi, it was simply what we were paid to do. In twenty words or less, he gave me my mission—outwit the wily Russian, take whatever chances were necessary but none that were not, win the game for America and don't fuck up.

I texted my flight details to Luz, but there was no sign of her at Ezeiza, as the *porteños* called the Ministro Pistarini International Airport. It was after midnight when I cleared customs. If Luz was still in the mood in which I had left her, I didn't want to deal with it, so I took a cab to my own apartment. None of the ingenious traps I had set to detect clandestine entry had been sprung. This meant nothing, since no professional burglar would have left signs of the intrusion.

I was dead tired. I had slept very little while in Virginia. I took a shower and fell into bed without bothering about pajamas. My brain went off the air. One second I was struggling to stay awake long enough to pull up the covers, the next—hours later in real time—I was wide-awake and in the grip of nameless dread. I called on my rational mind to come to the rescue. No answer. Dread gave me no hint as to where it came from, how it had gotten in, what it was warning me about. Was it in bed with me because I feared losing Luz? Because the gods were letting me know I had cooked my own goose?

I got out of bed, barely able to breathe and hardly remembering the way to the kitchen or where I kept the whiskey. I drank half a dozen glugs of Jack Daniel's from the bottle. The liquor went down the wrong way. I gasped, coughed like a tubercular, half-spat and half-vomited into the sink. Still coughing, I staggered into the bathroom and looked for a pill, any pill that would calm me down, but I don't take pills, so all I found were some morning-after tablets Luz kept in my medicine cabinet in case she ever needed them.

The phone rang. It was three o'clock in the morning. Luz's voice said, "I'm outside your door."

I opened it, and there she was, wearing an ankle-length maxi coat, long out of style but just the garment for what she had in mind. She was barefoot, her gleaming hair was loose. She slowly unbuttoned the coat's many buttons and dropped it to the floor. She was naked. Of course she was naked.

I had absolutely no sexual response. Never before in my life had such a thing happened in these circumstance. Because I, too, was naked, Luz saw this at once. Astonishment flooded into her face.

"*Jesús, María, y José,*" she said, "what have they done to you?"

Though Luz tried everything, nothing changed in the night or even in the morning after the dread had at last gone back into hiding. In her eyes I saw a question: *Who had I been fucking in Virginia?*

After a silent breakfast we went our separate ways.

That evening Luz did not return to my apartment nor did she call. Had the Luz I knew vanished? I knew this could happen without warning at any time. I had seen it happen. I relived with all five senses the time that followed my parents' final separation, a space in my memory that had been padlocked for twenty years. One day the two of them were married as they always had been, sleeping in the same bed, sharing a bathroom, appearing naked to each other, having breakfast together while reading different sections of the *Washington Post* just as they had done for half their lives and for all of mine.

And then one night for no reason I could understand, the film broke. A chalky squiggle appeared in the upper-right-hand corner of the screen, the sound track ran down, the screen turned into a square of blinding white light. They went on living in the same city, they shopped in the same stores, they went to the same restaurants and movie houses as always, but they never saw each other again. Chance never once brought them together. It was uncanny. They had put up with each other for twenty years. Now, in a moment, neither of them any longer existed for the other.

Was Luz, too, gone forever? Would she and I become invisible to one another in the same way as my parents had done? Already, lying wide-awake in the dark with an emptied mind, I could not picture her.

The next morning was the third Saturday that Boris had set as a dead-line for Headquarters's decision. He arrived at my door as usual at 5:57 A.M., the usual grease-spotted bag of *medialunas* in hand. I had set up the chessboard, and as soon as I let him in, we sat down to play as if this was a Saturday morning like any other. He won the first game, I won the second, and then he turned over the pieces one by one and crossed his arms and waited for me to break the silence.

Let him wait. I fetched a pot of espresso. I ate a *medialuna*. Boris, abstaining, watched wordlessly. My plan was to make him speak the first word. Winning that infantile contest of wills was the first step toward control. I had tried this tactic in similar situations and I knew it worked even with very smart people, especially if they were used to being the dominant one. Ask any frantic mother whose kid won't eat his oatmeal.

It worked this time, too, though it took a little longer than usual. As I poured myself a second cup of coffee, Boris, moving a muscle for the first time in minutes, swallowed his cold espresso at a gulp. I refilled his cup.

As if he were the one in control, he said, "Do you have a message for me or not?"

This was a small victory. I had made him ask the question, to let his anxiety show.

I said, "I do. There are conditions."

"The agreement was that there would be no conditions."

I said, "What agreement? It takes two to make an agreement. You made a proposal. It was received for what it was, a starting point for negotiations. If we have misunderstood you, if you don't like what I'm about to tell you, if you want to walk away, fine. That will be the end of it. You and I will stop playing chess and say good-bye forever and you can go back to Moscow and find some other way to live with the situation you told me you want to change."

"In that case you would get nothing."

"True, but we would be no worse off than we are now. Shall we continue?"

Boris waved a hand: *Suit yourself.*

The script for these farces is always the same, no matter what language is being spoken or who the target might be. The candidate for recruitment is a candidate because he wants something and he wants it now. The usual motivations are money, resentment over some personal slight, or disappointment. Boris wanted no money. That left disappointment and, unlikely as that seemed, idealism. Somehow Boris, in the face of his country's unbroken history of despotism, believed that Russia could be reborn as a better society. Or so he wanted me to believe. And so I had to pretend to take him seriously.

I recited Headquarters's conditions. I left the part about my mock recruitment by him till last.

He said, "You're insane."

He meant it. The arrangement violated every procedure he lived by. I said nothing.

Boris said, "This is an insult to my intelligence. It is impossible to accept the arrangement they want."

I said, "Then I'm sorry to say we're done."

Boris shook his head in disbelief. He got to his feet and walked to the window. Was he thinking, was he cooling off, was he showing himself to someone watching in the street below as a signal that the deal was done or the deal was off?

Everything I had planned for was in the balance. I should have been on tenterhooks. Actually, I couldn't have cared less whether or not Boris was playacting. Suddenly, in the middle of this scenario on which so much depended, Luz had walked back into my mind. As if she were physically present, I sniffed the faint musk of her heat, felt her glowing skin against mine, glimpsed her tiny, knowing precoital smile.

Boris said something. I heard his voice but not his words. I willed myself to come back from the elsewhere into which I had slipped and asked him to repeat. He still stood at the window, his broad back turned to me.

Making no attempt to conceal his annoyance—or maybe faking it for effect—Boris said, "All right. I will take this tomfoolery under consideration."

We were in business. I got out the standard secrecy agreement and the stamp pad on which Boris would ink his thumb. He did so without hesitation. On an impulse I inked my own thumb, too, and we both signed as if we were recruiting each other—as in fact we were, with strong mental reservations.

Boris said, "Helsinki, two months from today, same time, the sauna at the Scandic Park Hotel."

He watched my reaction. Would I follow orders?

I said, "No, not there, not then. The next morning at seven-thirty, the sauna at Maunulan maja in Central Park. Meanwhile, no more chess. No contact whatsoever."

After a flicker of hesitation, he said, "You know Helsinki. Good."

"Until then."

He nodded and departed.

Within minutes I was at Luz's door. I rang the doorbell instead of using my key. Minutes went by, and then she opened up. My intention was to rip off her clothes without wasting time by closing the door.

"No wonder I couldn't get you on the phone," she said. "You have a visitor."

"Who?"

"He's waiting for you in the living room."

She pointed the way with a jerk of her head. Her hair swung, then hair by hair fell perfectly back into place.

Diego stood at the window in exactly the same position, back turned, eyes on the street, in which I had last seen Boris a few minutes earlier.

He said, "How did it go?"

His face was blank. I thought at first he was asking about my trip to the U.S.

However, knowing Diego, knowing that Luz kept nothing from him, I said, "How did what go?"

Diego turned around and faced me. "Your meeting with Boris."

Oh, *that.*

I said, "He won the first game with Alapin's opening, I won the second, we skipped the rubber."

"You should be happy with the tie. He's a terrific player."

"Yes, he is, but then again he's a Russian, so it comes with the passport."

Diego said, "I wanted to have a talk with you. Do you have a moment?" He wore a serious look.

What did he have to say to me? *Can you support my little girl in the manner to which she is accustomed?*

He said, "As Luz has no doubt told you, her father entrusted her to me before he left us. He asked me to be a father to her, to protect her, to make sure that she was safe and happy. I promised I would do as he asked. Keeping that promise has been the chief preoccupation of my life. She is more than a daughter to me. In my mind she is also her father and mother. Within herself she carries their DNA, which used to be called the soul."

He paused, then said, "Does that sound overwrought to you?"

"No."

What came next didn't exactly surprise me. It did cause a knot of anger in my chest. I knew that Luz told Diego everything, that to her he was as much two persons—himself and Alejandro, not necessarily in that order—as she was to him. Her trust in him, trust that she extended to no one else, including me, was absolute.

Diego said, "Luz has told me the plan that you and she have to do damage to the primary enemy of mankind. From one point of view I find this frightening because you have put Luz in danger. From another viewpoint it's something I should have expected, given the blood that runs in her veins, and I'm proud of her. She is keeping something important alive. I am here to tell you that you had better keep Luz alive."

He paused and looked at me, as if expecting me to comment. I didn't comment.

Diego went on. He said, "I have known about this plot of yours for some time. Soon after you and Luz came together, she told me your plan and asked for my help. As it happens, I knew Boris when we were both young men. Alejandro knew him, too, but less well. Boris helped our movement in many ways. More than anyone except Alejandro, he kept it alive. After Luz told me you and she were looking for someone in the Russian apparatus who could help you, I spoke to Boris. He was intrigued. He instructed Arkady to have a party and invite you. The rest followed with no help from me."

I said, "Diego, you take my breath away. You just said I was the one who put Luz in mortal danger. And now you tell me this? What do you call handing her over to the Russians?"

Anger flashed in Diego's eyes, and then in an instant disappeared.

He said, "In this as in everything I do in connection to Luz, I am keeping my promise to Alejandro. I am protecting her. I will go on protecting her because she tells me she loves you and it's obvious to me that that is the truth. She is prepared to die with you or for you. She is her mother's daughter, and if anyone ever died for love it was Felicia. Because it is part of protecting Luz, I will protect you, too. I want you to know that, so that whatever may happen, you will not make the mistake of thinking that I would do you harm as long as Luz lives and loves you."

I said, "Let me ask you this. How exactly would you go about preserving Luz, and incidentally me, from harm?"

"Alejandro lives on in many minds in many places," Diego said. "His friends will protect Luz and protect you, too—rescue you both—if ever you are in what you call mortal danger. Luz will call me, I will call them, they will make Luz and you safe. You have my word on it."

He smiled. It was a charming smile. It almost made me like him. It was designed to make you trust him. Seeing that smile and reading what it said, any clinician would have made the same diagnosis I made. There was no cure for what ailed Diego.

19

Two weeks after our final game of chess, Boris left for Moscow. I was instructed to report to Headquarters forthwith. There was nothing left for me to do in Argentina except marry Luz. We had to hurry. One of Luz's Aguilar relations who was a judge expedited the marriage license. The ceremony was performed by him, as required by law, in the Civil Registry office. Diego gave away the bride and was also the best man because I didn't know another soul in Buenos Aires, American or Argentinean, well enough to ask him to do the honors.

Diego wept when he kissed the bride. The *abuelos* attended, proper but aloof. They took no part in the ceremony. In the eyes of the church, therefore to the Aguilars, this ceremony was no wedding because it was no sacrament. Only God could authorize a marriage that no man could put asunder. A religious wedding was impossible because I had never been baptized and declined to pretend to be a Christian even for a day. Thanks to her grandparents, Luz had been baptized and taken first communion, so she had genuine-false religious credentials even though she had no faith. Afterward we went back to the grandparents' house where most of the many Aguilars awaited us. Few of them were smiling as they drank the toast to the happy couple.

The next night, Diego hosted a more boisterous party at a restaurant. Speeches were made, everyone danced, some of the honorary cousins played and sang old revolutionary songs. When in his remarks Diego mentioned Alejandro and Felicia, the honorary aunts and uncles—eyes closed, heads bent—did whatever pious Maoists do at such moments instead of making the sign of the cross. Under the table Luz took her hand off my crotch and squeezed my hand, as if this were the more intimate gesture.

Diego's party lasted till dawn. We slept all day, and because I was required by regulations to travel on U.S. airlines, took Delta's evening flight to Dulles. As one of his many wedding presents, Diego had bought us an upgrade to first class. He wept again when he embraced Luz for a moment so prolonged that it was almost incestuous.

He shook my hand and said, "Remember, no matter where you are, you will always be among friends who will protect you. In case of emergency, call me on my cell phone. If I am operating and do not answer, leave a message. Speak these English words: '*My wife is homesick.*' Give me GPS coordinates for your location. Say nothing more than that. Help will come to you."

I said, "I can't begin to tell you how reassuring it is to know that."

"Luz's life is very precious," he said, ignoring the irony.

"Does she know about this rescue option?"

"She has always known. Remember, nobody else—nobody—has a right to know."

As we walked away from Diego, Luz was crying, too. She stumbled, also something new. I took her elbow to steady her. She shook off my hand as if I were trying to come between her and Diego and dried her eyes and walked a little faster toward the security gate.

With stopovers, the flight took eighteen hours. At our destination the climate was reversed. It had been autumn in Buenos Aires, it was late spring in Washington—green trees, flowers all over the place, equatorial heat when we walked out of the air-conditioned terminal at Reagan National Airport. When I unlocked the door of my apartment we found the unholy mess I had left behind many months before: dirty dishes in the dishwasher, soiled clothes in the laundry basket, moldy food in the refrigerator, half a glass of red wine that had turned to sludge. Sticky surfaces. Bad smell. Flies. Cockroaches. More heat.

I said, "Let's get out of here."

Luz said, "No. Let's get to work."

She turned the air conditioner to maximum, stripped to her underwear, and went to work on the kitchen. I cleaned up the other three rooms, a far easier task. She washed the kitchen floor on her hands and knees, her bewitching bottom moving in rhythm with the scrub brush. She sprayed insecticide and air freshener. In no time the flies were dead and the cockroaches had scurried into hiding and the house smelled like lemon zest. The appliances had been scrubbed inside and out and disinfected, the dishwasher and the clothes washer and dryer were running, the aged garbage had gone down the disposal followed by a large dose of Lysol. She stripped the bed, found clean sheets, and remade it, and then attacked the bathrooms I thought I had already cleaned.

She said, "If you ever make another mess like this one you'll need a new wife."

We tried out the bed.

As evening fell we ordered pizza and drank some of the beer I had left in the refrigerator. In the immemorial way of brides on their wedding night, Luz went into the bathroom and locked the door. I got into bed aching with fatigue. I heard the shower running, then the sound of a hair dryer. When she emerged at last, I was asleep. I was awakened by the scent of cologne and her tongue in my ear. When I opened my eyes, there was Luz, naked of course, but covering her pubis with an open hand.

She said, "Surprise."

She moved her hand. She had shaved. The little goatee that I loved was gone. This didn't exactly make a new woman of her, but the novelty made enough of a difference that I forgot for the next hour or two that there was any such thing as sleep.

The next morning, early, so as to catch Amzi before the daily routine swallowed him, I crossed the Potomac and reported for duty at Headquarters. Through the station I had already reported, leaving out my surreal chats with Diego, the full operational narrative.

Amzi wanted to talk about my marriage, not Boris.

He said, "So how did you get your bride into the United States?"

"She already had a tourist visa."

"Why?"

"She was planning to go to the ten-year reunion of her college class."

"Wellesley, right?"

I nodded.

"You do know you're supposed to clear marriage to a foreign national *before* you tie the knot, especially if you're the lucky girl's case officer and she also happens to be the daughter of a world-famous terrorist and still hangs out with his old buddies?"

"Yes."

"So why didn't you follow procedure?"

"I had other things to think about."

"Don't fuck around," Amzi said. "You have blotted your copybook. The Director is disappointed in you. Security is not pleased. They want you, and especially your bride, to be polygraphed cross-eyed."

I said, "Be our guest. Is it all right for me to mention that my wife is a trusted asset of this organization . . ."

"*Trusted*?" said Amzi.

". . . who has been polygraphed before and has always passed with flying colors? Or that Headquarters has been kept fully posted on our relationship and has given its tacit approval, including our intention to marry sooner or later?"

"Mention anything you want," Amzi said. "Anybody can beat the box if they take the right pills. I don't give a shit who you marry. But that ain't gonna turn down the heat from Security. And by the way, congratulations."

On what? I wondered but I nodded my thanks.

Amzi said, "Whatever, you get your wish. You'll be working out of Headquarters for a while instead of going back to Buenos Aires because as usual we don't really know what to do with you. Tom will keep you busy while you wait for Godot. We're done."

Tom gave me the same roomy office as before, a few doors down the hall from his own. He also, for a change, gave me things to keep me busy—meetings whose purpose evaded me and odd jobs that made use of my languages, mostly. There was nothing surprising about this: I still didn't know the routine, I had seldom been briefed on the subject at hand, I had no relationship with the other people who worked for Tom, let alone the hundreds who did not.

I wasn't exactly being welcomed to the club. Nobody invited me for a drink or a cup of coffee. In the cafeteria, people sometimes sat down at the same table and nodded but tended to study their cell phones rather than converse with me—or with each other, to be fair about it. There was no reason to take this personally. It was just the culture.

The bureaucracy dragged its feet when it came to documenting Luz. I did take this personally. By law Luz was entitled to American citizenship by virtue of our marriage, but since 9/11 the bureaucracy had processed applications very, very slowly. I gave Admin no peace on this issue, and though they were even more allergic than usual to embarrassment because like the rest of the federal apparatus they were haunted by the fear of being responsible for another 9/11, the process moved along.

Many Headquarters people were married to foreigners, some of them to Russians and Chinese and Iranians and others you might have thought represented a potential security risk. This had always been true. Cold War brides from hostile countries had often dined at our house when I was too young to join them at the table, but as I remember it, most of them were more American than some of the American wives. They were happy—maybe as cover, maybe not—to be in the land of plenty. Unless they were French they even thought the food was good.

Six weeks passed. My meeting with Boris loomed. No one had discussed this encounter with me. In theory, and I hoped in reality, only the Director, Amzi and Tom, and Security knew about it and all of them had more pressing issues to worry about. Besides that, what was there to talk about? Boris would either come through or he wouldn't show up.

No matter what, I was in no danger from the Russians, nor was Boris in danger from us. His own service might whack him and mine might send me to prison if it discovered the truth, but those were internal matters. The embargo on assassination applied throughout the Cold War and it continued to apply afterward. Neither side wanted to go to the mattresses. Mutual assassination was unproductive, uncontrollable. Once begun, it turned into a vendetta, and there was no end to it. Who knew what algorithm of mayhem might result from one reckless homicide?

Luz played house. She bought a new bed for the apartment and as only she could do, made it the focus of our existence. At auctions and thrift shops she bought paintings and drawings, Persian rugs and antique furniture and china and silver and more. These were frugal expenditures, but over time they added up to a hefty total. She never asked me for money. I never asked where her own money came from. Savings, Alejandro's share of the proceeds of banks that his freedom fighters had robbed for the Cause or ransoms of plutocrats they had kidnapped? An allowance from

Diego? What difference did it make? Had the taxpayers known what I was doing with their money they would have stopped writing checks to the U.S. Treasury.

Luz knew many more people in Washington than I did. Within two weeks of our arrival she was having lunch and going to matinees at the Kennedy Center and doing volunteer work with sorority sisters, accepting dinner invitations from Foreign Service people and diplomats of other nations who had passed through Buenos Aires while she was working at the foreign ministry, and signing up for advanced classes at Georgetown Law School. One of her honorary uncles, hitherto unknown to me, was counselor to the Argentinean embassy. He invited us to embassy receptions, my favorite thing, and dinner parties where we met his friends from other South American nations who had returned to respectability in everything except their hidden but ineradicable faith in the brave new world to come.

These people couldn't understand how she could be married to a reptile like me. None, least of all State Department people, believed for a minute my feeble cover story that I worked for the State Department.

At the office, to pass empty time for some useful purpose, I worked on Russian as a written language, reading newspapers and magazines and books and translating the columns and editorials in the *Post* and the *Times* into Russian. Because nearly everything I typed into the memory of a laptop vanished from my mind as if transferred to another human consciousness, I wrote all this out by hand. At first this unaccustomed exercise induced painful muscle cramps, but soon I was scribbling away as if I had traveled backward in time to the glory days before the invention of the keyboard.

On the long slow drives back to Adams Morgan through rush hour traffic I listened to pop music and tried to empty my mind, but often found myself thinking about Diego's parting words to me. He had sounded psychotic, and in the part of him that was the fossil of his bloodthirsty youth, I supposed he was psychotic. As far as I could tell, the rest of him, the visible Diego, the surgeon and doer of good works, was rational. So the questions were, which Diego had been whispering in my ear and had he been babbling or speaking in riddles? The more I thought about it, the more I tended to favor the riddles.

And if I was right about that, the invisible "friends" who would always watch over Luz and me and keep us from harm had to be terrorists for the simple reason that Diego was still a terrorist under very deep cover but still plugged in to the freemasonry of the revolution, and therefore the "rescue" he talked about would, in fact, be a kidnapping and the "protection" captivity.

And the end product of his protection, should I ever dial his number and speak the password, would be the end of me and Luz's return to him.

20

Precisely on time on the right day, Boris showed up at the Maunulan maja sauna in Helsinki. For the benefit of the bored receptionist we greeted each other as old friends—manly embrace, broad smiles, exclamations in Spanish. Neither of us resembled any native Spanish speaker who ever applied for a Finnish visa, but that was another issue. The sauna was crowded. As we sweated side by side among hungover Finns, Boris said next to nothing. I didn't interrupt. We hurried through the invigorating plunge into icy water, skipped the massage, and went for a walk in the all but deserted Central Park.

Without being asked, Boris told me he had in fact been promoted. He was now like a major general, the chief of his service's Directorate S, responsible for recruiting and running agents in the United States and the rest of the Americas. He was very busy. His service was hiring. After the fall of the Soviet Union, Russian espionage in the U.S. became more extensive and more intense than it ever had been during the Cold War. The intensification was a result of urgent need. The USSR under Bolshevism had been a chimera—a backward country with one foot in the Dark Ages masquerading as a modern state. The rest of the world, with America far in the lead, was inventing more technological wonders than the Russians could hope to invent for themselves. This had always been true and it explained why Moscow had devoted so much wealth and energy to the theft of secrets. It was the particular business of Boris's directorate to pilfer the fruits of capitalism. The need was urgent, the methods were ruthless.

Recalcitrant Russian expatriates living in the United States were bullied into recruitment by threats to their families, and in stubborn cases, by filing bogus charges that forced them to return to the Motherland and submit to prosecution with conviction and prison as a foregone conclusion. The class of Americans that regarded their own country as the evil empire and Russia as the holder of the moral high ground required no coercion. Such volunteers, when they were successful, were rewarded with large sums of money and diamonds and rubies and, to encourage the worker bees, secret decorations for their heroic service to mankind. This approach was remarkably effective, as the NKVD had discovered in the long-ago days of the Comintern when its operatives in the United States were complaining to Moscow Center that they were overwhelmed by the mobs of American idealists who were walking into their offices and volunteering to spy for the Soviet Union.

Boris fairly quivered with contempt for such gullible fools: They were in the grip of a collective dementia that made it impossible for them to acknowledge reality. Did they not understand that they would be the first to be shot if the kind of America they so passionately wanted should ever come into being? This contagious mania to reject their country and all they thought it stood for left few sleeping beauties for the Borises of this world to awaken with a bear hug. This was frustrating! How could such intellectual weaklings ever be trusted?

How much this tirade represented Boris's true opinion and how much of it was secondhand marijuana smoke was an unanswerable question. Either way, I suspected that I would be hearing it again. And again.

Boris said, "I have brought you a list of names."

He handed me a flash drive.

I said, "Who are these people?"

"Americans who are betraying their country by working for us."

"Are any of them inside Headquarters or involved with someone who is?"

"Their handlers don't think so."

"Are any of them connected to terrorism?"

Boris said, "They are mostly of the type we have been discussing, so probably they are sympathetic to suicide bombers. But as far as we know none of them makes bombs."

I handed the flash drive back to him. "Send this to the FBI," I said.

"It would be easier for you to do that, no?"

"Not without telling them the source. You are none of their business."

Boris shook his head. Americans! He put his hands behind his back, refusing to accept the flash drive. It was an incongruously peevish gesture.

I said, "Boris, hear me. This list is useless to Headquarters, which has no police powers and is prohibited by law from investigating U.S. citizens or running operations against them on American soil."

"Ha! No exceptions?"

He already knew, or thought he knew, the answer to that question.

Boris said, "But you can recruit your fellow Americans, turn them, give us a reason to punish them."

"It's seldom worth the bother. And wooing them only makes them feel important."

Boris and I were speaking Russian now, but softly, and for the benefit of anyone who might be watching we wore jovial expressions and sometimes for effect, Boris laughed loudly.

I handed the flash drive back to him. Again he refused it.

He said, "Why are you doing this?"

I said, "I came for product. This is not product."

"Then tell me, please, what would you call product?"

"Paté de foie gras is product. This stuff is the same color but it comes from the other end of the goose."

"You look like a nice boy, but you are very uncultured. Again, why are you here if not to receive information?"

"To begin the work we agreed to do together," I said. "I want the names and the current locations of your service's most effective officers who are targeted on the United States."

After taking this body punch, Boris closed his eyes—no movement, no sign of life. He didn't seem even to be breathing. Then he held out his hand, palm upward. I put the flash drive on his palm. He made a fist.

He said, "What would you do with this list of our most valued officers?"

"Find a way to make it look like I have turned them and they work for us."

"To what end?"

"Then your service will kill them all. You want to damage the system. I want to do the same. Your side will think it is penetrated. My side will think the same. Panic will lift its ugly head. They will start to destroy themselves."

"The dog will bite itself, is that the objective?"

"Dogs, plural."

"Then both of us will die."

"What if we do?"

Boris said, "How much goose liver do I get in return?"

"Payment in kind. The names of our most effective people."

"Your service has no effective people where Russia is concerned. Every single source your service has ever had in the USSR or the Russian Federation has not been recruited. He has been a traitor who volunteered."

Just like Boris.

I said, "True enough. Another good reason to save the American taxpayer a hundred billion dollars a year."

Boris went on the alert. "That's Headquarters's budget?"

"No, a figure of speech. I have no idea what it costs to breed dinosaurs. Boris, if you want to go on with this, I need to take something useful home with me. For now it doesn't have to be one of the crown jewels, merely a sign of good faith."

He reached into his breast pocket and pulled out a different flash drive. This one had a tiny red dot on it. The other had not.

Gazing at a long-legged young woman in athletic garb who all of a sudden was running in place within earshot, he said, in barely audible tones, "We must be very careful. The next time I'm available I will mail you a postcard of a city. Prague means Sofia, Budapest means Bucharest, Trieste means Berlin. Date is fourteen days after the date written on the postcard, not the postmark. Same time as today, place is always in front of the local parliament building. Opposite sidewalks, you on the parliament side, me across the street. From there you will follow me to the place where we will do business."

"Fallback?"

"No fallback. Be there the first time, on time."

Another girl caught up to the one who had been running in place and they took off together.

Boris had nothing more to report or demand. Without so much as a nod, he stood up and took his leave.

On the morning I got back to Washington, a Saturday, I slept until noon, then read the mail at the breakfast table while Luz showered and decided what to wear for the weekend outing she had planned. She had made arrangements to go to colonial Williamsburg, dine, and spend the night making the bed squeak at the Williamsburg Inn. Williamsburg was not far from the Plantation, so the weekend would give me an opportunity to meditate about Father.

Among the junk mail and the bills on the kitchen counter I found a letter with an actual postage stamp on it from a lawyer in Eugene, Oregon, advising me that my mother had died two months earlier of pancreatic cancer and bequeathed me her entire estate. For details, call the following number.

This was the first word of her I had had for ten years. I told myself I felt nothing. I lied. I stopped breathing. I smothered the sob that rose from my chest.

The picture that came into my mind at this moment was not Mother the cool beauty but Father the jaunty hobo, smiling wryly as he welcomed her to eternity or wherever it was that people like them went to shun each other after death.

21

At Headquarters, the flash drive Boris had given me was treated with the utmost caution. The computer techs assumed, as they were conditioned to do, that the drive had been loaded with an undetectable virus or worm or some other as yet unnamed thing designed to infect the entire Headquarters system. The fact that they were unable to detect any such virus or worm in this particular flash drive only intensified their suspicions: If it was undetectable, it must exist. While waiting for them to think of just inserting the flash drive in a cheap laptop off-premises and then dissolving the hard drive in a bucket of acid, I summarized the meeting in Helsinki to a noncommittal Tom Terhune.

He said, "I guess it's a start. Amzi wants to talk to you. But not till he's read the material."

Finally the flash drive was deemed to be free of viruses and worms or any other insidious threat. I had taken it for granted that Boris was not stupid enough for it to be otherwise, but as Amzi always said, you can't assume a fucking thing. On Thursday he summoned me to his office, with Tom tagging along as usual—why he tolerated these humiliations I don't know—and delivered an Amzi-style précis of the contents.

The information on the flash drive, he said, had turned out to be interesting. One of the secretaries in the Bogotá embassy had been photographing cables and dispatches and the officers of the station and the license plates of their cars with her cell phone and handing the images over to a Russian case officer who was her lover. She had been driven into the Russian's arms by what she now regarded as the sexual harassment by the political officer she worked.

"She was the PO's Monica and his wife found out," Amzi said. "Lucky break for her. According to your friend Boris's report, this Russian's got a twelve-inch dick—he's famous for it. Early in his career, so as to maximize his capabilities, he underwent intensive training in its use on a TDY at a sparrow school."

Tom said, "So what now?"

"Dirty Harry, here, goes to Bogotá after the meeting on Friday."

Tom said, "How soon after what meeting?"

Amzi said, "How about Monday?" He didn't answer the rest of Tom's question.

I said, "We're meeting with who on Friday?"

"The Director," Amzi said. "He wants to give you a token of appreciation for your good work. Eleven o'clock in his reception room. Be there ten minutes early. We're done."

That evening, on the drive home, I called the lawyer in Oregon. He said he would rather not discuss details over the phone. Could I come to Eugene to sign papers and discuss arrangements?

"Why is that necessary?"

"Your mother had certain wishes, so it is not just a simple will," he said. "Your expenses would of course be covered by the estate."

"You can't put this in a letter?"

"It was one of your mother's wishes that we not do that."

In other words, how about a few billable hours at your inconvenience? I said, "Then you'll have to ignore her wishes."

I told him I would not be free to travel for weeks, perhaps longer, and to overnight the documents before the end of the day to the lawyer in McLean my parents had always used.

The meeting on Friday in the Director's reception room was short and to the point.

He said, "Good to see you again. And once again, brilliant work and sincere congratulations. On behalf of the president and all your colleagues, thank you."

The short man materialized at the Director's elbow and handed him a leather box. It was a lot larger than the medal case had been.

Using my first name, the Director said, "I present this to you as a token of this agency's appreciation and admiration for your outstanding work."

He opened the box and handed it to me. Inside, nestled in velvet, was an exact duplicate of the anthracite-black, custom-made .45-caliber snub-nosed pistol I had left in the trash can in the men's room of the Sana'a airport after using it to kill three human beings—four if you counted Faraj.

I said, "Thank you, sir."

"Thank *you*."

He shook hands with me again, very firm grip, and vanished.

"The world's second-most powerful handgun," Amzi said. "I told you he likes you."

The short man reappeared and handed me a sealed, blank manila envelope. I opened it when I returned to my office and found a document granting Luz citizenship and a U.S. passport in her name.

I waited until morning to present Luz with her new identity. I didn't mention the .45. It was not a festive moment. She tapped her Certificate of Naturalization, a document that looked something like an enlarged dollar bill that bore her passport photo instead of the picture of a dead president.

She said, "Ugh."

She struggled to prevent whatever it was she was feeling from showing on her face and lost the contest: disgust, resentment. As far as she was concerned, she was living behind enemy lines.

What else would you expect? She was the daughter of Alejandro and Felicia Aguilar, who in her mind were victims of U.S. imperialism who had died for their political virtue.

She never forgot that, but she did not really remember her heroic parents. Early in our affair she had told me that she could not summon their faces, their voices, the way they smelled. When she thought about them, what she remembered was their absence after they chose revolution over their only child. Tangible proofs of their existence escaped her.

She left the room, leaving the passport and naturalization certificate lying among dirty dishes.

What with the accolades and satisfying Luz's appetites I had not had time to tell her about my forthcoming trip to Bogotá. This did not seem to be the right moment to break the news, and anyway I knew none of the details she would expect to be told.

I had no idea how long I would be in Colombia or what I was expected to accomplish after I arrived—try out my brand-new .45 on the stupid little spy in the typing pool? Order her to break up with her Russian and promise never again to violate the espionage laws? Nail the Russian?

That evening Luz and I dined with one of her Wellesley sorority sisters and the latter's wife in a posh house on Kalorama Circle. Luz and her classmate, a Department of Justice prosecutor, talked about little besides their reunion, scheduled—this had slipped my mind—for the following weekend. The wife, a very tall black woman who had gone to the University of Connecticut on a basketball scholarship, feared that she would be walking into a den of mean girls who would look down on her school and her student aid.

Luz and Portia reassured her—*"Oh, no, never at Wellesley!"*

But how right she probably was.

On my way to the office on Monday morning I visited the family lawyer in McLean at the unusual hour of 7:45 A.M. His name was Lester Briggs. He was alone in his firm's movie set of an office suite: polished mahogany desks and leather chairs, shelves of leather-bound law books, Persian carpets, portraits of dead partners who looked in the pictures as if they, the partners, were the work of a taxidermist.

Lester Briggs—surprise—was yet another classmate of Father's. They had lived in the same college. As I began to notice when I was about twelve, Briggs's wife had showgirl legs and cleavage and a high giddy laugh, a silly combination that drove Mother to distraction. I hadn't seen him or his sexy wife in twenty years. In those days he had worn the tiny perpetual smirk of the man who had everything and knew he was entitled to it.

He was almost elderly now—mane of white hair, horn-rimmed reading glasses perched on the bulb of his nose. He had learned to suppress the smirk.

He looked me up and down and in a mellifluous voice said, "Amazing resemblance. Have a chair."

A large loose-leaf binder lay on his desk blotter. He lifted it an inch or two, then dropped it with a thump.

"This is the documentation of the Stanford J. Lucketts Revocable Trust established by your mother's second husband. I am given to understand by her lawyer in Oregon that control of the trust passed to her when Mr. Lucketts died two years after they were married. Just before she died she amended the trust, naming you her successor as trustee. Therefore, complete control of the assets of the trust passed to you at the moment of her death."

"Why did it take two years for me to find out about it?"

"The lawyer in Oregon couldn't locate you, though he conducted a diligent search which will cost the trust about ten thousand dollars in legal fees. My advice is to pay the bill and be done with it. I don't much care for the way this firm practices law."

"Can you handle that?"

"It would be simpler if you just wrote a check. We can send the check to the lawyer. The checkbooks for the trust are in this binder."

Briggs went on. "You have the same powers over the assets as your mother had when she was alive," he said. "The trust eliminates the need for a will and avoids probate. It is a well-drawn document. It spares the estate the inconvenience and expense of probate. It is as tidy an arrangement as an inheritance can be. There is nothing else you need to sign except signature forms, which we will notarize and forward to the banks and brokerages that hold its assets. They already know that you are the successor trustee, so you have only to register your signature to do whatever you wish to do with those assets. The total in cash, stocks, and bonds is just under two million dollars."

I was startled. I said, "How can that be? My mother had no money of her own."

"Actually, she did," Briggs said. "Her government pension, of course, and your father gave her the equity in their house and practically everything else they jointly owned as part of the divorce settlement. She liquidated those assets before she went west and invested the proceeds, about two hundred thousand, in U.S. Treasury bonds. She hadn't touched this nest egg. Mr. Lucketts seems to have been pretty well off. The initial value of the trust was well over three million, but she had been drawing down on capital for ten years before she passed away."

"Lucketts had no children of his own?"

"I don't know. Anyway it's immaterial. They are not mentioned in the trust and have no claim on it."

"Do you know anything about this man Lucketts?"

"Apart from what I've just told you, no."

"So what do I do now?"

"Sign the paperwork I've mentioned."

"That's all?"

"For the moment, yes." He handed me the notebook. "Read this and follow the instructions. If you have any problems, call me. Are you married?"

"Yes."

"Children?"

"No."

"You may want to amend the trust to make your wife or someone else your successor as trustee. Otherwise the residue will go to the IRS when you die. If you need help, feel free to call on me."

Briggs paused, steepled his fingers, weighed words.

At last he said, "I think often about your father. After the debacle I tried to locate him, I wanted to help, but he had covered his tracks and the investigators could find no trace of him. Of course, he was a professional who knew how to disappear, so that came as no surprise."

A pause.

After a moment Briggs said, "His life, the way it went, as if there actually is such a thing as malign fate, was a surprise. It baffles me. It baffles everyone who knew him before whatever went wrong, went wrong. . . ."

I made a gesture.

Briggs said, "Am I upsetting you?"

"There are other subjects I prefer, Mr. Briggs."

"'*Lester*,' please. I can understand that, but I must ask you this. Did you see him before the end? Did you communicate?"

I said, "I saw him. As for communication, not really."

"Too bad," said Mr. Briggs. "Damned shame, all of it."

Wasn't it, though?

I didn't tell Luz about the Stanford J. Lucketts Revocable Trust. Three days later I flew to Bogotá. She stayed behind for the Wellesley reunion. I didn't ask whether or when she might be joining me, but on my last night in Washington we made love from midnight to dawn and she was as enthusiastic as ever.

"Every time," she whispered afterward, in Spanish.

"'Every time' what?"

"I die and go to heaven."

I didn't know whether that was her way of saying "good-bye" or "hello again." My inventory of uncertainties was growing by the day.

22

Dwayne Scoggins, the Bogotá chief of station, wasn't a bad fellow, but he was no happier to see me on his turf than his counterpart in Buenos Aires had been. He was a ruddy, unsmiling man who seemed to be holding the invisible barking dog of his exasperation at arm's length.

He said, "I'm in the dark. Why are you here?"

I said, "I speak Russian."

"Ah-ha. The scales fall from my eyes. You're tasked to seduce the seducer."

I said, "Something like that. Does the young lady know she's under suspicion?"

"She's not smart enough to figure that out."

"Has her boyfriend figured it out?"

"If he has, he hasn't told her."

"We'd know that?"

"We might. Her cell phone and her apartment and her car and her purse and everything else except her IUD have been bugged."

"Has the Bureau been clued in?"

"Not by me, but diplomatic security, whose case it is, will have to brief the legal attaché pretty soon. I'm curious. How long do you expect to hang around here?"

"I have no idea. It's up to Amzi."

"And in the meantime, what can I do for you?"

"I'd like to read the product of all those bugs you mentioned."

"Be my guest. You'll be fascinated."

Dwayne looked at his watch, rose to his feet, and put on a jacket.

He said, "Gotta go. Melanie will show you where to sit. Do you have a place to stay?"

"I'm at the Holiday Inn."

Dwayne pushed a button. Melanie appeared. She was an owlish young woman with a voice full of Mississippi—real friendly even if she hated your guts. It was dress-down Friday in the station. She wore jeans, Keds, and a polo shirt with the Ol' Miss Rebels logo. With the exception of Dwayne, everyone in the office, including me, was dressed for a backyard barbecue.

She handed me the file on the suspect, whom I decided to call Sally. In photographs, she resembled a coarser version of the character Sally in *When Harry Met Sally,* so you could understand why the political officer, who was now quite likely en route to Ouagadougou, had forgotten all about the mother of his children when Sally fell to her knees before him. There were no pictures of her lover.

There was nothing interesting in the logs, which consisted largely of transcripts of the taps on her phone and her purse. There hardly ever is. People with something to hide, a broad category of humanity that includes Russian intelligence officers, usually are careful about what they say over the telephone.

The next day I followed Sally when she left the embassy parking lot at quitting time. She drove a centerline-yellow Beetle, so keeping her in sight was not a problem. She went straight home, parked the Bug in its numbered parking space, and went upstairs.

Eating a tuna sandwich from the embassy cafeteria and an apple for supper and drinking a bottle of water and pissing into a plastic jug, I watched Sally's door until three in the morning. I did the same, each time in a different car borrowed from the station's motor pool, the next night and the night after that, catching glimpses of her through the windows of her flat. On the fourth night, at 2:47 A.M., she emerged, wearing a miniskirt. It was raining. She dashed in a clatter of heels to her car and drove away without turning on her headlights, a precaution guaranteed to attract attention. I expected that Sally would soon be stopped by a couple of horny cops who had been hoping that a blond *gringa* in a miniskirt would happen by with her lights off.

Out of necessity she stayed on lighted streets, so I had no difficulty keeping her in sight. There was virtually no traffic, and even though she seemed to be oblivious to her situation, I had to stay way back to minimize the risk of being spotted. My own headlights were on. There was nobody behind me.

I seemed to be the only one following her. After a mile or so, Sally turned on her lights. She drove into a parking lot and pumped the brakes three times, then twice again. A signal! I parked a block away and walked back to the parking lot.

And there she was in the arms of her Russian. They wasted no time on foreplay. No doubt anticipation had taken care of that for Sally on the drive to the rendezvous. The Russian picked her up, slid her onto his rigid penis, which was indeed impressive, and laid her down onto the slope of the Bug's hood.

It was still raining. The Bug's hood was slippery, and all that kept Sally from sliding off was the feature of the Russian's anatomy that Amzi had mentioned. I took some video with sound.

As I watched this pornographic moment through the camera lens, the question was, what to do next? Time was of the essence because Sally would soon be going away for a long time and there was nothing I could do to delay that. The tryst ended as abruptly as it had begun—elapsed time, seven minutes. Sally, disheveled but happy, drove away. I let her go and followed her lover home. If he noticed I was on his tail, as he surely must have done because we were practically the only two cars on the street, he was too professional to give himself away.

He lived in—or at least entered for my benefit—a large apartment building not far from the Russian embassy. He probably walked to work. I considered bumping into him when he emerged the next morning and starting a conversation—"*That was some crazy blonde in the parking lot, Tovarish!*"—then told myself to stop kidding around and start thinking.

Immediately, so as to avoid running into Sally in the embassy corridors the next morning and having her see my new face—she would likely take a good long look at any new man—I visited the station and identified the Russian from a blurred photo taken on the street in Bogotá. The stuff I had read the day before referred to him by the code name Headquarters had bestowed on him, so I didn't know the cover name he was using in Colombia, only the cryptonym we used in correspondence about him.

Now I discovered he was calling himself Kirill Sergeivich Burkov. The residential address listed for him was the one he had led me to, so it was possible he actually lived there. I composed a report to Headquarters, attaching the feelthy pictures. The camera, a Nikon I had bought with eight hundred dollars of my own money at the Pentagon City Costco, delivered clear video images despite the dim lighting along with a soundtrack that did justice to Sally's aria to delight.

I composed a cable to Headquarters, footage attached, and handed it to Dwayne Scoggins for transmission. He grimaced at the material, and though he clearly didn't like my stalking one of his targets, he voiced no objection.

I asked to see anything about Kirill Burkov that the DAS, the Colombian Security Service, had shared with the station. Melanie brought me the all-but-unreadable handwritten files made by sidewalk men. These included photographs, blurrier than the ones made with my Nikon, of open-air encounters with a couple of women—both now missing persons—who had worked for important men in the Colombian government. One of these women, a homely plump person in photos, had been the personal secretary of the minister of foreign affairs. The other, younger and prettier with vacant eyes, was the *chica* of a general of military intelligence.

Several of the DAS surveillance reports placed Burkov in a nightspot for singles called El Paradiso in Zona T, the Pigalle of Bogotá, where he trolled for lonely women with interesting bosses. Around midnight I went to El Paradiso, bribed my way in, and found a table in a dark corner. No sign of Burkov. Sex workers of both genders made me offers that might have been of passing interest to him. That night and for two nights afterward, I said no thanks to them all. The bouncers began to look at me as if I might be a candidate for an interview in the back alley. I carried knockout spray and my brand-new as yet unfired .45—after all this was Bogotá, the most dangerous city in the Western Hemisphere. I had no wish to baptize the weapon. On the third night I left early.

As I started the car—talk about coincidences—I glanced at the rearview mirror and saw Kirill Burkov crossing the street, holding hands with a laughing woman. She was a blonde and for a moment I thought she might be Sally, but then she turned her face in my direction and I realized that she looked nothing like her. She got into Burkov's BMW—him gallantly holding the door open for her—ankles demurely together. I followed the car to another deserted parking lot, where the routine with Sally replayed, except this time he seized the hem of the woman's dress and peeled it off over her head before he went to work. The blonde, her face hidden by the inside-out dress, wearing nothing below the neck but sequined red shoes that somehow stayed on her feet, screamed so wildly in her delight that Burkov had to clap a hand over her mouth.

Afterward he drove her home to a very small concrete house on a mean street. The next day I checked out her address. The house was occupied by three hairdressers, so unless the Valkyrie was cutting the hair of an in-the-know Colombian, the encounter had been recreational.

These sightings were leading me nowhere. Though I would have preferred to make do in some other way, I called on Dwayne for assistance. Glumly, he arranged for me to be invited to a reception at the Chilean embassy later in the week. The station had information that Burkov was on the guest list.

I continued to work the case, but all the while my mind had no room for anything but Luz. Five days had passed since we parted and I hadn't heard from her. My brain provided a slide show: Luz's image in the mirror that first day, in the surf in Patagonia, in strips of sunlight that fell through a venetian blind onto her nude body as she slept. On her back under the weight of a man I had never seen in reality.

So much for the aftereffects of lurking around parking lots and seeing yourself in others.

Usually I had no trouble standing alone and unnoticed at embassy parties, but the Chilean ambassadress was a conscientious hostess who introduced me into a circle of South Americans who treated me to the customary remorseless first-meeting grilling into my background and status. Then, one by one, they drifted away.

Soon thereafter Kirill Burkov entered the room. In no time he was deep in conversation with one of the wives, a prematurely gray *jolie laide* with the figure and complexion of a twenty-year-old who seemed to be lubricating by the syllable. Why? Did she somehow sense Burkov's endowment? She held herself and dressed and gestured and enunciated like an aristocrat. Burkov was a peasant: watchful pale eyes with epithantic folds and Slavic cheekbones, and almost no facial expression. Years ago I had read a biography of H. G. Wells, who had an enviable sex life though he was physically ugly. One of his mistresses was asked why he was so yummy. "It was the way he smelled," she replied. Maybe Burkov exuded a similar pheromone and women knew in the primitive brain what that meant.

When Burkov broke away from the woman, who kept her eyes on his broad back until he melded into the crowd, I broke away and searched for the Russian. He was nowhere to be seen, but apparently he saw me. He entered the men's room while I was washing my hands, used the urinal, and then stood beside me at the sinks and scrubbed his hands. He seemed to be unaware of my presence. Then he made eye contact in the mirror.

He said, in English, "Hello again. I have a question. Are you a collector of cars or do you steal a new one every night?"

A straight answer seemed to be in order.

"I borrow them," I said in Russian. "Now I have a question for you. Did you bang that ugly hairdresser for the pleasure of it or to see if someone was watching from the shadows?"

We were speaking to each other's mirror images.

Burkov jerked his head.

"Let's go," he said. "I'll lead. You'll recognize the car, I think."

23

Burkov's BMW was parked at the end of the driveway. I followed it to a bar on a dark street in a part of town that tourists were advised to avoid. To understate the reality, the bar, called La Sombra, lived up to its name: "Darkness." You couldn't make out the faces of the other customers. The booths were lit by night-lights, one per booth. These tiny bulbs were the only illumination apart from the dull glow of the bar's small fluorescent tube.

On the sound system Karen Carpenter sang "Close to You."

The waiter, old enough to remember Miss Karen, shone a penlight on the table and said, in Cockney English, "Eat or drink?"

"One Stoli, one black Jack, both doubles," Burkov replied in English.

He waited until the waiter went away.

Then he said, "That woman sings from the vagina. She's the one who starved herself to death, am I right?"

"Something like that."

"Very American—your women are so unhappy. What's the problem?"

"Disappointment."

The waiter came back with the drinks—British pub quantities, twenty drops in the bottom of a red wineglass.

Burkov paid in American dollars and said, "Two more. Doubles."

"Those are doubles, sir."

"Quadruples, then."

"So," Burkov said to me in English, "why are you following me?"

"Why do you ask?"

"Frankly, I am wondering why you're being so obvious about it."

Burkov was even quicker than Boris to come to the point. The new version of the Cheka must have revised the field manual along with its acronym.

I said, "Just impetuous, I guess."

Burkov lifted his glass and threw the vodka down his throat.

I didn't touch my glass. I did not like the idea of drinking, even in the line of duty, with this particular Russian.

In seconds, the waiter emerged from the dark with the second round. I tried to pay but Burkov was quicker.

"You can pay next time we meet," he said.

"There's going to be a next time?"

"Why not? But I'll have to drink a little more with you to learn to trust you."

For the rest of the evening—five quadruple vodkas for Burkov, five undrunk splashes of what purported to be Tennessee whiskey for me—we talked about football. He was a fan of Spartak Moscow—the old great Spartak clubs, not the feeble imitations that now wore the Spartak jerseys. Since the demise of communism, the only world powers with worse teams than post–Cold War Russia were the United States and China. Americans didn't even know the proper name of the game.

Sally was not mentioned. The fact that she was being watched—no doubt he had spotted earlier tails as easily as he detected mine—told him all he needed to know. I didn't think he had serious regrets about losing her. The stuff she was feeding him was junk, so he must have considered the possibility that she was a dangle that the station controlled. That thought had also crossed my mind, but alas for Sally, the fact was that she was in heat but thought she was in love. For Burkov's purposes, same difference.

For my own reasons I hoped that the State Department, the Bureau, and Headquarters would jointly decide to let her run a little longer and that Burkov's masters would let him continue to service her so I would have time to get to know him better. I was as indifferent to Sally's fate as he was.

As Burkov and I talked and talked and told each other nothing, Karen Carpenter sang her greatest hits over and over again. After an hour or so the Russian began to feel the vodka and fell silent.

Around midnight he got up and walked toward the men's room with the deliberate steps of a man who knows he's almost drunk. He never came back. He left no tip. Because I did not wish to be remembered by the waiter, I tucked a banknote under his empty glass and left.

It was at least as dark in the street as it had been inside El Pub. I walked to my parked car with my hand on the .45 and hair rising on the back of my neck. I was somewhat surprised when the car started instead of exploding. It wasn't Burkov or anyone from his organization I feared, but there were more terrorists per square mile in Colombia than in Iraq and Yemen combined, and no matter where they lived or which splinter cause they served, they all knew about one another and did one another favors as if they were a new unique nationality, and who knew which lunatic might owe a favor to the friends of the Yemenis I had blown away? When you can feel risk as though it is right behind you, expecting the worst is not a bad idea.

In a certain sense, in certain ways, I had enjoyed the encounter with Burkov. It had been relaxing to spend a quiet hour with a disciplined professional who worked to Cold War rules and killed only people who could not possibly be useful to him or the Motherland.

What I needed to know now was whether Burkov's first priority was the Motherland or Burkov or—God forbid—an ideal like the one Boris wanted me to believe motivated him.

The next morning I drafted a cable to Headquarters reporting the contact. After reading it, Dwayne called me into his office.

"I was warned that you work in mysterious ways," he said, "but this baffles me. What are you up to?"

He was a shade ruddier and his voice was a bit louder than usual. He glowered. I knew why. I was stepping on his toes in a serious way.

I said, "Just doing what I believe I was sent here to do."

"Which is what? Blow your cover to the Russians?"

I said, "Dwayne, I'm puzzled. I was sent down here to try to work on Burkov. You were informed about this. You arranged the invitations to the Chilean embassy. The whole idea of that was to make it possible for him and me to meet. We met. Were we then supposed to gaze longingly at each other across a crowded room and let it go at that?"

"This station selects its own targets and works them on its own territory using standard procedures," Dwayne said in a tightly controlled voice. "We didn't ask for outside help, we don't need outside help. This is Bogotá, where people end up dead every day for making smaller mistakes than you seem to make every time you go out to play."

I said nothing in return because there was nothing I could say that would mollify him—just the opposite.

Visibly telling himself to calm down, Dwayne stared at me in silence for longer than his tantrum had lasted. Maybe he was counting to fifty. Gradually his face reassembled itself.

Then he surprised me. He waved an apologetic hand.

"Sorry about that," he said. "I know you mean no disrespect and even though I think your methods are off-the-wall, I know they've worked for you in the past and that you're just trying to do whatever you think you were sent here to do. But thanks to you this guy Burkov is now a spoiled target for the station and the cunt that started all this hoohah is a sex-crazed idiot who has probably done us a favor that's going to land her in federal prison until she reaches menopause. We could have handled her and this guy Burkov in our own lackluster way. Bottom line, it ain't your fault but I can't live with this situation unless it's clarified."

Again, silence seemed the best answer to this. Dwayne added a footnote in longhand to my cable. He handed this across the desk for me to read. It consisted of two sentences. The first employed kind words about the work I had done while making pointed reference to the unconventional methods I had employed. The second sentence recommended that I be called home for consultations before proceeding further with the operation.

That was fine by me. Luz awaited me, or so I hoped.

I said, "If you don't mind my asking, what do you have in mind for Burkov while I'm gone?"

"Hands off until the situation is clarified," Dwayne said. "The sooner you go, obviously, the sooner we can decide what to do and how to do it."

Half an hour later a cable arrived from Tom Terhune ordering me to take the next available flight to Virginia. Melanie had made the reservation even before I read the cable. I gave her the .45 and the rest of my kit and asked her to hold on to it in case I ever came back.

"And if you don't?"

"I'll let you know where to pouch it."

Not counting time in the terminal, the flight to Dulles took eleven hours. As I commanded myself to fall asleep, I tried to picture Luz. Again I couldn't do it. Maybe her own inability to reimagine her parents was contagious. Maybe this was a sign that when I got back I would find her gone. Two weeks had passed since last I saw her. For the first week I had thought of little besides her. In the second week I gave her barely a thought, and pixel by pixel, I had somehow lost the images of her that had haunted my memory since the moment we met in Los Bosques de Palermo. I loved her and lusted for her as much as I ever had, but my brain refused to access her image. Had she found some psychic means of hanging up on me? Was I going to spend the rest of my life listening to a dial tone?

From the Bogotá airport I had sent Luz a text telling her my time of arrival.

I had little hope she would be at Dulles to meet me. But when I emerged from customs at one in the morning, there she was. She gave me a chaste wifely kiss, placed a palm on my unshaven cheek, pinched my nose, grinned, showed me the animal look in her eyes.

In the parking garage she got out her car keys and pressed a button. The headlights flashed on a silver Mercedes cabriolet and its hardtop folded into the trunk.

Luz said, "How do you like it?"

No words came. The sticker price of a car like this was around a hundred thousand dollars.

I said, "Borrowed or rented?"

"Bought," Luz said. "A birthday present to myself. You can pay for it if your conscience still bothers you. It's slightly used. I got a good price."

I shut up. She drove. We left I-66 at the wrong exit, the one for the Key Bridge.

Before I could point out the mistake she said, "I have another surprise for you."

In Georgetown she turned into the driveway of a house I had never seen before and pressed another button. The garage door opened. My pathetic old piece of junk was already parked inside. She drove in, punched a number into a keypad, and led me into the house: fresh flowers, soft music played, low lights. Paintings on the walls, a sculpture or two, good Persian rugs, a bottle of Champagne in an ice bucket.

I started to speak. Luz put a finger on my lips. She said, "This is ours, too. Don't say a word. Open the Champagne. I'll get the caviar."

24

Amzi said, "I see you've pissed off another chief of station."

He was in a jocund mood. It was 6:00 A.M.—early in the day for that. He and Tom and I were practically alone in the building, except for Rosemary, who noiselessly entered the room in her flat-heeled shoes bearing a tray with three cups of coffee and a box of sticky buns.

Amzi said, "So what happened in Bogotá, exactly?"

I told him about my audience with Dwayne. As Amzi listened, a small smile formed on his lips. His eyes were opaque as usual.

When I came to the end Amzi said, "Nothing else you want to tell me?"

"Like what?"

Amzi's smile had vanished. He said, "Oh, I don't know. Let's try what you think our chances are with Don Ivan, the great Slavic lover."

"I think he wants us to think the chances are pretty good."

"Meaning what?"

"Meaning that it's not impossible that he genuinely wants to defect and that he seduced poor Sally, who is a no-value target if ever there was one, as a way of attracting our attention."

"That's your favorite possibility?"

"No, just one possibility What do you want to do about Burkov while you figure out what to do about him?"

Amzi said, "Let him marinate for a while. Then we'll get together with Dwayne, like we should have done in the first place, and put his nose back in joint."

"And what do I do in the meantime?"

"Help Tom with the dishes. We're done."

I spent the rest of the day in my office, reading about Colombia. The whole country was a Hieronymus Bosch painting come to life. Our fingerprints were all over the place. The list of Headquarters operations was long, and nearly every one of them was a mission impossible. It seemed to me that Dwayne had enough to do just keeping an eye on this circus without worrying about small fry like Burkov and me. But large issues spring from small resentments. I took it for granted that Amzi would choose Dwayne if the choice was between him and me. How could he not? Dwayne was right—I was trespassing on private property.

That evening Luz threw a catered dinner party for ten. The guests were Luz's American friends—some old, some new. Nearly all the women had jobs—lawyers, activists, scholars—and lamented the fact that they didn't see enough of their kids, who turned for love, comfort, and advice to their illiterate Latina nannies. A couple of the males were househusbands. One of these was a poet, married to an oncologist whose one-thousand-word poem on global warming (rhymes in the middle of the lines) had just been published.

Neither the men nor the women took an interest in me: Luz was the one with the money and the sainted parents. They all loved her—loved the house, loved the food, loved the wine, loved the display of riches and good taste. Hated Republicans.

They stayed until midnight. Luz went upstairs as soon as she had kissed the last one good-bye. I followed the trail of her clothes, which began at the top of the stairs and ended at the bathroom door, which stood open. Naked, she stood at the sink, vigorously brushing her teeth. In the mirror she gave me a smile through the toothpaste.

I said, "We've got to talk."

She took the toothbrush out of her mouth, rinsed, spat, met my eyes in the glass, and said, "Serious talk or pillow talk?"

"Serious talk."

"Then I won't hurry."

She closed the door. I heard the shower running, the hair dryer humming. Half an hour later she emerged, modestly wearing a bathrobe and to all appearances cold sober.

She said, "Let me answer your first question before you ask it. Yes, we can afford this place."

"How?"

"I got a good price."

"How good?"

No answer. The house was worth millions. Divide its market value by two and it was still worth millions.

"How come the price was so good?"

"A man from Buenos Aires lost his wife, an American girl much younger than he was. It was sudden—an aortal aneurysm. He was crazy about her. He didn't want to be reminded of her, he didn't need the money, so he let me have the place for a song and went back to Argentina."

"Why the special price?"

"He's rich. He was a friend of Alejandro's. He's a friend of Diego's."

Of course he was. I said, "How much is the monthly payment?"

"Zero."

"You paid cash?"

"Yes."

"You have that kind of money?"

She said, "Not to worry. If we go broke we can sell this place for a lot more than I paid for it. I hate the apartment, I hate that phony neighborhood and its snooty nobodies. I hate this soulless, heartless city and its ridiculous copycat architecture and its one-note babble in fifth-grade English. I hate being alone in this nowhere when you go away. I am a *porteña*. I need something in my life that reminds me of Buenos Aires."

"The seller was someone you knew in Buenos Aires?"

No answer. *Enough questions.*

Luz turned off the lights. The drapes were drawn. It was as dark in the bedroom as it had been in La Sombra. Within seconds I had a naked woman straddling my body. I couldn't see her face. I put my hands on her. I knew her name, I knew her body, I knew the way her skin felt, I knew her scent and the texture of her hair. I wasn't sure who she was or why she seemed to love me. For all I knew, her passion was a pantomime. I had never been sure of her and now I knew I never would be. Before I stopped thinking altogether I realized that her elusiveness was the reason for this sweet apology.

At four in the morning I was still wide-awake, but my mind was elsewhere. Breathing softly, laughing, murmuring in her dreams, Luz slept the sleep of the just. There was no point in remaining where and as I was. I got out of bed, dressed for a run, and went downstairs, about as sure of where I was in this strange house as a sleepwalker. A crack of light showed under the kitchen door. I opened it and spotted keys suspended from hooks beside the door to the garage. I took the set that included the keys to the apartment and my old car, figured out how to open the garage door, and backed out. I had no destination in mind. After the interminable plane ride, the interminable day at Headquarters, and the long, long evening with Luz's one-mind-fits-all dinner guests, plus an hour of desperate sex, I was barely capable of thought, let alone conscious intent.

I rolled down all the windows. This turned the car into a sauna. Minutes later I found myself parking on our gentrified street, or what used to be our street, in Adams Morgan. A snowdrift of mail blocked the door.

I found a garbage bag and stuffed junk mail into it. I threw a cheap square envelope with a handwritten address into the bag before realizing what it was. I retrieved it and opened it. Inside was a postcard of a lighthouse in Trieste. The date was written in the European style on the back of the postcard, day and year in Arabic numerals and the month in between in Roman numerals. I decoded this to mean that Boris wanted to meet in front of the Reichstag in Berlin in two days' time.

But wait. How did he know my street address? I had given him the address of a post office box in Bethesda. Was this a trap, was the whole operation a trap, was Boris in cahoots with Al Qaeda in the Arabian Peninsula? Then I realized that Boris had probably gotten my address from the Internet, plus directions to the apartment, just as any marketing chiseler or terrorist could do.

While driving up Wisconsin Avenue I called Tom Terhune and in the obligatory telephone double-talk, told him I was going away for a few days for that chess tournament I had told him about.

In a sleepy voice he said, "Good luck." And disconnected.

When I got back to the house Luz was still asleep. I went into the bathroom and used her cell phone to book, at outrageous cost to the taxpayer, a flight to Berlin and a hotel and a car. I packed a carry-on bag and left a note for Luz on the refrigerator door. If she had meant what she said the night before about hating to be left alone, she would be infuriated by the callous way I chose to say good-bye. Or not say good-bye.

I had no key to this house. When I came back and rang the doorbell would I be admitted?

The flight to Germany didn't leave until five in the afternoon. I couldn't face a visit to Headquarters that might include a meeting with Amzi, but I didn't want to be alone. I wanted to unburden myself. It would have been nice to have had the option of dumping my guilty secrets onto a retired spy who was now a bartender—somebody who didn't give a rat's ass about the psychic wounds inflicted on me by Mommy and Daddy and Luz Aguilar but knew enough about the difference between psychosis and tradecraft to understand, as my mentor Fred of Moonshine Manor had mentioned, how little difference there was between the two.

The solution to this problem was as obvious to me as it had been to Alejandro all those many years ago in Buenos Aires. I called Father Yuri on his cell phone and asked in Russian if he was up to a walk in the woods.

We met as we used to do on the half hour at TR's statue. Father Yuri had brought two large navel oranges, and as we walked we peeled and ate them. We spoke Russian—or rather, I did. He listened in silence. I told him everything in minute detail. The relief of laying down this burden overwhelmed me. The talking cure was working.

At length but in what had seemed mere seconds, we arrived back at TR's statue. I was feeling a lot better. By now, though it was still very early in the day, the sun was bright. Father Yuri glanced at the shadow the statue cast upon the ground. I realized that he had always done this when we got to this place. Owing to his vow of poverty, he owned no watch, so this must be the way he told time.

He took a deep breath. We could hear the traffic across the river. Smell it.

I said, "Any suggestions?"

"Maybe you should ask yourself," Father Yuri said, "whether it might be possible that the things you doubt are exactly what they seem to be instead of what you fear they might be."

Then he walked away, leaving me to ponder the riddle.

25

In Berlin at the appointed time I walked across the open space in front of the Reichstag and at the precise minute he had specified, saw Boris jog by. I followed him. He slowed down enough, timing the stoplights and running in place, so that I could keep him in sight. After a few blocks he came to a Burger King and went inside. I sauntered around the block and entered. He was still in line. I got into a different line and by the time I bought a cup of coffee and sat down with him at a tiny table for two he was halfway through a King Sundae.

We didn't exchange a word or so much as a nod. He ignored me while he finished his ice cream, wiped his lips on a napkin, and bussed his debris except for a second, clean napkin, rolled into a cylinder, which he left on the table. He left. I finished my coffee, palmed the napkin, and went outside. There I unrolled the napkin and found a flash drive. In violation of good sense and Headquarters regulations and probably the National Security Act, I went to an Internet café and read it on a public computer. It contained a list of three Cheka officers—true names and official aliases and résumés, mug shots, home addresses and cell phone numbers and

214

past and current foreign postings with dates. Appended were the complete texts of contact reports filed by each of the subjects after meetings with their American case officers and a sampler of the secrets they had sold to the suckers. One of the names on the list was Kirill Sergeivich Burkov.

Boris had given me what I had asked for in Helsinki—maybe. It was a fine opening move. Absent the ability to read Boris's mind there was no way to be certain and there never would be.

I booked a morning SAS flight to Washington and got home in time for dinner. As if a spell had been broken, Luz was once again the woman she used to be. When she was in the mood she was a good cook, and while we drank prosecco she cut tomatoes and mozzarella and basil for caprese and made a new kind of pasta from a recipe she had found on epicurious.com. It was delicious.

We went to bed without doing the dishes. After the lovemaking, I couldn't fall asleep. Luz had no such problem; she never did after the fifth orgasm. I went downstairs and watched *Casablanca* with the sound turned off. I wondered, as I always did, what a woman like Ilsa saw in a funny-looking dimwit like Rick. Soon after Sam played "As Time Goes By," I switched off the TV and looked around at the paintings and sculptures and wondered again if money the friends of Alejandro had robbed from banks and collected in ransoms had been used to pay for them, and then executed them anyway. I knew the answer: *What else could it possibly be?*

At four o'clock on the dot, my cell phone vibrated. It was Tom Terhune. Amzi wanted to see me in his office at five-thirty.

On the way upstairs Tom warned me to step carefully. Amzi was in a foul mood. I took this advice seriously, though it was hard to imagine how Amzi could contrive to be any more foul than the Komodo dragon we all knew so well. I soon found out.

Rosemary pointed to Amzi's office door. Tom knocked. Amzi said "Come!" Tom opened the door and made an after-you gesture, and then withdrew.

The chairs in which Amzi's supplicants usually sat had been removed, just as they had been on that long-ago day in Moscow when he sentenced my father to the death of a thousand cuts.

Amzi said, "Thanks for the turd soup, you fucking idiot."

I held up a traffic cop palm and said, "Hold it right there."

He blinked. "What? Who the fuck do you think you're talking to?"

"You, you fucking bully. If you want to talk to me, keep a civil tongue in your head. If you can't do that, we're done."

Amzi looked me up and down. "Gee willikers," he said, "don't we got balls."

He pressed the intercom button on his phone and said, "One chair. Tell Terhune to go back to bed."

The secretary brought the chair.

"Please sit," Amzi said. "With due regard to your wounded feelings and watching my language, I want to discuss this material you brought back from Berlin. Would you find the word *bizarre* objectionable?"

"No. Puzzling."

"You are familiar with the contents of this particular flash drive?"

"I read it. But all that's in the contact report."

"So it is. That's why we're having this chat. If I may, I just want to confirm that you actually inserted the flash drive into a computer in an Internet café in Berlin and read its classified contents on that screen while a roomful of strangers in a strange land read it over your shoulder. Have I got that right?"

"Yes, just as I reported."

"Ah-ha. May I ask why the obscenity you did a thing like that?"

"Curiosity."

"You're aware what curiosity did for the cat?"

I said, "Amzi, I'm just guessing here, but I suspect you've got a problem with my report. Maybe if you come right out and tell me what it is, I might be able to help you."

Amzi said, "Let me explain. There are two complementary problems. The first is that you made an obscenity shambles of mandatory procedure by doing the stupid obscenity thing you did in an Internet café, and number two, by carrying the flash drive home in the toe of your obscenity shoe or you concealed it instead of securely pouching it home and cabling your contact report from the Berlin station. As a result I had to wait an entire weekend to know how completely you had obscenitied up. Does that answer your question?"

I nodded.

He said, "Do you have anything to say to me that might make me feel better?"

"I doubt it."

"Do you and your Russian friend the modern major general expect us to believe this fairy tale?"

I said, "It's usually a good idea to take everything that comes out of Moscow with a grain of salt. But there is a chance this information is authentic."

"Did you recognize any of the names on the list?"

"One name I recognized. The others, no."

"Did it occur to you that they might be telling us who supposedly works for us because they want to get rid of the people named?"

"Why wouldn't they just get rid of them?"

"Maybe because they want us to think these guys are ringers."

"*What*?" I said. "Amzi, you've lost me."

He studied my face as if he saw in it something only he could see, then spun around in his desk chair and looked out the window. The sun was coming up. He watched the pinks and golds deepen.

"Nice sunrise," he said. "What I want you to do, if you're still working for us . . ."

Still working for us?

". . . is go back to Bogotá and recruit Kirill the Well Hung."

"That wouldn't be redundant if he already works for us?"

"If it's redundant he'll just think he knows something you don't."

"And then?"

"Force some money on him and thumbprint him and develop the relationship as only you can. Find out what he knows about Boris and about the guys on the list."

I said, "What about Dwayne?"

"Dwayne has been mollified. He understands the underlying reasons for what we're doing. He is now your best friend in Bogotá. If you need operational money or a Stinger missile or anything like that, he's your man. But make nice. He's still a little bruised."

"When do I leave?"

"Yesterday would have been good. You'll be there for a while, so if you want to take your wife with you, that's fine. We'll even pay for her ticket."

As he spoke he went on admiring the sunrise. It was even more dramatic now—J. M. W. Turner might have painted it.

Amzi said, "If you do take Luz I'd think twice before introducing her to the target. But that's up to you."

He spun around in his chair and silently studied the sunrise.

"We're done," he said, with his back still turned to me.

I had no idea what this encounter was all about. No doubt that was the whole idea.

26

That evening I broke the news of my imminent departure to Luz. Did she want to come with me? You bet she did. She was delighted with the prospect of a holiday in Colombia. She had always wanted to see the backcountry, travel up the Orinoco in a canoe. She longed to swim again in a warm and salty sea of Spanish. Diego knew people in Bogotá, friends of Alejandro. She would get on the phone with him and have him tell the right people she was coming. As for the Georgetown house, we could turn the key in the lock, set the burglar alarm, and walk away. It would be waiting for us when we returned.

When would we leave?

"Me, tomorrow," I said. "You can follow whenever."

"Oh, no. Whither thou goest, baby. I will not be left alone again in this hick town."

"You'll have to use your U.S. passport. Argentineans need a visa to enter Colombia."

Even that didn't faze her.

She spent the rest of the evening packing, cell phone at her ear all the while, talking to Diego. I stayed out of earshot by going for a long run along the C&O Canal. I tucked tubes of secret agent-strength knockout spray in both pockets of my shorts, so I could induce temporary blindness and several layers of pain in a would-be mugger. After dealing with Kirill Sergeivich and Boris and Amzi all in a single day, I was far enough gone to half hope I *would* be attacked. Maybe I could release my frustration along with the spray.

Outside customs at El Dorado International Airport in Bogotá we were met by a gray-haired man who held up a sign that read LUZ. He had intelligent eyes and from the look of him was a former athlete.

"I'm Damián, a friend of Diego's," he said in English. "I have a car. I will drive you to your house."

I didn't know him from Adam and neither did Luz. This was Colombia. If I had had the .45 on me I might have reached for it, but Luz put a hand on my arm. She was unconcerned. She had known what to expect. Diego again.

In English she said, "Hi, I'm Luz. Very kind of you to meet us like this. Thank you."

"My pleasure. Really," said Damián, drinking my wife in as if I were just some guy waiting for a taxi.

Damián, if that was his true name, looked as if he was in his fifties, the right age to have been a friend of Alejandro's. Waving me away, he picked up our bags and put them into the trunk of a gleaming black Audi S8, then held open the back door for Luz.

The house he drove us to was in Salitre, an upscale suburb where people with inherited wealth or serious drug money or both tended to live. Damián filled us in. This neighborhood was as safe as money and the right friends could make it, Damián himself lived just down the street, Simón Bolivar Park was not far away. It was a good place to run if we liked to run, or to just go for a walk and be in the presence of nature.

The house had a swimming pool and a tennis court. The owners were abroad, living in Europe for the time being, and they were happy to have someone enjoying the place and making it look occupied.

"Especially," Damián said, looking at Luz in the rearview mirror, "the daughter of your parents. They knew your mother and father years ago, when all of us were young."

The car in the garage, a spotless S500 Mercedes, was for our use. The wine in the wine cellar was for drinking and would be replenished by the wine merchant who came and counted the bottles once a month. A maid and a gardener, her husband, came in once a week and if we wished, would cook and serve dinner parties. Armed men from a very efficient security firm kept watch on the house at night and checked the property several times a day. The alarm system included a panic button in every room. Damián was just down the street. Call him day or night, regardless of the hour. He and his wife hoped we could join them soon for dinner.

He gave us his business card and scribbled his cell phone number on the back. He was a surgeon.

"Like Diego," Luz said, speaking Spanish.

"We were together in medical school, and we had other interests in common."

"Ah," Luz said. "I thought so. You sound like a *porteño*."

Damián smiled a sad smile. His quick eyes searched her face.

"You resemble your mother," he said. "She was the most beautiful woman in Argentina."

Luz touched the back of his hand with a forefinger.

While Luz unpacked I called Dwayne and left a message. Fifteen minutes later he called back and invited us to dinner that very night.

The Scogginses lived in another swank suburb called Chico. They were a study in contrasts. Dwayne was about six foot four and slow to smile. His wife, a sweet-faced smiling woman, was from Montevideo.

While Dwayne and I talked business as if listening devices had never been invented, the women went outside. They got along famously. Clearly Luz was not going to lack for chums in Bogotá.

Dwayne, too, made a friendly gesture. "Your friend Kirill Sergeivich looks like a lost soul since you vanished," he said. "Good sign."

Throughout dinner, eyeing Luz, he was the soul of geniality, telling comical stories about his tiny hometown in Kentucky where they hitched mules to the parking meters and played football without helmets and always married their cousins, so all the kids in town looked alike and no adulterous wife had to worry if her baby didn't resemble her husband.

After dinner Dwayne invited me into his study for a cognac—Peyrat XO. It was organic. I had never heard of it. Chiefs of station lived like pashas wherever they were and wherever they came from.

At last we talked a little business. During my absence Dwayne had kept an eye on Kirill Burkov. Naturally he had used Colombian sidewalk men. Burkov spotted them almost immediately, identifying each new team as it came on duty.

"He's good," Dwayne said. "I called off the surveillance before we had exposed all our local gumshoes to him. By then we knew what we needed to know."

"This guy *wants* us to know where he'll be at any given minute between nightfall and dawn," Dwayne said. "His routine never varies. He only comes out at night. I guess he wants you to know where to look for him when you get back in town. The Russians watch the airport, so by now he probably knows you're back. So *buena suerta*. And this."

He handed me my .45, and as a gift from the station, a new quick-draw holster—the latest gun-nut thing, Dwayne said. He used the same holster himself, but he preferred the compact 9 mm Sig Sauer P290 to my heavy revolver. I should give the Sig Sauer a try, the station could loan me one.

"I know you've had pretty good luck with the weapon you've got and I know John Wayne used it to win the West and all like that," he said, "but technologically speaking, it's the bow and arrow of handguns."

When we got home Luz and I blessed our new dwelling in the usual way and as usual she fell into a deep sleep immediately afterward. By the half-light that filtered into the huge master suite I watched her in the teeming country of her slumber. I was overcome by my love for her. The memory of her fingertip on the back of Damián's hand made me growl.

At three in the morning I rose from the bed, dressed, stuck the .45 in its new holster in the waistband of my pants, and drove the purring Mercedes to La Sombra. According to Dwayne's timetable, Kirill Burkov dropped in every Wednesday at 3:45 A.M. and ordered vodka. He seemed to be waiting for someone, but no one ever showed up. At 3:50 my cell phone made the sound it makes when a text message is delivered. The message was a confirmation from a watcher in the shadows that Burkov had just shown up at La Sombra.

Ten minutes later I parked the Mercedes, an irresistible temptation to thieves in this dark neighborhood, and walked around the corner and went inside. The chilled recycled air reeked of raw perfume, liquor, and secondhand marijuana smoke. In a booth at the back of the room a cigarette lighter ignited, then went out for a few seconds, then flared again. *Burkov.*

I walked toward the extinguished flame and sat down.

In English Burkov said, "I have already ordered your black Jack."

He pushed the glass across the table.

I said, "Save the Kremlin's money. I don't drink whiskey."

"So I noticed. What do you want?"

"Ginger ale."

He knocked twice, loudly, on the table. The waiter appeared.

Burkov said, "So how was Mother?"

"A little forgetful but hale and hearty."

"Did you tell her about me?"

"In passing. She has her doubts about your intentions."

"Of course she does. Mothers are always suspicious."

The glow from the tiny bulb was too feeble to make it possible to read Burkov's face. That was the point of La Sombra's perpetual midnight. No doubt it was also an asset to the not very tempting hookers of both genders who worked the place. This lack of visual clues turned the conversation into something like talking on the telephone to a person who has reason to lie to you.

Burkov switched to Russian and lowered his voice. The sound system, which had been switched off, came to life: Tonight, Willie Nelson sang "Red Headed Stranger." Customers in adjoining booths raised their voices to be heard above Willie's reedy tenor. Burkov spoke two or three rapid sentences in a normal tone. I caught only half the words.

I said, "Speak up, Kirill Sergeivich. I can't hear you over the music and the panting."

"Then follow me."

He gulped his whiskey and walked out of the place. I followed him as instructed. The full moon was reflected like a very realistic photograph in the windshields of the parked cars. There was more light in the street than there had been inside.

Burkov was speaking up now—barking, actually.

He uttered the Russian equivalent of: "So are you going to shit or get off the pot?"

The vulgarism triggered something within me. I had heard enough insults without listening to more in Russian.

I said, "Good night to you, too." And walked away.

Burkov took three rapid steps and grabbed my arm. He had a grip of iron.

In melodramatic tones, in English, he said, "I am in danger."

I said, "Come on. This isn't the movies."

Speaking Russian now, he said, "Please take me to your car. Mine is not secure. We must talk."

"You want to talk to an American agent in an American car?"

"If there is a recording of what I say to you, so much the better."

I said, "Kirill Sergeivich, you are a most unusual Russian spy."

Now Burkov took me by both arms and squeezed. Speaking through his teeth he said, "Listen to me. Moscow thinks I work for you."

"Really? Do you?"

"No, I do not. You already know that, of course you do, but what does it matter? It's what they think. That means it's as good as the truth even if it is false—better. They don't have to prove anything. All that's necessary is that they believe it. Do you know what they do to traitors in my service?"

"Live cremation is what I've heard."

"That's right, but that's just the way it ends. By the time they nail down the coffin lid all you want to do is die. If you help me there is much I can tell you. But I have to go with you now—this minute."

He looked around, as if a squad of Russians snipers was watching him through night-vision scopes. He was sweating, trembling. He was a little drunk.

I said, "Why should I believe this story?"

"I don't require that, only that you give me the benefit of the doubt. I am putting myself in your power. What more do you want? Are you working for Moscow? I don't understand you. I am offering jewels—*jewels.*"

"Like what?"

"Like who a certain important person in Headquarters belongs to Moscow."

"Name?"

"First, you help me."

I said, "This is not a good place to linger. Let's go back inside."

Burkov didn't like this idea—clearly he wanted to get as far away from La Sombra as possible, as quickly as possible. But he followed me in.

Our glasses were still on our table. We sat down.

We heard a scampering sound. The other customers, all of them, were dashing for the exits as if the place was on fire. There was no smell of smoke. I drew my .45—it practically leaped out of its slick new holster—and held it under the table.

An instant later, I understood the panic. Two thugs with guns in their hands appeared at our table. Neither spoke. One of them, a scowling hulk, leveled his weapon at Birkov's head.

I shot this man in the foot. He screamed in pain. My Moonshine Manor firearms instructor had been right—a .45 caliber slug to the big toe is enough to immobilize anything that walks. The man dropped his cocked pistol on the table—miraculously it didn't go off—and still shrieking and writhing, sat down on the floor as if the tendons in his knees had been cut.

For a fraction of a second the other desperado took his eyes off Burkov. Burkov took advantage of this—hands across the Elbe—by delivering a karate chop to his Adam's apple. He, too, collapsed, choking and fighting for breath.

We stepped over our victims, the hulk still howling and rocking back and forth, the other fellow unconscious but fighting for breath and losing the battle, and went out the back door. We both held pistols in our hands.

We found ourselves in a dead-end alley that opened onto the street where the Mercedes was parked.

I said, "Who were those guys?"

Burkov, behind me, said, "Who knows? Where's your car?"

"Nearby. Will it blow up when I turn the key?"

"You'll find out when you turn the key. In case you are now willing to believe they are planning to kill me, I am formally asking for political asylum in the United States of America."

He tapped me on the shoulder and when I turned around, handed me two pistols, the Makarov he held in his hand and a smaller hideout weapon, also a fighting knife and a blackjack and aerosol tubes of knock-out spray and—I'm serious—a strangling cord. In a way this was reassur-ing. He had been standing behind me in the dark for almost a minute and I was still breathing.

I opened the trunk and gestured him inside. He climbed in as if this was the only way to travel—which in his case, it was. The lid silently closed itself.

By now it was almost six in the morning. The car started with its usual discreet purr.

I called Dwayne, already wide-awake, and asked him where I could drop off a large package.

He said, "The office. You will be met."

27

Fifteen minutes later, Kirill Sergeivich Burkov went through the looking glass. One of Dwayne's people, a paunchy middle-aged officer I knew by sight but not by name because we had never been introduced, awaited us inside the embassy gate. He wore a rumpled corduroy clearance-sale suit and a wide paisley necktie that had gone out of style well before the turn of the millennium. We exchanged no words. I popped the trunk. Burkov unfolded himself and Dwayne's man led him to a waiting van. Both men got in. A young fellow I had never seen before was behind the wheel. While the door was still sliding to its closed position, the gate opened and the van drove through it.

All this happened in seconds. I left Burkov's weaponry in a heap on the passenger seat and went inside the embassy. The armored door to the station, which looked like an ordinary door, was locked. I rang the bell. No response. I called Dwayne's cell phone. He didn't answer.

I went home. This took a while because the city was awakening and traffic thickened by the minute. One of the CDs stored in the Mercedes's player was a Rolling Stones album. I hate the Rolling Stones. I pressed PLAY and turned up the volume until I couldn't hear myself think, which was the whole idea.

At home I transferred Burkov's arsenal to the trunk, unloading the firearms and stuffing the clips into my coat pockets. I found Luz as I had left her, sound asleep, muttering under her breath to someone in a dream.

I locked up Kirill's weaponry. I took a shower, taking my .45 with me into the bathroom, and shaved even though I knew that washing away pheromones and removing stubble would displease Luz, who liked to smell the full aroma of the male who was in bed with her and be scratched by his beard. When I went back to bed, she was still asleep. I didn't wake her.

I didn't even try to sleep. My brain was releasing so much adrenaline that I couldn't possibly have done so. What I wanted to do was get my mind off the events of the previous evening, off everything that had happened since the day I played golf with Karim.

To that end, I recited poetry to myself. I memorized the entire text of *The Ancient Mariner* in eighth-grade English and ever since have silently recited it to myself when trying to overcome periodic fits of anger and regret and shame so strong that they could have been mistaken as epileptic seizures.

> *The very deep did rot: O Christ!*
> *That ever this should be!*
> *Yea, slimy things did crawl with legs*
> *Upon the slimy sea.*

And so on through the cornfield of middle school English: *Evangeline,* "The Song of Hiawatha," Hamlet, Shelley, Tennyson, gobs of Kipling.

Finally I fell asleep. My dreams were just as bad as I had expected. In the morning Luz woke in her usual fashion. After a sufficient number of orgasms she picked oranges from a tree in the garden and squeezed them. She made a dish, new to me, out of crumbled corn bread, butter, and white cheese that she said was called *arepa con quesito*. Diego had gotten the recipe from his fellow medical student Ernesto Guevara—it was Che's grandmother's recipe, therefore the manna of the revolution. Diego had taught Luz to make it when she was a child and she had forgotten all about it until she woke up this morning in Colombia.

I waited till late afternoon before presenting myself at the station. As usual, no heads were lifted as I passed by, not even—or maybe especially— that of the man in the corduroy suit who had taken custody of Burkov.

Dwayne's secretary gestured me into his office. He was reading a cable. He did not look up when I entered but held up a just-a-minute hand. He finished, signed the document, and rang for his secretary.

Dwayne said, "Take a pew."

I sat down. I was calm again.

"Mariana and I really enjoyed meeting Luz last night," Dwayne said. "She just loved her. Beautiful woman, great personality. How did you get so lucky?"

"I might ask you the same question," I said. "I have something for you."

I had dumped Burkov's stuff into a string bag I found in the kitchen, and now I dropped it on his desk.

Dwayne turned the bag upside down and the arsenal spilled out onto his desk. The noise was considerable.

He said, "You took all this away from him?"

"He made me a present of it."

"Your prints are on it?"

"Yes. So are his and now, yours."

Dwayne's outward manner was a blank.

I said, "Where is he now?"

Dwayne said, "Beyond the reach of those who might do him harm."

"That's a comfort—he's such a vulnerable soul."

Dwayne said, "You look pissed off. What's the problem?"

"Where's my Russian?"

"We took him under our wing. That's what procedure dictates and Amzi insisted upon. Don't worry. He's safe, he'll always be safe in our hands no matter what he turns out to be. I'm real sorry, and I know Amzi will be even more contrite, that you didn't get to say good-bye. But that's the way it works."

"OK, but where is he?"

"I don't know. My guys handed him over to some people at an airstrip and away he went. I never laid eyes on him and I never will. Case closed as far as this station is concerned. Your work here is done. Go home."

"I just got here."

"So you're a fast worker. Keep your perspective about Burkov. All's well that ends well, and he's in good hands. The chief negative is that Mariana and Luz won't get to be girlfriends."

"That's a shame."

"Yeah, but so many things in life are. You should be happy. You did your job. You'll never see Burkov, or whoever he really is, again. But if you've been reporting what was truly in your heart, you didn't like the bastard anyway, so what have you lost? Any questions?"

"What happens to Sally?"

"She's not our problem. Diplomatic security handed her over to the Justice Department. If she's smart she'll spill her guts and cop a plea and take her medicine. Conjugal visits from her well-hung boyfriend probably won't be part of the package. Bon voyage."

28

In his brightly lit office at Headquarters, chilled to an arctic temperature, Amzi said, "Home again, home again, jiggedy-jig. You didn't waste any time in Bogotá."

We were alone—no Tom, seemingly nobody at all in the empty, hushed building. Amzi's wall of clocks said it was 3:41 A.M. Eastern Standard Time. He was wide-awake. I was dead tired. Amzi's secretary had called me while my flight was taxiing to the gate after landing at Dulles and told me to come straight to Headquarters. I had had no sleep for forty-eight hours, every one of which, this one especially, spent in places where I would rather not have been.

I said, "Give Dwayne some credit for my swift return. After he kidnapped Burkov there wasn't much left for me to do in Colombia."

"He mentioned that you didn't seem to grasp the finer points on that one. Can I be of any help?"

"No need."

"But you were miffed," Amzi said. "Don't be. It's SOP. We have people who handle walk-ins like your guy. They quarantine the subject. Nobody but them goes anywhere near him. The idea is for them to become the only friends the lost soul's got in the world."

"Thanks for the explanation. Why am I here?"

Answering a direct question wasn't Amzi's strong suit.

He said, "Where's your wife?"

"Still in Bogotá. She has family friends there."

"The usual, 'Wow, I got-away-with-it crowd'?"

Well, yes. But I saw no reason to comment.

Amzi said, "*I've* got a question. How are you doing?"

"I'm a little tired after the flight."

We had already been together for more than an hour. It was 4:28 in the morning.

"I meant all in all."

"OK."

"You like the work?"

"It has its moments."

"You're better at it than a lot of people thought you'd be."

"I'm glad you think so."

Amzi said, "I wasn't one of the doubters. You've got the genes. Your father had a gift for this work, as much as anyone ever did, and the apple doesn't fall far from the tree. He had a lot of bad luck. You seem to specialize in good luck."

This was the first time Amzi had ever mentioned my father, whose final stroke of bad luck he had arranged.

I said, "Good luck? Me? For example?"

"For example, you should be dead. The way you operate, it was a miracle that you didn't get yourself castrated and decapitated in Sana'a or somewhere else in holy Islam or that your Russian buddies didn't put something left over from the KGB poison store in your coffee."

"You're worried about me?"

"No, but you need a rest," he said. "It's a management situation. If you don't get some rest your luck will run out. I want you to take a vacation. This time I mean it, so don't try to wiggle out of it. Leave your cell phone in your safe and take Luz, when she's through hanging out with her father's jolly old comrades, to some romantic paradise in the Pacific. Bali would be good. No station there. Sunbathe, walk on the beach. Eat nonorganic fatty foods. Drink drinks with umbrellas in them. Sleep. Do what young couples do when there's no television and they don't have anything to read."

I said, "No thanks."

Amzi said, "Oh, really? Then maybe we should think about the options. You need sleep? The French used to have a treatment called the sleep cure. I'm not sure what it was supposed to cure—unhappiness, probably. They'd pump people full of drugs and feed them through tubes, change their diapers, and keep them asleep for I don't know how long—weeks, months, maybe years in serious cases. It was like space travel. A robot gives you a shot, you wake up happy and refreshed a thousand years later somewhere in Andromeda with everybody you knew back on Earth long since dead and muscles so weak you can't get out of your capsule. We probably even know a French shrink we can recommend."

I said, "No thanks."

The real Amzi awakened.

"Wrong fucking answer," he said in his sandpaper voice. "You're fucking done with this case. You need a rest. Starting now. Get out of this building within fifteen minutes and go somewhere for not less than thirty days. We're fucking done."

When I got to the house in Georgetown, which still smelled of the people who used to live there, I found a postcard from Boris.

It read: "Budapest. Three days hence."

Fuck Amzi.

29

This time, Boris was wearing a navy blue blazer with brass buttons instead of his running togs. Following him through the streets of Bucharest resembled a guided tour of the city's landmarks. I had never been there before and the unexpected—the unsuspected—beauty of the city took me by surprise. The language, which sounded like gargled French, surprised me, too, because I half understood it. Before World War II, according to the guide to Romania, Bucharest had been called "Little Paris" because of its eclectic architecture, its broad boulevards, and its many parks. It had its own Arcul de Triumf that looked a lot like the one in the Place de l'Étoile, and its own Seine, the Dâmbovita River. After half a century of communism the architecture had some Stalinist monstrosities, such the monumental Palatul Parlamentului. According to the handbook this was the largest administrative building in the world. It was the monument to himself that the psychotic dictator Nicolae Ceauşescu completed shortly before he was deposed in 1989 and shot, along with his wife, by a firing squad.

Boris's destination was the Cişmigiu Gardens, a former royal pleasure park in the city center that was said to contain one hundred thousand

CHARLES McCARRY

species of trees and shrubs and plants. At this early hour it was virtually empty. Boris headed straight for an outdoor chess table, sat down, and fished a set of chessmen from the bag slung from his shoulder. I had been keeping a discreet distance between us, so by the time I caught up with him and sat down, the board was ready.

Boris got the white pieces, so he made the first move. He opened with the bewildering Stonewall Attack. Neither of us said a word during the minutes it took him to destroy my defense and my illusions about ever becoming his equal at the game.

After I tipped over my king he said, "So where is Burkov?"

"Somewhere in the United States, I think."

"You *think*? But where?"

"I don't know."

"How can you not know?"

"By having no need to know."

"You will overcome that problem."

I said, "I will? Who says so?"

"I do. Don't be so touchy. Burkov is very good. He will charm his keepers. They are nice American boys who will learn to like him and trust him enough to make the one mistake it is necessary for them to make, and as soon as he has planted whatever lies he has been ordered to tell them, his superiors will order him to walk away."

I said, "'His superiors'? I thought you were in charge of the Americas."

"He belongs to a different directorate," Boris said. "This kind of switch has happened before, when your people took a man they thought was a defector to lunch in a restaurant in Washington, and can you imagine, let him go to the w.c. all by himself and never saw him again."

Assuming that Headquarters had turned the escapee and was sending him back to the Russians as a penetration agent, yes, I could imagine such a parody. And so could Boris.

"In Moscow," Boris was saying, "these fools would have been shot, and rightly so. It may look to Amzi like Kirill Sergeivich was kidnapped or murdered, but he will be alive and well and fucking some stupid woman during lunch hour and laughing his head off. He's a psychopath, yes. But a very, very smart psychopath."

For Boris, a man of few words in any language, this speech was the equivalent of reading *War and Peace* aloud.

He said, "Help me. Please tell me exactly what happened between you and Kirill Sergeivich."

Boris was turning the tables again, acting as if he was the handler and I was the asset. But he did have a right to know, and if we were partners, as our pantomime of an operation was supposed to suggest, he had a need to know. Besides, once he knew, what would he know that had the slightest value as intelligence? He and his superiors already knew that Burkov was in the hands of Headquarters and they knew everything that Burkov knew.

I told Boris as much as he needed to know.

When I was finished, Boris said, "So you're telling me he just disarmed himself then disarmed you in another way by leaping into your arms crying '*Save me*'?"

"You could put it that way."

"This did not arouse your suspicions?"

"Boris, please."

"But why did you let the other Americans take him away?"

"Why would I object? How could I stop them? In theory we were on the same side."

"The fact remains that now he's of no value to us. We must restore his value."

"Oh? How do we do that?"

"We kill him before the eyes of his minders. It's the only way to make Amzi believe Kirill Sergeivich really was a traitor to Russia, that he was working sincerely with the Americans all along because he is a secret democrat, that he knew so much he had to be killed by evil Moscovites."

This made sense—perverse sense, demented sense, but the only kind of sense that mattered to the Borises and the Amzis of this world. And increasingly, to me.

Trying to make a joke of this joke of an idea, I said, "Then you'll have to find some weird Russian way to kill him, like the polonium you so cleverly used on what's-his-name in London. Radiation poisoning is detectable, so even American fools should get the message."

Boris said, "Listen to me. There is no such thing in assassination as too obvious. To be obvious is the point."

He picked up the chessmen and in the process dropped a flash drive onto the board.

"That's for Amzi with love," he said. "Find out where Kirill Sergeivich is being held. I will invent a death for him that will make the newspapers happy."

30

Ten minutes later I texted a summary of this conversation to Amzi so that there would be no future misunderstandings about whose side I was on—an important distinction, since I was on nobody's side.

A couple of days later, back in his office, Amzi said, "How does your Russian buddy propose to do what a Russian's gotta do?"

I said, "He didn't say, just that it would get your attention."

Amzi said, "Find out."

"Any suggestions about how I do that?"

"You think like a fucking Russian," Amzi said. "So think. Let Tom know your insights. We're done."

He had taken the last sip of his coffee and spoke these words as he put down his cup. Suddenly I realized that this was the way Amzi timed his meetings—they lasted exactly as long as it took him to drink a cup of coffee.

In the elevator, Tom Terhune, who had been sitting beside me in his customary silence during the entire dialogue with Amzi, suddenly regained the power of speech.

He pressed the emergency stop button and the cage braked its fall, causing the two of us to stagger as we caught our balance. I grabbed Tom's elbow—he was sixty years old, after all, and I was afraid he might fall and hurt himself. This annoyed him: Did I think he was on his last legs? He shook off my hand.

"What Amzi really wants," Tom said, "is for you to somehow circumvent protocol and sit down with Burkov and talk this situation through."

"Then why didn't he say so?"

"When did Amzi ever say what he means?"

"Then tell me, please, what you think he means?"

"That's what I'm trying to do. He doesn't want to wait for Burkov's minders to ask the right questions."

"Why not? Is there something he doesn't want them to know?"

Tom ignored the question. Was he trying to be opaque? Of course he was. It was the habit of a lifetime.

The elevator's emergency telephone rang. Tom picked up the handset, spoke his own name, and said, "Everything's fine. Give me a minute to work the problem. I'll call if we need help."

He hung up and turned to me. "You *will* do it," he said.

I said, "What makes you think that?"

"You're under orders. You're under discipline."

"Improper orders. If I do this, I'll be thrown to the wolves."

He said, "Maybe, but you've got an insurance policy. The Director likes you. Anyway, it's already all arranged."

"What's already arranged?"

"Your meeting with Burkov."

"Not my pardon?"

Tom brushed this fly away. He said, "You will meet Burkov in the parking lot of the Giant supermarket in Warrenton, Virginia, at twelve noon tomorrow. Allow yourself two hours to get there from the District. You'll see a white van that has Russ and George we do it all and do

IT RIGHT painted on it. Park to the right of the van, your car headed in the opposite direction, and roll down your window. Turn the radio up to the max. Russ or George will get out of the van and approach your open window. They'll knock on the roof of your car and shout, 'Can you turn that shit down?' You'll say, 'Sure thing. Real sorry about that, buddy.' Then they'll walk away and you'll get into the van. Burkov will be inside."

"And if I don't show up?"

No answer. This was not the Tom I had, until now, thought I knew. But then, in all fairness, I was not the man he thought he knew. If I said no to this incomprehensible scheme, I'd be fired and the day I lived for would be lost forever. Father would never be avenged.

Tom said, "Well?"

I didn't say no for a third time. The only way I could find out what was going on was to proceed as ordered. Tom gave me a brisk nod to show me he recognized capitulation when he saw it.

He punched the red emergency stop button, the elevator came back to life with a shudder, and down we went.

On the way to Warrenton the following morning I drove in and out of rain squalls, some of them so violent I couldn't see the road and had to stop and wait out the downpour. I arrived at the Giant parking lot five minutes late. The white van was parked well away from the shops. Ignoring the rain, I tuned in a hip-hop station and turned up the volume until it hurt my ears and rolled down the window. It was still raining. In seconds the left side of my body was soaked. A young man who looked like he could walk onto the practice field at the University of Alabama, run one play and make the team, got out of the van. He approached the car and spoke the recognition phrase. I gave the reply. Rainwater spilled off the peak of his John Deere cap. He paid it no mind.

He said, "Are you carrying?"

"No."

He handed me a plastic bag. "Put your cell phone and anything else electronic in the bag, also any ID, false or genuine, and everything else in your pockets. I'll hold it for you. You'll find the bag on the driver's seat when you get back into the car." He handed me a device about the size of a bottle cap that was suspended from a black cord.

"Hang this around your neck under your shirt," he said. "I'll be nearby. I'll unlock the door so you can get into the van. I'll lock the door behind you. You won't be able to open it from the inside. When you're ready to go, press the button on the gizmo, once only, and I'll let you out. If you're in trouble, press the button twice. You've got fifteen minutes."

The interior of the van was rigged like a boat: seats that unfolded to make beds, a stowaway kitchen, a latrine. There were no windows. Burkov wore incongruous baggy NBA-length shorts, a Celtics T-shirt with Larry Bird's name and number 33 instead of POW on the back, no shoes or socks. No chains or manacles.

Burkov said, "Ah, you. Would you like a Coke?"

"No thanks. How's it going?"

"As you see. American methods of interrogation differ from the Russian system."

"So far."

"Yes, I know the worst could happen at any moment. I've heard your people will sometimes go so far as to deprive their victims of sleep, or make them hold their arms over their heads for minutes at a time or listen to loud rock music or have ferocious attack dogs snarl and slaver and bark at them. Or go even beyond that and spread a towel on some poor soul's face and pour water on it. It's worse than a sorority initiation."

"Try to tough it out."

"I'm trying. So, my friend and rescuer, what brings you here?"

I said, "Curiosity. In ten words or less, what exactly was the purpose of that comedy in Bogotá?"

"I told you the reason—to save my ass."

"They were going to kill you?"

"Yes. As you saw."

"That's the question. What exactly did I see?"

"What you saw is what happened."

"Can you tell me who you believe controlled the killers and the reason why they want to kill you? You seem to be good at your job."

He leaned across the space between us and whispered in my ear.

"Who do you think?" he said. "Your friend Boris is using you. You think you recruited him. But he was recruited many years ago by somebody else in your Headquarters, a powerful man who will do anything to protect him because he is the best source they have ever had. I know this is true, I have proof."

"Name of this source?"

"Why should I tell you what I could sell for any price I name?"

"You're sure about this?"

"Does the sun rise every morning? Boris is the only possible suspect. He has already killed one man who knew too much. He will kill you if necessary."

"Just like in the movies."

Burkov said, "You should take this seriously, my friend. I like you. I am grateful for what you did for me. I am trying to repay you. But no more talk. Go now. Don't come back. Get out of this business. Go back to being a human being."

"What proof do you have?"

"I've told you enough. The rest, your government will have to pay for. Go."

I was only too glad to do so. I pressed the button on the device. The lock clicked, the door of the van slid open. I got out and heard the door lock behind me. There was no sign of the athletic young man. The rain had stopped. I moved my car closer to the Giant, went inside, and bought some cooked Buffalo wings, a peach, and a bottle of spring water.

When I came out of the supermarket the white van was still parked in its isolated parking space at the far edge of the parking lot. This surprised me. Why were they lingering?

Behind me I heard a loud *pop*, a *whoosh*. I glimpsed a fiery flash, smelled acrid smoke, saw or later on imagined that I saw the track of a rocket-propelled grenade headed straight for the van. When the missile struck, the vehicle convulsed like a living thing, then exploded and spat the shrapnel of its burning parts in all directions.

I got into my car and drove away. As usual, Boris was right: There is no such thing as too obvious where assassination is concerned.

Its whole purpose is to advertise, to be remembered. To let you know your fate is up for grabs.

31

My brain woke up in the kitchen in the house in Georgetown. It took me a moment to realize where I was and how I had got there. I had driven the sixty miles from Warrenton in a trance. Witnessing the fiery death of Burkov, watching as he was cremated alive and taught the lesson his murderers had wanted to teach him and me and teach the world—achieved what I had never been unable to command my mind to do: *Shut down, leave me alone.*

I had to urinate—badly.

I was standing in front of the toilet bowl, emptying my bladder, when I heard someone pounding on the front door. It sounded like he was using a sledge hammer. I heard a crash and the sound of shattering glass as the door came off its hinges and crashed onto the floor in the front hall. Then, in the mirror, shouting men with guns in their hands. An instant after that, while urine still spurted, someone with the strength of a gorilla grabbed me from behind and dragged me backward into the hall. I pissed all over the floor. I was still too out of it to feel shame. It is almost impossible to stain a good Persian carpet. In my mind I watched a memory: rug makers in Kurdistan dragging Bijar carpets fresh from the loom into the street to "season" them. If passing camels trampled and pissed on them, so much the better.

That was the first coherent thought, if you could call it that, I had had since I drove out of the Giant parking lot three hours ago.

The gorilla was subduing me school yard fashion, his bony forearm against my windpipe and with his other hand bending my arm between my shoulder blades. A second man was frisking me and throwing the contents of my pockets on the floor as he went.

The frisker said to me, "Put your dick away, for Christ's sake." His face was inches away from it.

His partner said, "Help him out, why don't you?"

The frisker said, "Very funny. He's clean."

The gorilla took his forearm off my throat.

I said, "Who the fuck *are* you guys? Why are you doing this?"

There was no need to ask, really. Both men wore sateen warm-up jackets with the Bureau's famous initials emblazoned on their front and back in large DayGlo yellow capital letters.

A third agent grimly watched the procedure. Apparently he was the agent in charge. He made a gesture. The other agent let go of me. I put my penis away and worked the zipper.

Answering my question, the agent in charge said, "We'd like to ask you some questions."

I said, "I'd like to do the same. For starters, who's going to pay for a new front door?"

"Don't push it," the agent in charge said. "We can do this nicely or we can do it some other way, your choice."

I said, "Do what nicely?"

"Ask you a few questions."

I said, "Questions about what?"

"Where were you at twelve forty-two this afternoon?"

I didn't answer the question.

"Is the Giant supermarket on Lee Highway in Warrenton, Virginia, a possibility?"

I didn't answer the question.

He said, "Did you see anything unusual?"

I said nothing.

"What did you do after you left the Giant?"

I said, "You first. Who's going to pay for a new front door?"

"OK. That does it. You're coming with us."

"Am I under arrest?"

The agent said nothing.

I said, "Do I get a phone call?"

"Yes, if you think anyone will take the call."

"Can I have my phone back?"

To my surprise, he handed it over. Because I assumed that Headquarters already knew what was going on and would not interfere as a matter of interagency courtesy, I called Lester Briggs, the lawyer who had handled my legacy from Mother—he was the only lawyer I knew—and described my situation.

He said, "Go with them. Quietly. Answer no questions—none, no matter how trivial or irrelevant they seem. Make no small talk. Control your emotions. I'll be there as quickly as I can. Let me talk to the agent."

"They ripped the front door off the hinges. Can you get somebody to fix it?"

"Yes. Now, the agent."

I handed the phone to the agent. "It's for you."

He put the phone to his ear and said, "Special Agent Hathaway."

The call lasted less than a minute. I could hear both ends of the conversation. Lester Briggs asked where they were taking me. Special Agent Hathaway told him. Then he put my phone into a plastic evidence bag and said, "Let's go."

To my surprise they didn't read me my rights or put cuffs on me or even take hold of my arms, and during the ride to Pennsylvania Avenue they ignored me. I might as well have been deaf, dumb, and invisible.

This adventure didn't last much longer. Lester Briggs was a competent lawyer. He talked to somebody offstage while I sat at a table in silence in front of a large two-way mirror. A steely female agent kept me company by fixing me with an unwavering stare and tapping a pen on the table (Moonshine Manor wisdom: *When conducting an interrogation, make the subject wait and distract him with some small but annoying mannerism.*)

She got a call on her cell phone.

She listened, disconnected, and then said to me, "You're free to go. I'll walk you out."

On the way out I collected my belongings, which included my Headquarters credentials and the pendant the athletic young man in the parking lot had given me. Being as ostentatious about it as possible, I counted the money in my money clip, a 1908 Saint Gaudens twenty-dollar gold piece that Father had given me on my thirtieth birthday. It was all there.

As for my cell phone, I assumed that it had been bugged even though I was sure the Bureau just didn't do things like that without a warrant.

Lester gave me a lift back to Georgetown.

I said, "What was that all about?"

"They didn't go into detail," Lester said. "But they're suspicious of the company you keep—all those Russians—and that you inherited three million dollars from an impecunious mother out of the blue and Luz spent almost twice that amount in cash for a house in Georgetown and has charged fifty thousand dollars' worth of clothes and various other items to her credit card since you hit town. None of these things are crimes, so unless they have something they're not disclosing, as they probably do, they have nothing on you. However, watch your step. You have become a person of interest. That means they think you're guilty of a crime but they don't yet have enough evidence to book you. Do not relax. Confide in no one."

"Is what they did today the way they usually operate?"

"They're not paid to be gentlemen. Technically they were within the law. They had a warrant. They say they thought you were armed and dangerous. Were you?"

"No."

He pulled into our driveway. Dusk was falling. The lights were on in every room in the house. A couple of handymen were fitting a new door.

Lester said, "The agents did that to your door?"

"Yep. Are these the guys you hired to hang a new door or are they Bureau surveillance in disguise?"

"I don't know, but here's some advice. Don't send the Bureau a bill. Don't provoke these people in any way. They're mad enough at you already. And they don't especially like the agency you work for. I'm not going to kid you. This is a witch's brew."

No fooling? I said, "Thanks."

Lester said, "Call me immediately if they make further contact. If they come back, the same rules apply doubly. Answer no questions. Do not even shake your head yes or no unless they ask you if you want to use the men's room. Sign nothing. If they read you your rights do not acknowledge that you understand. Do not smile. Do not frown. Show no emotion. Be cool in Kabul."

To avoid the handymen or whatever they were, I went in through the garage. Luz was in the kitchen, standing up at the counter, drinking wine and eating cheese and a large peach, which she had cut into eight segments and arranged on a white plate like the petals of a daisy with the pit in the center.

She asked me no questions. She had never looked more ready for bed. She said, "Want some?"

The answer was yes, but there were witnesses on the doorstep. For the next hour we ate our cheese and peaches and drank most of the wine. We listened to the vintage country music the handymen were playing on their radio. We did not kiss, we did not dance to the George Jones songs, we did not touch, we barely spoke. This was effective foreplay, but it did not erase from my mind what I had seen in the Giant parking lot or what I now knew in my bones was the truth about my father's ruin and the fate of Luz's father and the connections between the two.

The handymen finished what they were doing. That included fitting a new door that matched the old one exactly and painting it the exact same color. Their work was expert. The bill was enormous. Luz wrote a check without demur. The handymen—exercising their cover, maybe—were as suspicious of the check as I was of them, but they pocketed it and drove off in a mud-splashed white van that had no name or address or phone numbers painted on its sides.

For two hours Luz and I made love as if we might never have another opportunity—not such a remote possibility, given the way things were going at home and at work—then fell asleep on sweat-soaked sheets. I did not wake up until nine the next morning. It took me a while to remember where I was. The room, the entire house was strange to me. Luz stirred and groped for me in her sleep. I evaded her grasp, she subsided. I went into the bathroom and shaved and got into the shower. Luz joined me, but not for her usual reasons.

She murmured, "Something bad happened."

"How do you know?"

"I felt it in your body last night. What? Have they found out?"

"I don't think so. I'm not sure. But that's not the point."

"Then what is? Tell me."

I told her.

The shower beat down on us. Luz's hair was plastered to her skull. As I talked all expression erased itself from her face.

She said, "Did they intend to kill you?"

"No."

"How can you be so sure?"

"I'm not dead."

"Not this time," Luz said, "not yet."

She began to cry. I tried to embrace her. She evaded me. Sobbing spasmodically, eyes tight shut against the tears, she reached blindly for shampoo and rubbed it into her hair. I left her alone.

Still dripping wet, I used Luz's cell phone, a fifty-dollar Walmart special that the Bureau and Headquarters theoretically did not know existed, to text Father Yuri, asking him to go for a walk with me on Roosevelt Island that afternoon. Before I left the house I wrapped my own compromised cell phone in aluminum foil and put it in the freezer. This was a ridiculous act that accomplished nothing, but it was the prescribed thing to do in the world I lived in.

I drove to work, assuming the all-seeing eyes of the Bureau or of Headquarters Security, or both, followed me. As I walked through the door of my office, the phone rang.

It was Rosemary. She said, "He wants to see you now. Immediately. Alone."

Instead of having his feet on his desk as usual, Amzi was standing up when I entered. He was angry, or feigning anger, who could tell the difference? There was fury in his eyes, color in his face, his right fist was balled. He looked more than ever like one of the great apes.

He said, in a voice somewhat louder than usual, "Where the fuck have you been for the last twenty-two hours? It's twelve o'clock."

I said, "I overslept."

"You turned off all your phones and slept all day yesterday after you fucking disappeared and disobeyed orders?"

I said, "Not exactly. Amzi, you already know the answer to your question. So what's going on here?"

"I do?" Amzi said. "Let me summarize your insubordination. You witness the assassination of a defector under our protection I had personally told you to stay away from. You don't report in, you vanish, nobody knows where you are or if you're fucking dead or alive or if you're the prime suspect or if you've been snatched by persons unknown and are spilling your guts in a torture chamber. And *you* ask *me* what's going on?"

Amzi being Amzi, I didn't know whether this was role-playing or reality. I wasn't betting on reality.

I said, "Just to save time, what don't you know?"

"I just told you. So indulge me. Where were you between the explosion and this minute? Why did you go silent? What the fuck did you think you were doing? Start with the minute you left this office yesterday. Leave nothing out. "

Despite Lester's advice to confide in no one, I left nothing out, not even my thoughts, such as the fact that I had expected that there would be a sniper on the roof of the Giant, which is where the RPG round came from, and that he would blow my head off as I walked back to the car. Or that in my mind there were no nonsuspects in this crime—none.

Not even Amzi.

All this took awhile. Amzi did not interrupt. Suddenly he cared nothing about time. He drank no coffee. He did not glance at his clocks.

One element in the story interested him greatly.

He said, "Let me get this straight. Terhune stopped the elevator and told you I wanted you to pay a call on Burkov?"

"Yes."

Amzi went to the window and looked out. He asked me no more questions. With his back turned he said, "We're done."

I said, "Oh, no we're not. What happened to the young guy I met in the parking lot?"

"He's got some flesh wounds but he's OK. His partner, the driver, was killed. Did you see him?"

"No. The driver's compartment was separate."

"The cops found an arm with a wristwatch that belonged to him a hundred feet away from what was left of the van."

"Did they also find Burkov's wristwatch?"

Amzi said nothing.

I said, "One more question. Who sent Special Agent Hathaway and his friends to break into my house and how did they know where I was living?"

"Not me," Amzi said.

"Security?"

"I'll have to get back to you on that." His back was still turned.

Amzi had become less anthropoid. You might even have said there were signs of human feelings in his eyes and in his posture. But also resentment, reluctance: He had the look of a man who has been forced to know something he did not want to know.

I said, "Amzi, did you keep the bargain, did you get Alejandro and Felicia out of Argentina, did you relocate them? Are they alive? Did they survive?"

Amzi remained silent. He went to the window again, hiding his face.

"In a manner of speaking," he said.

"Meaning what?"

"There was a wild card."

"Who played it?"

Amzi held up a hand. He said, "That's all you get. We're done. Get the fuck out of here."

Later in an otherwise empty day, I parked my car in the short-term lot at Dulles, rented another car, and at five o'clock by TR's shadow, met Father Yuri on Theodore Roosevelt Island.

I said, "This is about Alejandro. I know you were his confessor and what restraints that involves, but I'm not interested in anything he may have told you. I want to tell you something, then ask for your opinion."

He nodded.

I told him what I knew—or more accurately, what I had been told about Amzi's dealings with Alejandro. Father Yuri listened in his usual deep silence, eyes averted as if we were in some invisible confessional booth.

He said, "What do you want?"

I said, "First, is that an accurate account?"

"I cannot answer that."

I took that to mean it was an accurate account, something that Alejandro had told him. It wasn't all I wanted to know.

I said, "In payment for what Alejandro gave him, did Amzi save his life and the life of Felicia? Are they alive?"

Father Yuri said, "You should talk to Diego about this."

He walked away. I would never see him again. I was sure of that.

32

That evening at dinner Luz listened as I recounted this conversation.

She said, "Why talk to Diego? We've always known they could kill you. They can kill anyone, whenever and wherever they like. They were just reminding you."

I said, "If it just confirms what we always knew, then why the sudden change of heart?"

Luz, who never apologized, never explained, ignored the question. She cleared the dishes and carried them into the kitchen and returned with a salad bowl in one hand and a cheese board in the other. In silence, like a dutiful wife from the twentieth century but without the dazzling smile, she mixed the salad. She poured more wine into my glass.

She smiled as if for the camera and pressed the tip of my nose with a fingertip and said, "Do you ever get tired of vinaigrette and the same two cheeses?"

"No."

"Delice de Bourgogne and gorgonzola night after night, olive oil, lemon juice, mustard on your lettuce over and over again. You wouldn't prefer ranch or Eyetalian right from the bottle and a well-aged Velveeta?"

Now she was smiling a *Midwich Cuckoos* smile. I put my hand on her bottom and said, "Don't make fun of American culture."

"Why not? Answer the question."

I said, "No, *you* answer the real question. What's going on here?"

The smile vanished.

"I thought you'd never ask," Luz said. "I wish I could tell you I'm pregnant and I don't want to bear a child that's condemned to relive the life I've lived because her father was just another Alejandro and her mother was another Felicia and she will never be sure if they are dead or alive. However, I'm not pregnant, and if I ever become pregnant I will put an end to it on the day I find out because I couldn't condemn the child to live the life I led, and one ruined lifetime waiting for the dead to come home in the night and wake you up and give you a kiss and a wonderful new doll pays the taxes on political insanity."

"You think they may still be alive?"

"Not anymore. But what difference would it make if they were? The damage is done."

She was dry-eyed, angry, immovable.

I said, "I still want to talk to Diego."

"About what?"

"The past."

"You're going to Buenos Aires?"

"Yes. Interested?"

"No. I've already talked to Diego about the past."

"I'd like to have your help. He may need encouragement."

"Diego? He's immune to encouragement. He does what he wants, nothing else."

I started to speak. She stopped me with a gesture. This was a new Luz.

"Enough," she said. "In three weeks my grandparents celebrate their sixtieth wedding anniversary. I'll come then."

Her eyes said, *If you're still alive three weeks from now.*

As if nothing out of the ordinary had happened, we ate our salad and finished the cheese and the wine. We left the dishes on the table and went upstairs. For the first time ever she did not make the first move. When I touched her she submitted, but she did so in silence, and when it was over she turned her back to me. She slept in silence, too—no murmured conversations with the people in her dreams, no laughter of delight.

Oh yes, Luz had changed. Whatever happened to her had happened in Colombia. That was where I needed to go. In the morning I called Amzi. Rosemary said he was traveling and unreachable.

I called Tom Terhune and told him Amzi had suggested I go on leave and I was leaving today.

"Good idea," Tom said. His voice was flat. "When do you want to start?"

"Now."

"Fine. Go. Take Luz with you. You won't be bothered. Turn off your cell phone."

He didn't tell me to call when I got back. He didn't ask how long I would be gone or where I was going.

He merely disconnected. I was not the only one who had been talking to Amzi. Everyone was leaving without saying good-bye: Amzi, who had probably never said good-bye to anyone in his life, Father Yuri. And now, Luz. It didn't take a mystic to read the signs.

From the office I went back to the house to pick up my passport. Just as I was leaving—no note for Luz, no good-bye, she would either be there when I got back or she wouldn't be—she returned from wherever she had been.

She said, "Do you plan to come back?"

"Is that what you want?"

"Not exactly. What I want, what I have to have, is for you to leave your other wife and do it today and lock her up and never see her or think about her again."

"What other wife?"

"Let's call her by her true name. The witch."

"Stop talking in code. Spit it out, Luz."

"I mean that thing that introduced us has been living with us ever since, hiding in our minds, lying between us when we fuck, which is why I fuck like a psychopath, because I'm trying to get past the witch to give myself to your self. I can't live with the witch any longer. You've got to burn her. Kill the bitch. Now, this minute."

She didn't have to tell me what she meant in plain language. I knew what she meant. The witch was the plan, the prank, the revenge for our fathers.

I said, "How do I do that? And if I do, will you believe me?"

"Yes. Decide. Now."

"What do you burn in return? Your parents?"

"They burned themselves at the stake long ago. They threw me away just like yours threw you away. My mother made her escape by dying rather than go on with the life to which the Aguilars' money had condemned her. She must have been glad to be thrown out of that airplane and realize she was free of her prison. Not the one the army ran. The one with the invisible walls."

"And your father?"

"He made his choice, too, didn't he? To die without actually dying. How clever. No wonder he's the saint of fools. He didn't care enough about me even to let me know he was alive. I may have been his own flesh and blood, but how could he care about that when I was the child of a woman he never loved, just something he fucked whenever he had nothing better to fuck? For twenty years he was dead to me, dead to the *abuelos,* dead to everyone who ever trusted him except Diego, who was the only one who was too smart to trust him, and now I discover from a stranger in a hellhole in the Colombian jungle that. . . ."

Luz stopped herself.

I said, "Discover what?"

Silence. She remained dry-eyed, absent, in complete control of herself.

"No more," she said. "I'm out. I'm through being your companion in lunacy, through being a spy for Diego, tattling on you, telling him everything because he acts like a father to me for the purposes of cover because he wants to give eternal life to the lie that has ruined my life. It wouldn't have cost the bastards a peso to tell me the truth. My truth to you is, I can't love you if you don't give up volunteering to be murdered."

This was a performance, not an outburst. She was perfectly composed— not a hint of expression in her voice or her face. Her voice was cold, measured, as if she had learned her lines.

"So what do you want from me?"

"I just told you," she said. "You have to burn the witch, give up avenging someone who deserved what he got. Yes, he did! Delete the bastard. It's easy—one keystroke. I am filthy rich—literally. The money is filthy. Diego paid me off on my thirtieth birthday. We can go anywhere, be anyone, love for the sake of love."

"And if I don't give it up?"

"Then good-bye. If you want to die for the sake of a pile of the shit deposited in your mind by liars and fools instead of loving me as I love you, go right ahead. Yes or no?"

"I'll have to think about it."

"'*Think* about it?'" Luz said. "You don't know whether to choose the witch or me?"

"Luz, stop."

"Too late, my friend. It's over. Get out of my house. Go. Die alone." Luz!"

"*Go.*"

I remembered Sana'a: the look on Faraj's face when he felt the knife.

33

If Damián was surprised to hear from me, I didn't hear it in his voice when I called him from the airport in Bogotá. A more suspicious man than myself, if such existed, might have wondered if he had been forewarned.

Like Tom, like Amzi, like Father Yuri, he asked no questions. Nor did he offer any invitations.

I said, "I need to talk to you."

"You do? About what?"

"A personal matter. Can we meet?"

Silence. I thought he might have hung up on me.

He said, "Does Luz know you're doing this?"

"No."

"Does anyone?"

"No."

"Are you doing this in the line of duty?"

"No."

"It's four o'clock in the morning. I have a surgery at six-thirty. You have no manners."

"I know. Is the house where Luz and I stayed still empty?"

"Yes, but the security people will shoot you if they find you on the grounds at this hour of the night. Park five houses away, to the east but headed west. What kind of car do you have?"

"A small gray Mazda."

"One hour, exactly. I will drive by. Follow me. Don't be early or you might very well be shot. This is a dangerous neighborhood after dark for strangers lurking in cheap automobiles."

Precisely on the minute, Damián's Audi passed by. I followed. He turned into the drive of the house where Luz and I had stayed.

We did not go inside. In the garden, in the dark, he said, in English, "I have half an hour. What do you want?"

"Information."

"I thought you were off duty."

"I am. As I said, this is personal. What happened to my wife while she was in Colombia?"

Damián considered the question. His thoughts showed on his face: Should he ignore me, should he lie, should he tell me the truth even if I had no right to it and anyway, being a stupid Yanqui, I could not possibly understand it? Should he escape from this dilemma by calling security and reporting an intruder in the house? Should he shoot me and leave my body where it fell for security to get rid of?

He said, "What do you suspect?"

"That you told her something she didn't know about Alejandro."

"You suspect this on what basis?"

"Her behavior, your history, intuition."

"Intuition has been defined as the way your brain warns you when you're wrong about something."

"Her behavior and your history don't suggest that."

Damián said, "One day when you were at work, I took her to Leticia, Colombia. Have you heard of it?"

"No. Where is it?"

"A two-hour flight from Bogotá. It's a hellhole on the north bank of the Amazon at the point where Colombia, Peru, and Brazil come together. Half the town is in Brazil under another name. Its economy is based on drugs, murder, and kidnapping. The surrounding jungle is home to terrorists who want to be drug millionaires and drug millionaires who used to be terrorists. Leticia may be the most dangerous place in the world outside of the Afghanistan. Once you are there no one can find you and no one can rescue you and you have no place to go."

"So why did you take her to such a place?"

"To visit her father's grave."

I said, "Why is Alejandro buried in Leticia, Colombia?"

"His burial is relatively recent. Leticia is where he went when everyone thought he was dead because it's the last place on earth and that's where Mr. Amzi Strange, mad genius that he is, thought he would be safe because the terrorists would protect him, and because once he was there he could not leave because the terrorists would not let him leave because he was the Jesus Christ of the revolution and they would be unable to protect him if he did. And besides, Alejandro was already in business in Leticia."

"Doing what?"

Damián snorted—what did I *think* he was doing?

He said, "Let me say this: Luz is a very, very rich woman for the daughter of a man who once chose poverty as a matter of principle and didn't have a peso in his pocket when he escaped from Argentina."

"He was a drug trader?"

"A drug lord. One of the biggest. In his own mind, twisted as it was, he was still a terrorist, incognito for the cause, who believed that he was filling up a treasury for the revolution that must inevitably come to pass."

"And Luz's mother?"

"They were betrayed at the last moment by the North Americans, or maybe just one American. The military took her."

"But not Alejandro?"

"That was the deal. He had already handed over everybody in the movement except the cadre. The junta didn't know who the cadre was. Probably they still don't know for certain, and if they do, they now work for what used to be the cadre, because the cadre now runs the country. Felicia did know all the names, so to the military, having her was almost as good as having Alejandro. Amzi negotiated the substitution. She was supposed to be a hostage to guarantee Alejandro wouldn't start a new movement. Diego was the brains. He was always the brains. And the treasurer."

I thought, *And what were you?* But said, "You're telling me Felicia survived, too?"

"Alejandro may have thought so. They had released her to Amzi, but then they took her back at the last moment as a guarantee of his good conduct. But she didn't talk. So just as the legend says, they threw her out of an airplane after taking a lot of photographs of her in different clothes and different hairstyles, always with a current newspaper in her hand. Every three months or so until the junta was overthrown they sent Alejandro a retouched picture to show that his wife was alive and well and just as beautiful as ever. To verify a fictitious date, they Photoshopped the front page of the newspaper edition of that day into the picture. Someone from your organization had shown them how it was done."

"If Amzi betrayed Alejandro and Felicia, why would he save Alejandro?"

"He didn't betray them. Headquarters was supposed to take custody of Felicia, protect her, keep her alive. Amzi was a swine, but he was a man of his word. The military grabbed her at the airport at the last minute, when she was already aboard a plane. They grabbed Alejandro, too, but Amzi made them a deal and they released him in his custody."

"Then who did sell them out?"

"A young Headquarters guy in the Buenos Aires station who thought all terrorists should die. A zealot, like us, but on the other side."

"His name?"

Another snort from Damián. Had I no manners at all? The eastern sky was vivid—Renoir pink, Gainsborough blue—and became more so by the minute.

As the colors intensified I said, "You know everything else. You must know the name of the informant."

Damián said, "There's no end to your curiosity, is there? All right. What harm can it do after all these years? His name was Terhune. Maybe you know him."

He looked at his watch. He said, "Four-thirty. I have to go. Don't contact me again, ever. Do not go to Leticia. Go home. Don't come back to this country. You are not welcome in our past."

34

Back in Washington in the apartment in Adams Morgan, I woke from a bad dream about Luz and got out of bed before I fell back to sleep and the dream continued. The mail still lay on the floor in the front hall. I gathered it up and took it to the kitchen—twenty pieces of junk, a depressing bank statement, a bill from Lester Briggs. A cheap square envelope with flecks of wood pulp caught in the paper and a Stockholm postmark.

Enclosed was a postcard of Republic Square in Prague with a date scribbled on the back. Prague meant Sofia. I had a feeling that Sofia, combined with Boris, would make me wish that Prague meant Prague.

I set the alarm on my cell phone for five and put it in my shirt pocket, then closed my eyes. When the phone vibrated and woke me up I called Amzi. He was back from wherever he had been.

In gobbledygook I told him where I was going and whom I was meeting.

He said, "Forget about it."

"Skip the meeting?"

"You're on vacation. Stay on vacation."

"Why?"

"Because you need the rest and so do I."

He hung up.

Amzi was right. I needed a vacation. I booked a ticket for Buenos Aires. Then I called Diego and told him I would be arriving the following evening.

He said, "I understand you had a conversation in Bogotá."

"Yes. That's what I want to talk to you about."

He said, "I'll be in my office at five-thirty the morning after you arrive. Can you make it?"

"Yes."

In his white coat, Diego looked like a different man—competence itself and far less genial. His office at the hospital was a hideaway—ostentatiously small, austere, windowless, no decor, not even diplomas.

Diego said, "Did Damián tell you everything you wanted to know?"

"No."

"I have a surgery in thirty minutes, so this will have to be brief."

"Does that mean there's not much more to tell?"

"It means I have decided to trust you."

I doubted that.

Diego said, "I know what you're thinking. When somebody tells you that, it usually means he has decided to prepare you to believe the lies he is about to tell you. But if I hurt you, I hurt Luz. I know her. She will never stop loving you, and I think you know I would never do anything to hurt her in any way."

I said, "Luz and I . . ."

He interrupted with a gesture. He knew. Of course he knew.

I said, "Why exactly are you so protective of Luz?"

"Because she is my daughter."

"Adopted daughter."

"No. Felicia and I were together. In love."

"Your best friend's wife?"

"This happened before the marriage."

"Your best friend's girl, then."

Diego said, "His betrothed, bought and paid for. My girl. She was pregnant when they married. They didn't have sex before that. She refused him. She and I didn't have sex after the wedding."

"Does Luz know this?"

"She might suspect. I thought she would realize the truth when she was old enough—look at her, look at the pictures of her mother, imagine me as I was back then, then look at Luz and you will see."

"Who else knew this?"

"Felicia, who is dead. And because she told him, Alejandro, who is now also dead. Now you."

"Why me?"

Diego said, "I'll tell you that, and more, when you're ready to believe me."

"Why do you want to tell me anything? If you know about Luz and me, you also know I have no need to know."

"Don't be so sure about that."

Was he offering me hope as Luz's go-between? Did he think this was a weakness he could use to his advantage?

I said, "Why should I believe you?"

"Because I'll give you no choice."

He pressed a button on his phone. A nurse entered with a syringe in her hand. Diego was rolling up his sleeve. Expertly, the nurse swabbed his arm, inserted the needle in a vein, and drew blood. She handed the vial to me and then left the room.

Diego said, "Send this and a sample of Luz's DNA to a laboratory that compares DNA. There are several of them in Buenos Aires. When you get the results—they'll move you to the head of the line if you pay a premium—we'll talk again." He looked at his watch and stood up. "I have to go now." He left.

The lease on my old apartment in Buenos Aires was still in force. I was staying there. In the bathroom wastebasket I found what I needed— menstrual blood on a sanitary napkin.

I Googled a DNA laboratory and walked the samples over, paying the fee and a substantial extra sum to speed the process, and then went for a walk in the park where I once ran with Boris, who in theory was waiting for me in Sofia. Where, I wondered, would he fit into whatever it was that Diego, the fox of the revolution, was dying to tell me.

Bribe or no bribe, it took seven working days for the DNA lab to complete the test. In the meantime I had nothing to do. There was no reason for me to get in touch with the station and many reasons not to do so.

In dreams I made love to Luz. In my waking mind she was dwindling into some blurred alternative world. Maybe Diego would advise her to give me another chance and she would turn around and come back and everything would come up roses as in some pastel replay of our meeting in Los Bosques de Palermo. I knew that this could not happen. The film had broken.

My powers of concentration weakened. I couldn't read ten pages of a book—I was trying once more to get through the fog of *Ulysses*. Not a single word registered. I tried to play chess and even such a simple thing as solitaire on the iPad. Same result. Movies were the same: I sat in the dark for two hours, eyes on the screen every minute, and emerged from the theater with an empty memory. Music, too: it went in one ear and out the other. Luz had packed up my mind and taken it with her.

One morning as I ran down a path beneath the great trees in the Parque Lezama, someone behind me spoke to me in Russian. I knew the voice. I stopped in my tracks. Arkady caught up.

"You're back in town! What luck. What brings you?"

"Nostalgia."

"Then you're free. Or are you?"

"Apart from chance meetings with Russians, yes, mostly."

"Then can you come to dinner on"—he got out his cell phone as if he didn't know his schedule by heart—"Friday, my house? Does that work?"

"Who else will be there?"

"Just the two of us. *Viernes. A las ocho.*"

It had been months since I last saw Arkady. I had half forgotten him along with nearly everything else, but at dinner with a few deft brushstrokes he restored the John Singer Sargent portrait he had made of himself: elegant, well tailored, fit as a fiddle, witty, condescending but infinitely agreeable. The bastard great-grandson, one was supposed to imagine, of a Russian prince shot by the Bolsheviks that fateful October, and a lovely ballerina, quivering with passion, whom the prince had abducted from the Bolshoi.

Dinner was delivered by a caterer, who put it on the table and left. Throughout the meal it was conversation lite. Arkady was just back from a trip to Europe. He had seen a terrific *Magic Flute* at the Wiener Staatsoper, a fine *King Lear* in French, in Paris—and he still savored that left-footed goal I had sneaked by Boris. He, Boris, would never recover. Not many people ever got the better of him.

What had he been doing in Paris?

A stopover. He had had business in Sofia. Had I ever been there?

"No. What's it like?"

"Kafka's dream, Stalin's architects. They have a national museum in the former royal palace with fifty thousand works of Bulgarian art, nothing foreign allowed. The star of the collection is the great Bulgarian artist Vladimir Dimitrov, known to Bulgarians as the Master. He painted women—happy peasant girls picking apples, babushkas looking like they were embalmed, standing up with their eyes open."

And oh, speaking of Sofia, this was for me. Arkady handed me a blank sealed envelope. I took the envelope and smiled and said thank you, very kind of you, and laid it unopened on the table.

"Coffee? Cognac?" Arkady asked.

He had a bottle of French cognac, also from Paris. It was organic, if you could believe such a concept, so it would make up for the goose that had suffered on our behalf. It was called Peyrat XO. Had I ever heard of it? His cunning, his subtlety, his mastery of information were meant to be noticed. Admired.

While he fetched the coffee and the Peyrat XO, I opened the envelope. Inside was a duplicate of Boris's previous postcard of the Náměstí Republiky in Prague, but on the back, instead of a date, a message in Boris's all but illegible hand. At first it seemed to be gibberish but, shades of the famous Greek cipher last used by the Brits in India in 1857, it was English written in the Cyrillic alphabet. It decoded as: *"Believe the surgeon."*

35

When I handed Diego the lab report, he scanned it, holding it at arm's length, then nodded briskly.

I said, "You've seen these results before."

"Not these particular results. But the same results."

"There was a doubt in your mind?"

"For many years, before DNA was sequenced, I knew that I might be wrong. We made love the night before Felicia was married, and for several nights before that. She and Alejandro consummated the marriage the following night. Luz was born two hundred and eighty-four days later. How could she be sure?"

He was calm and collected as always. But I had no difficulty imagining how he had felt on the wedding night, how he raged, wept, imagined murdering the man who was raping the girl he loved and who loved him. How hatred took command of his whole being, every corpuscle.

Diego said, "So doubt is now banished from your mind?"

"On this question, yes. As far as I know there's no equivalent of a DNA test for whatever else you're planning to tell me."

Diego said, "Arkady tells me that the two of you dined together." A pause. Then he said, "Also that he delivered a message from Boris."

I said, "True. But why would you tell me that you know that?"

"I am still trying to build trust between us, to show you that I conceal nothing," Diego said. "It's an uphill struggle. So I now tell you this: During the revolution we had help from the Soviet intelligence service. We were the enemy of their enemy, so they were generous, despite the fact that Alejandro called himself a Maoist. Money, advice, information, encouragement, weapons."

I said, "Why am I not surprised?"

Diego said, "Boris was the go-between. Is that also no surprise?"

"The go-between or your case officer?"

"A friend."

"Who was Alejandro's control?"

"We'll get to that. That's the fundamental purpose of this operation. But not now, there is no time. This Saturday I have two surgeries in San Antonio Oeste. We can fly down on Friday and have dinner at the house and on Sunday go for a walk on the beach, where we can speak freely."

"Why not?"

"Sunday is Alejandro's birthday. Every year the *abuelos* have a party for him and light twenty-eight candles for the number of years he lived, or rather that they believe he lived."

Luz hadn't mentioned this. I said, "Will Luz be there?"

"Yes. She is already coming for the *abuelos's* anniversary."

I said, "All right. I don't want to be in Buenos Aires on that day, either."

"The Aeroparque at four, then. Takeoff at five. Bring warm clothes, a jacket, a hat that won't blow off. It's closer to Antarctica there than here."

He got to his feet: "Until then."

I longed for Luz. There was no escaping it, I carried lust in my chest like a sleeping animal. Trying to turn my mind away from this, I remembered something Father had told me for no apparent reason, as if he were talking about the weather or a movie, namely that he had not married for sex.

I was about eighteen. It was the last trip we ever took together. The two of us were in Kyoto, looking at the rocks and the meticulously raked sand of the famous Zen garden in the Daisen-in temple. My parents were still married.

Despite her good looks, he said, Mother hadn't especially appealed to him—she never had.

"Everybody was getting married," he said. "It was the season for it. My generation did everything in unison—birth, school, college, politics, job, career, marriage for the supposedly unlimited sex, kids, and after a decent interval, death, with the wife pushing the husband who had outlived his usefulness into the grave with a rattle of dry bones and then cashing the life insurance policy."

Mother married him, he said, because she thought he was going places. "Basically," he said, "we married for purposes of display."

I said, "I don't really want to hear this."

Then he had said, "Sorry about that. But I'm telling you this for a purpose. Don't make the same mistake. Love the woman you marry, be crazy to fuck her all night, every night until death does you part, and make sure she feels the same about you, that it's a case of genes calling out to genes. Sex isn't everything between a man and a woman, but it's the basis of everything and the only thing worth having in life."

How right he was.

On the flight to San Antonio Oeste I occupied the copilot's seat. We were flying far above the cloud deck, and the setting sun shone through the glowing cumulus. I had Googled this Beechcraft. Its price, new, was in the millions. I asked Diego why he needed such a large, expensive airplane.

"I don't need it," he said. "Alejandro did after he started his second life. He paid for it. Every now and then he would send a pilot to pick it up. He would keep it for a week or two, then send it back."

"He used it to transport drugs?"

"Transporting drugs was what Alejandro did. A sacred duty to the revolution."

I said, "Wasn't that risky for you?"

"The right fees, I supposed, were paid to the right authorities."

"You supposed? I was told you were the treasurer of Alejandro's enterprise."

"Damián told you that? Once a man starts telling secrets he doesn't know when to stop. Yes, it was risky. But someone had to do it, and I could hardly refuse. Alejandro wouldn't let a dollar touch his hand. He lived in Leticia like a hermit saint: bread, soup, water, a fish from the river on Friday."

"Why?"

"Take your choice. Cover. Madness. Maybe even penance for Felicia. Instructions from the late Chairman Mao."

I started to ask another question.

Diego said, "Not now, please. I have to visualize the surgeries."

He switched on the automatic pilot and closed his eyes and seemed to enter into a state of meditation.

After landing we drove directly to Diego's house. It was dark when we got there. He warmed up a dinner his cook had prepared and packed in a picnic cooler.

As we ate, he said, "On the plane you started to ask a question."

"Never mind. It was off the subject."

"Nothing is off the subject."

"All right then. Why do you do these pro bono surgeries? How do your patients find you?"

"I find them. They are the kind of people, sometimes the actual people, Alejandro betrayed to the military, while the rich ones were chosen to sit at the right hand of Alejandro."

"The ones who survived, they know who you are, who you used to be during the revolution?"

"Not usually. I did not make myself visible in those days. I was called by another name, it was part of the romance. Alejandro gave them the opportunity to die for the cause. The revolution was profoundly class conscious. They were the invisible ones, the expendables who did the dirty work. They were told nothing, they counted for nothing. Now, long afterward, they have no idea what Alejandro did to them. In their minds he coud do no wrong. They're Alejandro worshippers even now. Good night. I have to be up at four."

36

Sunday was a windy day. Surf pounded the beach and the black-and-white gulls of Patagonia were blown around like paper airplanes. Diego had to shout his secrets in order for me to hear them. The inventory was heavy: love, death, betrayal, the loss of illusion, the slow realization as things fell apart that illusion is not necessarily another name for virtue. I asked no questions because I did not need, and in truth did not want, more information about this tawdry *Iliad* of a failed revolution.

Like Homer, Diego started in the middle and did not always stick to the point.

"These gulls—*Larus dominicanus* after the holy order's vestments—are suspected of killing the right whales by landing on their backs, dozens, even hundreds at a time, and pecking and ripping off bits of flesh," Diego said. "To Alejandro, the revolution was the gulls, the oppressors were the whales who were too stupid to dive because they thought they were invulnerable."

For once Diego was slow to get to the point. He began with the Damon-and-Pythias childhood friendship between him and Alejandro.

He told me little that Luz hadn't already told me. The boys lived in adjoining houses, one of them with a rich father, the other with a failure for a father. They were inseparable from the sandbox onward. Felicia lived two doors away. Felicia's father had gambled away his inheritance, millions of pesos, at the roulette tables. She was younger than the boys. They saw her go by in her stroller, pushed by her mother, the haggard relic of a belle. Later on, when she was a toddler, Felicia would appear out of nowhere and watch the boys in silence as they played with a football or wrestled. They would tell her to go away. She would remain where she was. She had enormous unwavering brown eyes and shining hair to her waist. She always wore a dress—made, she later told Diego, by her mother from the elegant gowns she had worn as a debutante.

When Felicia was seven, her father, while blind drunk, shot himself while he was having sex with his wife. She went into a trance from which she never afterward emerged. Felicia went to live with her grandparents.

"They came and took her away to their ranch on the pampas," Diego said. "We never gave her another thought."

When she was seventeen and Alejandro and Diego were twenty-one, Felicia's maternal grandfather died. She and her grandmother moved into the house with Felicia's crazy mother.

"We knew who she was the minute she reappeared," Diego said. "But she was no longer a child. Now she made your heart ache and your blood rush to your manhood. Neither of us had ever before seen or even imagined such beauty, such sexual magnetism. I fell in love with her at first sight. Alejandro fell in lust. Neither of us confided his feelings to the other, but I knew Alejandro. He wasn't interested in how I felt. Or how Felicia might feel. He was the irresistible one. She was his, of course. Girls fell at his feet. They had always done so. Women in their thirties had taken him to bed when he was fourteen and he had taught *them* about pleasure. This innocent beginner would be no different."

Alejandro pursued Felicia. She ignored him. He thought this was flirtation, that she was luring him on. Diego, who loved her too much to touch her, became her friend—her only friend. No man could be alone with her for five minutes and remain just friends. Out of love, Diego managed it.

Felicia was always alone. She was too beautiful to have girlfriends—no female who was merely pretty wanted to be compared to her. Her beauty frightened men.

She entered the university, Alejandro's father secretly paying the fees. She and Diego were often alone together. The two of them studied together, bicycled together, went to the movies together. It was a chaste friendship. She told him nothing about herself. Diego asked her why. She replied that there was nothing to tell. There was no Felicia. Her life was the death of her father and the madness of her mother. And inescapable aloneness. There was nothing else in it. The two of them studied together like brother and sister at Diego's house, in his room.

One day, without warning, she kissed Diego—not the chaste kiss of a young girl, but a full, long kiss with an open mouth. He was amazed. She gave him her tongue. He thought he would ejaculate. They sank to the floor and became lovers. Both were virgins, so their instincts taught them what Alejandro had planned to teach Felicia. And more.

Diego said, "For a year we made love every day except when it was her time of the month or she was ovulating. I was a medical student. I taught her how to count the days and gave her a fever thermometer and explained how to use it. For once, angels watched over her and the Vatican roulette worked. All the while Alejandro pestered her without mercy. She continued to ignore him. At last, desperate to have her even though he thought she was incurably stupid like her father and would soon be ugly like her mother or as crazy or both, he asked her to marry him.

Diego said, "He thought she'd have to let him fuck her if they were engaged and then he could get rid of her. He told me this. Whatever Alejandro thought, Felicia wasn't stupid. She said no to his proposal of marriage. A week later Alejandro's father, Luz's kindly, beloved *abuelo*, offered the grandmother a dowry of fifty thousand U. S. dollars—at the time, half a million pesos. He reminded her who had paid Felicia's fees at the university. A day after that, Alejandro proposed again and Felicia accepted him.

"My heart broke," Diego said. "Hers, too. I said, 'Marry me tonight, we'll go to Uruguay and never come back.'

"She said, 'If I do that, my family will starve. What else can I do but marry him? But you and I will still be together in our real marriage. We'll find a way.'

"But I knew we could never do that. We weren't characters in a pulp novel for lovelorn women. I couldn't share her. This had nothing to do with my friendship with Alejandro—Felicia and I had burned that bridge. I hated Alejandro, I would have killed him with my bare hands if I could. But then Felicia and I would have been lost to each other forever, so instead I encouraged him to make his stupid revolution in the hope that the junta would kill him. On that last night together we both knew she was fertile.

"She counted on her fingers to make sure. I did the same. There was no doubt. This last time we were together was clinical.

"Afterward, she said, 'What shall we name him?'

"It was the only joke Felicia ever made in my hearing. She was wonderful in every other way but she had no sense of humor—none. How could she have? Life had made her sad to the bones. How else could she have been, with her history and now with this loveless future, this mortgage on her life that the *abuelos'* money had made possible?"

All this Diego shouted into the wind as if making a speech without a microphone. At the end of it he showed no emotion. It was impossible to tell if this was a virtuoso display of self-control or if he actually was hiding his agony as he had hidden everything else all his life, or if in reality he felt nothing and was playing a role.

He said, "This was a bad idea, the wind is too strong. Let's go back. My throat is getting sore."

Back at the house, over the howl of the onshore gale, Madonna sang "Don't Cry for Me Argentina." Diego showed no sign of resuming his runaway monologue. At lunch he chewed his food and drank his wine, looking into the distance at nothing.

Breaking the silence at last, Diego said, "I'm tired. If I don't reappear in an hour, wake me up."

While he napped I watched *The Official Story,* an Argentinean movie about a child whose natural parents had been disappeared. The man whom the child, now grown up, believed to be her father was not her father but a policeman who had taken her as a baby from her murdered parents.

Halfway through the film, Diego woke from his nap. He glanced at the screen, his reaction to what I was watching, if he had one, was unreadable. I switched it off and removed the headset.

He said, "I'm rested now. Let's sit at the kitchen table. It's better to talk face-to-face. Do you have any questions about what I've already told you?"

"One. How did Alejandro get into the drug business and survive?"

"In the usual way, by killing people before they killed him and taking over their operations. When he bought his escape with the lives of the fighters, he didn't give the military everybody. The best killers, the ruthless ones, the ones who would die protecting him because he was the magic, those he kept for himself. When he got to Leticia he sent for them."

"Your people."

"You might say that."

"He actually ran drugs, corrupted the masses, to fund the revolution?"

"Without blinking an eye. To Alejandro the revolution was a way to go on killing the people who deserved to die. If he had to forfeit the lives of some of the people he wanted to rescue from capitalism, so be it. It was a small price to pay for the Maoist nirvana to come. That was his fixation, to defeat the antichrist or the anti-Marx or the anti-Mao, the aliases didn't matter."

"You're describing a psychopath."

"Aren't Messiahs usually psychopaths? Genghis, Lenin, Hitler, Stalin. The deity of the Old Testament behaved like an escaped lunatic, murdering and punishing and ordering massacres and the rape of widows and daughters and drowning whole populations because some of the daughters of man had fucked the Nephilim, the sons of God, and polluted the blood of the creatures he had made in his image. He only spared the Israelites divine genocide in the desert after his spies failed him in the Land of Canaan because Moses told him he would be ridiculed in Egypt, where people would ask what kind of a god this was whose people would not obey him. Why did he love Abraham, Job, Noah, David? Because they flattered him with their obeisance. That's why homicidal maniacs like Hitler and Stalin are obeyed. Their behavior is godlike behavior. Or perhaps you don't agree."

I didn't disagree. I said, "You put Alejandro in the same class with that list of names?"

"It doesn't matter where I put him. That's where he put himself."

"If lunacy is what you saw in him, why did you help him?"

"Two reasons. One, because I wanted to separate him from the money, put it where he could not find it."

"Steal it?"

"Sequester it. Without it he couldn't have his revolution."

"Why would a revolutionary like you want to prevent it?"

"Because I was no longer a revolutionary and profoundly regretted that I ever had acted like one. I was a convert from idealism. Idealism is the curse of man's existence. Nazi idealists slaughtered seventeen million. The Leninists, the Stalinists, the Maoists, the small fry like the puppets who ran the countries in the Soviet bloc and Kim Il-Sung and Pol Pot and Castro murdered ninety-four million of their own people worldwide. That was enough."

As Diego said these things, which sounded like words from the heart, he seemed as calm, as reasonable, as rational as ever. I had asked a question. He was answering it. But no human being could possibly be as calm and reasonable as he imagined himself to be. If he was telling me the truth about himself he was just as crazy as the mad Alejandro he was describing to me.

I said, "You thought you could control a psychopath?"

"No but I could block his intentions and get away with it. I was the custodian of the treasury of the dead revolution, the one Alejandro had killed by betraying it to save himself when all was lost to the enemy. He needed this capital to finance his new enterprise. If he killed me he'd never know where I had put it."

"How much money are we talking about?"

"Too much to run a total at any given moment because it grew, and still grows every hour of every day. There was a lot of seed money. During the revolution we robbed many banks, we collected some large ransoms. Operations cost practically nothing because we stole our weapons and explosives and lived like the poor."

"How did you get control of the money?"

"Alejandro handed it over to me from the start. It was beneath him to touch filthy lucre. He had never had to worry about money and he didn't want to start. He was busy thinking up a new Flood."

I believed him. Whatever Diego did, he did for Felicia. Control of Alejandro's money made almost anything possible. Felicia had been forbidden to him. He wanted to rescue her. He wanted her back. He would do anything, kill his best friend before betraying him, to accomplish this.

I knew how he felt.

I said, "You said you had two reasons for doing what you did. What was reason number two?"

"That's why we are here, to talk about that. There was someone I wanted Alejandro to die with. The two of them at the same time in the same way."

"A second man?"

He waved the question away.

I insisted: "Who was the second man?"

"We'll get to that, but not yet. I had no access to this man. He was out of reach, too dangerous to touch even for Alejandro. He's still alive. And still out of reach."

"But you still want him to die."

"I want to talk to him, to look into his eyes."

"What does this have to do with me?"

"He's not out of reach for you."

I said, "If that's so, and I doubt it, why would I get involved?"

"You involved yourself when you married Luz."

But our marriage was over. I started to say so. Diego held up a hand. You might expect a surgeon to have shapely hands. His were large, broad, with blunt fingers made for the wrench rather than the scalpel.

He said, "That's enough for now. We have the whole night and longer to talk. Meanwhile, let's drive into town and have a drink and dinner. I know a restaurant in Las Grutas where you don't absolutely have to order steak and chimichurri."

37

It was almost midnight when we returned to the house. We had drunk a lot of wine. I drove. Diego was in no shape to do so. I was astonished that he let me see this. First he reveals to a total stranger whom he knows to be a spy his secret hatred for his best friend and the unspeakable reason for it.

Now this. What next? Was this peeling-away process genuine or part of whatever convoluted plan he was executing? Needless to say I favored the second of these possibilities.

Diego said he was too tired to talk any more and tired also of remembering. We'd continue in the morning, maybe the wind would die and we could walk on the beach as planned. It was better to speak of these things when outside. He staggered off to bed. A better man than I might have been kept awake by what Diego had already told him, but the sound of the surf was soporific and I was not entirely sober myself. I fell asleep almost immediately and as far as I now remember, did not dream. When I woke I did not feel for Luz beside me in the bed. I knew before opening my eyes that she was gone forever.

It was full morning. I heard the whine of a coffee grinder. Over the speakers Selena sang "Bidi Bidi Bom Bom." I knew her extraordinary voice because I had bought one of her CDs as a study aid when I was learning Spanish. How fitting it was that a victim of murder should sing me awake in the house of Diego, manager of murderers.

I got up, showered, got dressed, and made my appearance. In the kitchen as he cooked breakfast, Diego, his back turned, was singing along with the next song on the album—"Amor Prohibido." He knew something about that.

I wished him good morning. He turned around, smiling. He was in a buoyant mood. How had I slept? Had I seen the sunrise? This was one of the best spots on earth for sunrises and sunsets. On certain evenings, especially after the autumnal equinox, you could even see the colors of the sunset reflected in the eastern sky and vice versa—light from halfway around the world, projected from a star.

The weather front had passed, the day was cloudless. The wind had died. The surf was gentle. Diego and I went for a swim that made the skin pucker. I hadn't swum in such cold water since the polar bear club at Camp Chingachgook. Afterward we trudged along the beach in our bare feet. For the first fifteen minutes or so, as the strengthening sun took the chill off the morning, Diego was mute. Nor did I speak.

Moonshine Manor: *Create a silence and the subject will fill it.*

Diego had wound his white towel around his neck like a scarf. This made his tanned skin look darker. You could see the younger man he had been—not an Apollo like Alejandro, but the rough-cut masculine type many women preferred, as Felicia had demonstrated. I had never seen him in the company of a woman. I wondered if he had foresworn sex when Felicia was kidnapped out of his life.

Diego was a romantic, or at least had been one when he was young, because otherwise how could he have imagined he could change the

CHARLES McCARRY

world or regain lost love, so it was conceivable he had lived in celibacy
ever since he lost Felicia. That would explain a lot, considering the use he
had made of all that surplus testosterone. I told myself to stop speculat-
ing, to wait for the facts.

He said, "You know, I always think of Felicia in this place, imagine her
in the house and on the beach, which is odd because she never came here."

The whales were gone. The gulls circled, eyeing us. Was each bird a
part of the flock's collective mind, and was this mind deciding whether
to land on our bare backs and peck the flesh from our bones as if we were
some smaller, paler kind of whale?

Diego continued: "If she and I had gone away that night, across the
river to Uruguay, we might have had a place like this in another country.
Everything would have been as it was meant to be."

Meant to be by whom? By the psychotic gods Diego did not believe in?

Before I had finished the thought, Diego said, "You know Amzi
Strange, I know you do. He was the one who rescued Alejandro, who
otherwise would have ended up falling ten thousand feet into the ocean
at nine point eight meters per second per second, just like Felicia. The
mathematical formula is vf equals g * t. Or do you already know that?"

"I used to know it. Please continue."

"Amzi also did his best to save Felicia and nearly did so, but he was
betrayed."

"Betrayed? By whom?"

"Again I say we'll come to that. And in a minute or two we *will* come
to that, so in the meanwhile please pay attention. I want you to know
the context."

"I'm listening."

"A second Yanqui was involved—better to say that he intruded. He
was a Headquarters man, like Amzi, like you. Younger then than you
are now. Quiet, smart, patient, ruthless. A gentleman. Destined for great
things. So many Yanquis give that impression, they are educated to give

it. He was the go-between for the Headquarters station in Buenos Aires and the people who were torturing and killing revolutionaries. His heart was in this dirty work. He *liked* the oppressors. He was one of them. He hated us, especially Alejandro, I think because he saw us as renegades, traitors to our class, which of course we were, and saw Alejandro as a danger to the life he had always led, which of course Alejandro was. He himself was the most dangerous foreigner in Argentina."

Diego paused for effect. "He was the one who was told by a traitor inside the revolution exactly where Alejandro would be at any given moment. He made everything that happened, happen."

"Who was this traitor?"

"Only the traitor and the Yanqui know."

On the horizon, a white sail broke the horizon. Diego stopped talking and watched it. The boat turned and sailed northward before the offshore southeast wind. It was a strong wind. In a remarkably short time it became a white dot, then vanished. While Diego watched the boat I watched his face. He looked like he might weep. How unbearable his feelings must be, I thought, having been bottled up since the day Felicia married his best friend. So maybe he wasn't faking it.

I said, "If only the traitor and the Yanqui know, how do you know?"

Testily, as if I were a patient who had inconveniently awakened on the operating table, Diego said, "Why do you constantly interrupt? Wait."

"Go on."

He said, "It was Alejandro's own fault. He refused to be protected. It was the keystone of his self-image. It was the cult of the personality. He wanted the world to believe he was afraid of nothing. He would die if he had to, but he would never fear the oppressor, never yield to tyranny. He was the only free man in Argentina. If the masses followed him, they would be free, too. It was said by his admirers that he had a cyanide pill he would crush between his teeth if the enemy found him. Or if that failed, blow up himself and his attackers with the powerful bomb he carried in his backpack. This was all fantasy, but the myth was useful. His bravado was a threat to the cause. I always had him shadowed by my best guys—the ones he didn't take notice of, the ones who did the dirty work, the ones I sometimes operate on now—in case the enemy tried to grab him. He was so hopeless when it came to even the simplest tradecraft that he never realized they were there. They were armed with Uzis with orders to shoot to kill."

"Uzis? How could they kill his kidnappers without killing him?"

"They couldn't. Their orders were to kill Alejandro in case he didn't have time to kill himself. Now be still."

Diego said, "If I may get back to the point, this Yanqui, Alejandro's case officer, was a shrewd reader of people. He pretended to be a sympathizer, an enabler. He found Alejandro's weak point and made a proposal. He would help the revolution. Alejandro was interested: He hadn't been told that the revolution already had a helper, Boris. The Yanqui proposed to Alejandro, who knew that the revolution was doomed, that he, Alejandro, had a duty to save himself for future work. He knew his man. This was an idea Alejandro could not resist. It planted in Alejandro's mind the seed of the second, new improved revolution, led by a resurrected Alejandro. That was a strange thing for a Headquarters man to do unless he was recruiting Alejandro, which of course was exactly what he was doing whether Alejandro knew it or not. . . ."

He interrupted himself, pointed out to sea.

"*Look, whales!*"

"Where?"

"Underneath that flock of gulls, south-southeast, about two hundred meters out."

I saw them now—a whole pod of them, adults and calves. Gulls wheeled overhead.

Then the gulls attacked, all at once and as a single creature, as if poured in their hundreds from a spout. The whales swam serenely on as if they didn't know the gulls existed.

"The whales are being eaten alive," Diego said. "Maybe the whales can't feel the beaks. The blubber must block the pain."

We watched the whales a little longer, as they became a sort of living, breathing Galapagos covered with squawking gulls. Over the years, according to Diego, hundreds of dead whales had been found along the coast. Gulls were the chief suspects, or so scientists believed. Protectors of the whale were alarmed, Diego told me, but this had probably been going on for millennia. Seagulls didn't suddenly decide, all at once, *Let's eat the whales,* so maybe, since there were still plenty of whales to eat after centuries of feasting on blubber, there was less to worry about than whale lovers feared.

Diego's mind worked in its own way. I listened patiently—with interest and amusement, even, and waited for him to get back to the point he was evading. Moonshine Manor again: *As long as they're talking, let them talk until they say something useful.* Sooner or later, in theory, Diego would get back to Alejandro's Mephistophelean Yanqui case officer.

In time, the whales swam out of our field of vision along with the hovering gulls. We walked on in silence for a while. There were few gulls left on the beach and presumably the ones in flight were glutted with blubber and blood, so it was quieter than usual. Diego spread his towel, the one he had wrapped around his neck, and sat on it.

As if there had been no interruption, Diego said, "This Yanqui's idea was to persuade Alejandro that there was no hope whatsoever for the revolution. Now that he had learned his lessons from its failure he should drown it like a litter of kittens, and having profited from its mistakes, start a new revolution that would succeed and justify the sacrifices of the one that had failed. He would save many lives, because there would no longer be any reason to kill our comrades, who no longer had a leader. A soul."

Did I follow? I said I thought so, but please continue.

"Alejandro was immediately seduced by this argument," Diego said. "It was an offer of immortality. Of course he knew exactly what would happen to those he betrayed. We had a source, one of the good people, one of us, a woman Alejandro had slept with for a while when we were all students. Now she was married to an army officer who, thanks to her political influence, had discovered that he had a conscience. He was the aide de camp of the general who was in charge of the torture. On inspection tours with the general this husband saw what was happening to the disappeared. He saw people he knew, people he had had dinner with, his wife's friends. They recognized him. This shook him up. He would come home and tell her everything. He thought the junta, which saw itself as the Fourth Reich in everything but name, was staining the honor of the army, of Argentina itself, in a way from which neither could ever recover. He would cry on her bosom, but he went on with his career. The wife would tell us everything this bastard told her. So the point is, Alejandro knew perfectly well what would happen to everybody else if he did as the Yanqui advised. Including Felicia."

"But?"

"Be patient. The Yanqui insisted on meeting Alejandro's wife. Felicia was hiding at the time like a good freedom fighter in Villa Cartóna, a shantytown, a *villa miseria*. She had become an operative—she had done enough and more than enough on her own to be wanted by the torturers. Even in rags in a room where rats ran over your feet, she was breathtaking. If the world was coming to an end, no man who saw her could be interested in anything but her. The Yanqui saw how invaluable Felicia was to his purposes. How Alejandro must love her! He wanted to give Alejandro an incentive to do what he wanted to do anyway. Rescuing this amazing woman was just what the doctor ordered. That could be arranged. It would make it possible to do anything he wanted to do, commit any outrage, and only enhance his mystique. But first Felicia had to be kidnapped. The Yanqui told the torturers where she was. That night they took her."

A pause. "The officer with the conscience saw Felicia in prison because the general particularly wanted to get a look at this beautiful wife of the famous scarlet pimpernel, Alejandro. She was spread out on a table, naked. . . ."

At this point Diego leapt to his feet and walked away and into the surf, where he stood, knee deep in the heaving water, gazing out to sea—assuming he could see anything besides the pictures in his mind.

When he came back—eyes averted, face ravaged—he started to speak even before he sat down.

"The Yanqui thought that Alejandro could now be blackmailed. It didn't work, of course. It didn't work because Alejandro didn't care what happened to Felicia. So when the Yanqui suggested that there was a way to rescue his beloved wife, he cut him off and stalked away, as if this heathen had no right to speak her sacred name."

"Your watchers heard and saw this?"

"How else would I know it happened?"

"You don't think Alejandro did know he was being shadowed and didn't want witnesses present?"

"No."

"For the sake of argument, suppose he did—"

"I suppose nothing for argument. Neither should you. Reality and only reality matters. "

"OK. What would your men have done if Alejandro, in a state of ignorance, had listened and agreed?"

"They would have killed him."

"On your orders?"

"On what they had heard with their own ears. They knew what his betrayal meant."

"Why didn't they kill the American?"

"Why should they do that? Headquarters would just replace him with someone we didn't know. Also, we already had enough powerful enemies."

"So then Amzi appeared out of nowhere?"

"Yes. It was him, not the Yanqui, who appeared at the next meeting with Alejandro. However, who but the Yanqui could have told Amzi where to look?"

"Why?"

"Orders, presumably. I have no firsthand knowledge of that. I can only tell you what I was told."

"By whom?"

"By Boris. He knew a lot about the Yanquis. He said Headquarters had been appalled by what the Yanqui had done. *Kidnapping!* They—don't laugh—didn't do things like that. They took the Yanqui off the case. Headquarters wanted to get Felicia back, to get her out of the country. The torturers wanted something in return."

"How did Boris know all this?"

"He didn't say, but everything else he ever told me was the truth. These questions are taking us off the subject."

I went back into priestly mode—a neutral listener, not a judge.

Diego said, "Amzi made Alejandro an offer. All he had to do was give him, Amzi, the true names and whereabouts and photographs when possible, of every fighter of the revolution, and Amzi would cover Alejandro's ass by giving him back his wife in such a way that everyone would believe that whatever he had had to do, he had done for love. Treachery would be seen as romance. His betrayal of everyone who trusted him and everything he said he believed in would be one more proof of his moral nobility."

At this point Diego closed his eyes and took a very deep breath.

Eyes still shut, he said, "Alejandro pretended to refuse. He walked away. Amzi stalked him. Whenever Alejandro ventured out of one of his safe houses, there was Amzi, waiting for him. He was very, very good at his work. He knew from the first moment my people were there."

"But your people did nothing?"

"Amzi's people had guns on them. The Yanquis had night-vision glasses so they could see our people but our people couldn't see them, just feel their presence. Please listen. I am almost finished."

He was annoyed, tired of reminding me how to behave. I shut up.

"Amzi sweetened the offer," Diego said. "He knew that Alejandro's problem was not a moral problem. He was beyond morality. It was a question of where he could hide, where he could continue what he called his mission. Obviously he couldn't stay in Argentina or ever come back without being tortured, shot, or hanged or all three. Amzi offered him sanctuary. Headquarters would get Felicia back because she would be of no further use to the torturers after they knew, thanks to Alejandro, what they had been trying to make her tell them. So he would have saved her life, a dividend. Headquarters, in the person of Amzi, would smuggle the two of them secretly out of the country, provide them with fully documented new identities and an annuity. Then he would forget they existed. But rescue them if necessary, even if this did not become necessary for fifty years.

"Alejandro dragged it out. He was a tactician if he was nothing else. But then, as you already know, he accepted. And then the moment came. The torturers appeared, a dozen thugs along with a representative of the general commanding, none other than the conscience-stricken husband of our friend the good woman. Felicia was with them, dressed up by her captors in the latest fashion, her hair done, her makeup perfect courtesy of the torturers' makeup artist. Felicia was drugged and only half-conscious. She was barely able to walk or talk or hold up her head.

"Amzi showed them the thick envelope he carried and said, 'We'll take her now.'"

"The officer said, 'And the information?'"

"Amzi said, 'First, the woman.' The officer said, 'No. First, him.'"

"The thugs grabbed Alejandro and manacled him hand and foot. Even if he had had a cyanide capsule in his tooth or a bomb in his knapsack they would have done him no good. Before they gagged him Alejandro screamed at Amzi: *'Cabrón! Hijo de puta!'*

"All this happened in the dark, so my men heard it rather than saw it. Their fingers were on the triggers of the Uzis. Somebody in the dark behind them—Amzi's men, who else?—blackjacked them. When they revived, everybody was gone. Also the Uzis. Amzi had saved them. Otherwise they would be in a cage or dead. They knew this. So did I."

I said, "So whatever happened next happened in the dark?"

"Everything happened in the dark."

"You say your people were unconscious. So how do you know that the famous deal that Amzi supposedly made—Felicia's life in exchange for the rescue of Alejandro and the revolution—actually happened?"

Diego let silence gather. How stupid could I be? Had I not been listening? Were the facts not self-evident?

He said, "I know because there were witnesses—Alejandro and the good woman's husband. Also, Alejandro was alive, Felicia was in the hands of her murderers."

"So the good woman, as you call her . . ."

"As she was."

". . . was your source."

"Yes, of course," Diego said. "But Amzi insisted they release Alejandro into his custody. They agreed. They could not do otherwise without bringing the imperial wrath of Washington down upon themselves. And after all, the torturers had what they wanted: the names of everyone they needed to torture and kill, the key to the final solution of the Alejandroista Question. They didn't need Alejandro. If he had no followers, if they were all soon going to be dead, what harm could he do? They would keep the woman. The gringos would understand that they must have a guarantee, a hostage. When at the last second they seized her at the airport, Amzi made no effort to protect her."

Diego looked at his watch.

He said, "Time is short. To answer your question, the name of the Yanqui agent who sent Felicia to her death is Thomas Terhune."

I was not surprised. The picture puzzle was coming together.

I said, "One more question. Why are you telling me this?"

"Because I want to talk to Terhune, and I want you to bring him to me."

Talk to him?

I said, "What makes you think I can do that? Or that he'd be stupid enough to do it?"

"Wait. Don't jump to conclusions. What is done is done. Doing more harm can't change that. Soon I will be old. I want to die in peace, and I realize that the only way I can have peace before I die is to reconcile with this man."

"Diego . . ."

"No. Let me speak. You know a Jesuit called Yuri, a Russian."

"I do. How do you know him?"

"How do you think? Boris introduced us."

"One atheist providing spiritual guidance to another?"

"An intelligent priest was what I needed at the time. This priest had confessed Alejandro, so he would know what he could not tell me and offer informed spiritual advice. Father Yuri made me see what I must do. I know what you must be thinking. But ask yourself this: Who introduced you to Father Yuri?"

Diego's move was crude. So what else was new? The home truth about the clandestine life is that it clothes itself in subtlety but lives by the raw truths of human nature. Diego wanted something. In order to get it he would tell me everything. He would do this because his spy, Luz, had told him that I, too, wanted something and what that something was. He knew I would pretend to believe his lies in order to get it, just as he pretended to believe mine.

Diego said, "Think about it. Ask yourself why should I do this Yanqui harm after all these years, what I can possibly have to gain in comparison to what I stand to lose—Luz, above all? You of all people know what it is to lose her, what it means, how incurable the pain. Besides, there are incentives. There is much I can tell him."

I said, "The revolution is old news."

"I know that if anyone does. However, terrorism is not old news. The drug trade is not old news. Washington throws away billions trying to penetrate its secrets. I know those secrets by heart—methods, names, connections, rivalries that can be exploited and how to exploit them. I know the politicians who are being paid in money and girls and protection to make all this possible. I know where the bodies are buried. Above all, I know where the money is hidden."

He also knew how good it would be for his business if the U.S. government eliminated his competition.

I said, "Amzi won't buy this."

"Why not? I think otherwise. Those two are enemies. Terhune betrayed Amzi in the Alejandro operation, saddled him with the blame and the guilt for what happened to Felicia. Terhune's got something to resent. He made the new, worse Alejandro possible. Amzi spoiled everything. He stole the credit that belonged to Terhune. He has probably done the same thing many times since. And as a result, he has overshadowed Terhune for the rest of his career. Terhune thinks that he should be the DDO, that Amzi cheated him of his rightful place. This is his chance to recoup. Amzi knows this. He will not hesitate to send him into danger and hope for the worst."

"You want Terhune to come to Argentina?"

"Where else?"

"If he's as smart as you think he is, he'll never do that."

"Then we can meet on neutral ground. I will fly to meet him anywhere outside the USA."

For a change, I was the one who snorted. Where exactly was this neutral ground to be found? Given their history, there wasn't a patch of it anywhere on the planet large enough for Diego and Tom to occupy at the same moment.

Many seconds later, Diego broke the bubble of silence.

He said, "There's only one way to find out—ask him. Will you do this for me?"

I said, "I'll deliver the message."

38

Amzi said, "It sounds like Diego has either made friends with Jesus or he wants to behead Terhune. All in favor of Jesus say aye."

No one spoke.

Amzi said, "OK, Tommy Tune, you're first on the dance floor."

"First principles first," Terhune said. "Once a terrorist, always a terrorist. This man in particular. He was the brains and the executioner of the movement, then of the drug operation. Alejandro was the dummy in the store window."

Amzi said, "So you don't want to take the bait?"

"I didn't say that. Maybe he actually has something useful to say. He says he knows everything and maybe he does. Everything he's told us so far is factual. It's a gamble. But we're supposed to be gamblers."

Amzi pointed a finger at me. "You?"

"If all he wants is to kill Tom," I said, "he doesn't have to lure him to Argentina to do it. Bill Stringfellow was less than five miles from his house when they chopped off his head. Diego knows where Tom lives. He has a stable full of assassins. He can whack Tom on his way home at any moment of his choosing or murder him while he watches TV or blow up his house during a family reunion. He could have done any of those things a long time ago if that's what he wanted to do."

Amzi said, "You think he might actually spill all those beans?"

"He certainly was pretty talkative with me. You both know the case. Did he say anything that wasn't true? Tom?"

"It doesn't seem so. He may have left unsaid some things that are true."

"Like what?"

Neither Tom nor Amzi answered the question. Nor did they exchange a glance, as a couple of men who knew the same secret might have done. I didn't follow up.

Amzi said, "So what do we do now?"

He pointed at me.

"It's Hobson's choice," I said. "In my opinion it would be wise to err on the side of caution. Let me handle it."

"He's your fucking father-in-law."

"In biological terms, yes. In fact, I have no idea what Diego is to me. And anyway, whatever he may say, the connection is irrelevant."

"Nice you're in such a cooperative mood," Amzi said.

The truth was, Diego really wasn't an enigma to me. Now that Luz and I were apart, why should his attitude toward me include so much as a molecule of trust or affection or good intent? To Diego I was a pigeon in training. If I pecked the right button I got a bread crumb.

Terhune said, "What he's told us so far concerns the past and matches what we know. That means nothing. As our young friend, here, told us in another context, this guy is way too smart to lie to us when we already know the truth. What he wants to do is give us a reason to yield to temptation. Can we do what he wants us to do and profit from it? It would be risky, but it could be done."

"And go on living?" Amzi said. "He ain't going to meet us inside the embassy with a bag over his head, and where else could we be in control?"

Tom said, "On neutral ground, as he suggests."

"Like where?"

They batted this ball back and forth for long minutes. Diego was right, these two did not like each other. However, they could read each other. They spoke over my head, as if I were a child who couldn't understand the language grown-ups spoke among themselves. I was fine with that. They were talking themselves into this folly, just as Diego had hoped and for the reasons he had stated. He knew the type. It was their job to be curious, to live for answers, to outwit all comers.

Registering reluctance, Amzi let himself be convinced. It was a weak performance. He might not want Tom to come to a bad end, but he wouldn't be sorry if he did. He just didn't want the responsibility. They decided to ask the Director's permission to take the risk.

Downstairs, Tom beckoned me into his office and shut the door.

"I want to clear the air," he said.

I thought, *Please don't confess.* I needn't have worried.

"There's something you should know," Tom said. "The Bureau has informed Security it has established that your mother died as a Medicare patient in a nursing home in Oregon. She wasn't destitute but she was no millionaire, either. Her second husband—it was a common law marriage—never had a trust fund. He was a substitute high school English teacher, a nobody. The millions she's supposed to have left you in trust was transferred from a bank in the Cayman Islands that's popular with the cartels if it isn't actually owned by them, to a bank in Lichtenstein they are also known to use, then to a bank in Denmark, then to the bank in Oregon, which presumably is clean. The Bureau thinks it's onto something. Security tends to agree. That means a spot of bother. Clearly, whoever set this up wanted to throw you to the dogs. It will be hard to get the gumshoes to believe that, because that means they'd have to admit they were wrong and start all over again. Security is a world unto itself.

Nobody, not even Amzi or your admirer the Director, can tell Security, let alone the Bureau, what to do or what not to do."

"Was my lawyer in on this?"

"I don't know, but he touched the money. That will be of interest to the Bureau."

Thanks, Tom, for the peace of mind.

I said, "What do I do now?"

"About what?"

"Diego."

"Nothing whatsoever until you hear otherwise. It'll take awhile for this to get through channels. Go back to Buenos Aires. If Luz is still there, she should stay there, out of the Bureau's jurisdiction. If Diego asks, and he probably won't, tell him the truth—we're thinking about it. We'll inform the station that you're in town and to stay out of the way. Report in to the station as soon as possible and keep in touch. If you need anything, they'll help you out in the usual ways."

I flew back to Argentina that afternoon. In spite of myself I looked for Luz among the waiting crowd outside customs.

It's no simple thing, giving up hope.

39

It took Headquarters a while to put the operation together. Tom would fly in on a Headquarters plane and fly out again the next day. He would be accompanied and protected by a special ops team. The meeting would take place at midnight in a safe house in Barrio Chico, a neighborhood in northeast Buenos Aires.

Because I was someone Diego could trust or would have to pretend to trust, I would drive him to the safe house. A lead car and a chase car would accompany us. Diego would not be told exactly where he was going. Tom would be waiting for us in the house. While inside he would be protected by one member of a six-man special ops team and me. The rest of the team would be deployed outside the house and out of sight.

Diego would pass through metal detectors and an X-ray chamber when he arrived. I would be armed with my .45 and other weapons and if necessary, would shoot Diego dead, as would the special ops man. The inside man was a former Navy SEAL who for this operation used the name Joe. In the next few days I rehearsed all of this many times with the team as a whole and with Joe. They went through the motions, but all made it clear they thought I was worse than useless.

Joe was a silent fellow in his forties, a panther, cold as ice, a trained killer like the rest of his teammates. While Diego was in the safe house he would be one breath away from sudden death, but Tom would be safe unless Diego was wearing a suicide vest. In which case, we'd all die, Diego included.

It was a mystery to me why Tom wanted to do what he was doing unless he had a death wish, and why the powers that be were letting him do it. He was a walking institutional memory of Headquarters. He was a prize. Any drug lord would pay a fortune for the chance to pump him out. If something went wrong, as I was sure it would because it almost always does, we would, as Amzi put it, be left with our dicks in our hands.

Diego had been told—by me, because I was the only possible liaison—that he would await me at 11:30 P.M. in a parking lot on the other side of town. I'd pick him up and drive him to the meeting place. He objected to nothing, asked no questions. And there he was, on time as always, sitting in his Mercedes.

We drove to the safe house in silence. I was bringing together two men who hated each other and who both wanted to see the other man dead. The only certain element was that there would be a surprise. The only question was, which one of them, Diego or Tom, was going to provide the surprise?

Two steps inside the house, after Diego had failed to set off the hidden metal detector, Joe waited.

He said, "Good evening, Doctor. I have to search you. Please raise your arms."

Diego did so slowly, reluctantly, and then in one swift expert movement, cut Joe's carotid artery with the plastic scalpel he held in his right hand. Blood spurted from the artery, just as it had done from Faraj's artery in Sana'a. He was dead in seconds.

Diego stepped over his body, entered the sitting room where Tom awaited us, and plunged the needle of the plastic syringe he held in his left hand into Tom's neck. Tom, frozen in wide-eyed surprise, dropped like a stone.

By then my .45 was in my hand, but I didn't shoot. I could not kill Luz's father and with it, all hope of ever seeing her again.

Two thugs with Uzis slung from their necks materialized as if they had been beamed down from the Starship *Enterprise*. No more than fifteen seconds had passed since Diego and I walked through the front door. Despite the .45, the men with the Uzis ignored me. The thugs produced a U.S.-issue body bag, unzipped it, and spread it out on the floor. They fitted Tom's rag doll body into it and zipped it up.

Diego said, "Let me have your weapon and your spare ammunition. These comrades are very protective and they hate Yanquis. We don't want any misunderstandings."

I said, "Is Tom dead?"

"No. That was Versed I injected, not a poison. He'll wake up in a couple of hours, remembering nothing. The gun, please. Hurry."

By now both Uzis were pointed at me. I handed it over, thinking I would be dead before I drew the next breath. I was not unhappy about this. The joke that was my life would come to an end. Good.

Maybe thirty seconds had passed since Diego murdered Joe. The whole episode had been soundless.

"Let's go," he said.

We walked out the front door together, Diego in the lead with my gun in his hand, the two comrades lugging the sagging body bag with Tom inside. A van pulled into the driveway at the precise moment we reached it.

Diego, unhurried, said to me, "Take the front passenger seat, please."

The comrades, Uzis at the ready, sat behind me. Diego sat in a jump seat. Inside his bag, Tom was curled up in the luggage space.

I searched the deserted street, but in the dim light of its lamps saw no sign of the special ops team. None. By now two minutes had passed, not more. Maybe the team was just around the corner, waiting for Joe to check in. Or maybe Diego's Uzi corps had killed them all, gassed them, shot them dead with silenced weapons like the ones the team itself used. I assumed I would not live long enough to find out.

We changed cars three times along the way and after a two-hour ride, ended up at an abandoned military airstrip somewhere in the country-side. Diego's Beechcraft was parked at the end of the runway, propellers spinning. He unloaded the .45, threw the spare ammunition away, and handed the empty weapon back to me. We climbed aboard.

A man I had never seen before sat in the copilot's seat. Diego sat down in the pilot's seat.

I went to the cockpit door. Behind me the comrades took Tom out of the body bag and bound him with a whole roll of duct tape into one of the seats. He seemed to be regaining consciousness.

In a loud voice I said, "Diego."

Studying the display of instruments, he said, "Yes?"

"Where are we going?"

"You'll know when we get there. I can't talk right now. Sit down and buckle up."

The engines revved, the plane lurched into motion and rolled down the runway. I sat down and buckled up.

Tom woke up. His arms twitched. His jaw moved as he attempted to make saliva. He looked old—lank gray hair falling into his eyes, gray pallor. His shirttail was out, his clothes askew. The right sleeve of his white shirt was bloodstained. I had never before seen him disheveled.

In moments we were airborne. The plane made a wide turn, climbed to altitude, and flew toward its destination, wherever and whatever that was. The window shades were drawn, so there was no way of locating Polaris or guessing which way we were going or what lay below.

Tom opened his eyes, looked at me as if he had never seen me before, saw that he was bound hand and foot and torso to his chair with fifty feet of gray tape, and then closed his eyes, as if reentering oblivion or trying to do so.

He said, "What's happening?"

"I'm not sure."

"Why aren't you taped like me?"

"I don't know."

"Like hell you don't. This is your work. I know it is."

His speech was thick, his eyes full of loathing. I had not foreseen this reaction, but Tom was right. This was my work. He may have made a stupid decision to take this reckless chance, but I had brought the temptation to him. Even when asked, I hadn't told him what I was sure Diego had in mind but chose instead to assume he was smart enough to know without help. Maybe I was right. It was just that Headquarters was no match for Diego. And never had been.

Tom, the Yanqui who handed Felicia over to her torturers, had given Diego a reason to lead the life he led—to avenge the rape of the love of his life, first by Alejandro, later by a roomful of common soldiers, to romanticize her and himself, to paint indiscriminate murder of the innocent as an act of virtue, to call money dripping with blood and suffering the treasury of social justice. In short, to do all the things he accused Alejandro of doing because Alejandro was a monster of pride.

With better luck, as he had said, he might have crossed the Rio de la Plata with Felicia by his side and lived happily ever after with her in his arms and children as beautiful as she was in their laps. Someone had to pay for that no matter the cost. Without Diego, Alejandro would have done something stupid and been arrested before he had done any serious harm. Dozens of the dead who had been collateral victims of bombs and bullets would have lived.

Yet when all was said and done, I and nobody else had made this ending possible. Now I had my own revenge by act of omission, by means I had never imagined. Just like Diego. Our politics, his as well as mine, was revenge, which we shared more deeply than any two fools who had ever shared communism or capitalism or religion or loved the same woman. When I set out to betray I thought I would be the only Judas in the picture. Instead, I had discovered that traitors were a worldwide fellowship—Mother, Faraj, Diego, Boris, Burkov, Tom. In his own fashion, Amzi.

Luz? She had typed a period on an empty page. Everything Diego had ever done, he had done for her. She had known that he was her father—of course she had—ever since she was old enough to know the truth and smart enough to understand it. She had lived her life in the power of that colossal secret. What greater romance can be imagined? How could I compete? Yes, she had deceived me. But if, five seconds from now, Diego or one of the comrades put a bullet in my brain, or if I lived to be an old man and like my own father was murdered in my sleep for pocket change, I would die loving not the real Luz, a being to whom I had never been introduced, but the Luz in the mirror. She had made love as if she loved me. What more did she owe me?

The plane descended and then leveled off. Diego emerged from the cockpit. He pointed at Tom. With razor-sharp fighting knives the two comrades sliced off the duct tape that bound him and stood him on his feet, gray tape still pasted to his clothes. This did not hide a dark stain on the crotch of his trousers.

To me, Diego said, "You're here because I wanted a witness Amzi would believe. All this is being videotaped, so you'll have documentary evidence to back up your story. I wish you all the best. I'm truly sorry about Luz."

Was he going to let me live? One of the comrades opened the Beechcraft's door. The other comrade regarded me with amusement—inspired no doubt by the startled look on my face. No matter what Diego said, no matter the sympathetic face he wore, I was sure that my life was about to end.

Diego, strong for a man his age, seized Tom, who was shouting in Spanish and resisting with all that remained of his strength, by the collar and the belt. He rushed him to the door and heaved him out of the airplane. Then, without a word, Diego himself turned around, smiled at me, crossed his arms on his chest, closed his eyes, and threw himself backward through the open door and into the night.

The comrades, impassive, tidying up, wadded the duct tape into a ball and threw it after Tom and Diego, then closed the door and went back to their seats.

The plane banked. There was a moon that night. By its light, before the comrades closed the door, I saw that we were over the Atlantic where, at last, Felicia rested in peace.

It was over. I had my revenge. All I had to do now was live with it.

They say that the dead know everything, so maybe Father was having the last laugh in some afterworld for souls consigned to an eternity of mirth. If so, he laughed alone, but he was used to that.

In time, I supposed, I would get used to it, too.